Surviving 10

John Page

ISBN: 1461095573

ISBN-13: 978-1461095576

A companion site, www.surviving10.com, contains illustrations, photographs, links, a bibliography and copies of all the electronic documents in the New Plymouth Clan survival archive mentioned in this book.

Credits, photo inserts:
Cover photo: courtesy of Donald W. Macy
page 35: courtesy of StoveTec, www.stovetec.net
page 46: Donna's farm map by author
page 48: photo of VITA stove by author
page 48: image of tin-can rocket stoves from video *coffee can rocket stove #2*, http://www.youtube.com/watch?v=_-BQMpaW-E0
page 49: photo of institutional stove courtesy of Aprovecho Research Center, www.aprovecho.org
page 49: photo of Justa stove from *New Rocket Stove Designs for Central and Southern Africa*, courtesy of Peter Scott
page 61: Donna's farm terrain map by author
page 85: drawing of Pontiac shelter in public domain, Daniel B. Beard
page 183: photo of VITA stove courtesy of Aprovecho Research Center
page 203: New Plymouth map by author

DEDICATION

For Jerina, Ben, Sherry, Zecharia, Nancy, Peter, Dean and Larry.

FORWARD

This book is speculative fiction, given that I write it in advance of the pole shift described. But it is inspired by and molded by the content of the ZetaTalk web site that figures so prominently in the story.

The character of Charlie in the story reflects my own thinking about ZetaTalk: strangely believable, yet more and more credible as events unfold worldwide that match ZetaTalk's predictions.

I have myself been up against the struggle to explain the possibility of a pole shift to skeptical friends and family. I also know people whose religious convictions are so strong that they will have real difficulty dealing with the propositions of Immanuel Velikovsky, Zecharia Sitchin, and ZetaTalk. I sympathize with their quandary, and I try to deal with it in the book.

The real message I hope to convey is that the world is increasingly plagued with natural and political disasters that warrant serious preparation for the end of the world as we knew it. If "prepare for the worst" is reasonable advice, then preparing for a pole shift covers the other possibilities pretty well.

I acknowledge and cherish the support, wisdom and editing skill my wife, Jerina, has applied to the creation of this book. And I am grateful for her wholehearted commitment to preparing for disasters of many sorts, a pole shift being the worst of them.

I do encourage you to prepare for disaster. The links and documents in the New Plymouth archive at the companion site, www.surviving10.com, will help you do that.

John Page
Cruso, NC
March 2011

ZERO HOUR

IN THE TRENCH

They'd been in the trenches for two hours. They didn't feel ridiculous anymore. This was what they had prepared for. It was still dark, the same as it had been for days by Mark's watch. Not like night. More like just before dawn, with a faint glow in the east.

What time was it? What did "time" mean now, after a lifetime of measuring life by sunrise and sunset, and uncounted mental calculations of what time it was in a city in a different time zone. Dawn used to be the daily reset of time, measured to the minute, that swept across the globe every "day," like "clockwork," triggering life, summoning the faithful, the drudges, the movers and shakers, the mothers, children and teachers to their places.

The days had gotten measurably longer over the last week. Way longer. There was no doubt the Earth's rotation was slowing. There was no doubt why, either. For weeks, now, when it was day and they could see the sun, they could see It too. That nasty, dragon-looking Thing in the sky beside the sun.

The news had called it all sorts of things. NASA had said it was a meteor, later said it was "planet-like," that it wouldn't get bigger, then it would get bigger but pass harmlessly, then that there might be an earthquake or two.

Then NASA just went silent.

Government officials stammered and mumbled, afraid to issue THE WARNING. Then they had nothing to say, either.

Or maybe nobody could hear them anymore.

In the last year, the earthquakes had steadily increased in number and intensity. Like popcorn. One here, one there. Then several together, then more. Then a roar of them.

The news had described the early ones—Haiti or Chile—as singular events, with planes flying in and supplies being marshaled. Then there were more, like New Zealand, and then the new ones became just "another one." When so many occurred in the United States, people talked of nothing else. This wasn't normal. This had never happened. This was unprecedented. This was God's warning. This was God's punishment. This was Armageddon. This was the End.

As the roads, buildings, and bridges crumbled, the vision of the world as a community of nations went out of focus, then faded. The world closed in day by day. News from New Delhi and Naples. Then some vague word about India and Europe. Then nothing.

The Internet was no better than the TV, which was another sign. Web sites came and went. Then just went. Sites in the U.S. disappeared as earthquakes shut down their servers or broke the cables of the Web between there and here.

Roads crumbled into a jumble of impassible flakes. Even walking on them was difficult. Bridges cracked. Trucks sat on roads and interstates where they were when the particular quake in that spot made farther progress impossible.

Loads of perishable food spoiled in the trucks that stood in the sun of 22-hour days. The grocery stores on their routes remained empty after panic buying and residual looting. After a few days, most of the trucks on the Interstates near cities gaped open, cargos jumbled on the ground.

Desperation had set in quickly.

Earthquakes harvested trees, which brought power lines with them to the ground. Lines that came down stayed down, because shattered roads froze repair trucks on their separate patches of asphalt, and the men who would drive them were home instead, guarding the family food.

Not that there was any point in repairing the power lines after the succession of 8+ quakes cracked the hydroelectric dams. Tangled rails halted coal transport, so the coal-fired plants shut down, too. At least that was the rumor.

The grid was gone. And it wouldn't be back for a long, long time.

Without power, wells and pumps quit, so there was either no water or too much. Refrigerators and freezers died, and their contents turned toxic. *Carne Vale*—farewell to meat. Cable TV would have turned to snow as cables snapped, if the power were on. TV satellites died in the hail of rock burning up in the Earth's atmosphere, as It stormed in the sky.

Radio stations on emergency power broadcast discouraging news and unhelpful advice, then stopped altogether.

If you weren't ready now, you were out of time.

Earthquakes mangled old dams around the country. Some just leaked their lakes. Others collapsed and sloshed walls of water into the valleys below where towns were. Had been. Quakes had brought down what brick buildings hadn't gone already. Mounds of brick towered along debris-filled streets, now covered in places by water. Lots of fires. The quakes had spilled the crude fires, candles, and oil lamps, which sometimes ignited leaking gas, which did for wood houses what the quakes did for the brick. The agony of Haiti was now universal. But without rescue. Those who might rescue were tied down trying to help their own.

Mark hoped that his children had listened and had prepared. He'd never know if they had.

It was no comfort that he'd never know if they hadn't.

His group had been at Donna's farm for six months, getting ready. The store of emergency food they'd saved back in the normal times was gone, used up when food distribution became sporadic after the New Madrid fault in the midwest went. The garden they'd planted had done well, considering the weather. Canned, packed, and buried nearby, so they had something to start with for the Aftertime.

They'd gone into the trenches when the moan began. Moan: that wasn't the best word to describe that sound. Like a very loud New York City subway passing underneath a sidewalk. But louder. And it never ended. Much louder. The earth vibrated with it. Deep down, you could feel little clicks, like something deep was breaking.

When it started, birds had fled to the sky all over the valley. The cloud of birds that rose from trees all over revealed more birds than anyone had ever seen at once. They added a high-pitched hysterical rattle to the low, menacing growl of the Earth. Every dog howled or barked. Except Jesse. Jesse, never the brave dog, had frozen, eyes dilated. Now he trembled inconsolably. The growling bear was digging him up and was about to eat him.

The people in the trenches with Mark were as ready as they knew how. They had tried to pay attention to the warnings and advice from a variety of web sites and books, while they had them. They'd expected the quakes. While the stores were still open, they knew there would be no more groceries. They'd avoided the looting and the looters. They'd expected the dams to go, so they weren't in town when the water came down and passed over the rubble from earlier earthquakes. They'd expected the Earth to growl. As each calamity followed another, they all knew more surely that Mark had been right all along.

They were all there in those trenches because of Mark.

In winter parka, boots, winter gloves, goggles and a motorcycle helmet.

Funny attire for August.

But not for what was coming.

TIME LEFT: FOURTEEN MONTHS

GARDEN PARTY

Couples sat in a circle of wobbly lawn chairs on uneven grass, newly dry, poking at potato salad or fumbling with self-constructed hamburgers. They had all been friends for years but seldom met all together. This picnic celebrated the end of rain and the start of the long, blue, dry Oregon summer. After almost eight months of rain each year, they always celebrated.

They caught up on activities the past winter, family, other friends, and summer plans.

Alice looked down at her near-empty plate, then looked around the group. “Does anyone else feel like the world is coming apart?”

Donna laughed. “Well, have a nice day! Whatsa matter? Plugged-up drain?”

“No. I'm serious. It just seems like the country...no, the world...is coming apart.”

The group joined in, talking so fast that you couldn’t tell who was saying what.

“Me, too. There are so many disasters now: floods, snow in odd places. A 110-degree swing in one day.”

“I thought you were talking about riots, shootings.”

“That, too. All of it. Life isn't the same as it was when we were growing up.”

“There are so many shows on TV about mega volcanoes, the big earthquake, the world after mankind is gone, and all that stuff about 2012.”

“Do you believe something will happen in 2012?”

“Yes. Or before.”

"Like what?"

"Let's see. The Big One in California."

"That wouldn't end everything."

"True. Financial meltdown."

"That's more likely, and it would trash the world."

Mark jumped into the conversation. "I read a book about that called *Patriots*. Civilization in the U.S. crashed after hyperinflation. The heroes headed for the hills. Ended up fighting and winning a guerilla war against the UN."

Then he added, "Or an EMP that kills all electronic devices, including cars and planes. That was the premise of the book *One Second After.*"

Donna frowned. "What's an EMP?"

Before Mark could answer, Bill, an ex-Navy submariner, joined in. "Electromagnetic pulse, a large jolt of electric energy put out by a nuclear weapon. Destroys the circuitry in radios, computers, anything electronic. Fries them."

Donna frowned even more. "A nuclear weapon would mean nuclear war."

Mark countered, "Or a terrorist attack."

Alice had just read an article about survivalists in Idaho who most feared the government. "What about the government taking over."

Donna laughed. "You mean more than they have?"

"No. I mean martial law."

Mark tried to regain control. "That's pretty far down the list of causes. If it happened, it would be because of something big like a terrorist attack or financial meltdown. And it wouldn't necessarily mean TEOTWAWKI."

"Is that an Indian word?" Charlie asked.

Mark shook his head. "No. It stands for The End of the World As We Know It."

"A meteor strike would do that. Is that likely?"

"Who knows? NASA has said one isn't likely."

"Would you expect them to say anything else?"

"They didn't until the last minute in the movie *Deep Impact*," Sharon noted.

Mark had also seen *Deep Impact*. "Well, what would be the point? Can't do anything about it. Can't hide. If everyone stops working, everything shuts down, and everyone starves or kills each other for the last food. If I were in charge and knew a meteor was coming, I probably wouldn't tell the world either. Telling everyone would just bring the end sooner, and it would be a lot nastier than a quick poof at the end."

"Yeah. Probably right."

Mark wondered if it was time to bring it up. He looked at Rachel. She rolled her eyes.

He could tell what she was thinking. *You're really going to bring it up, aren't you?*

His favorite subject.

Mark plunged ahead. "Well, there is one possible disaster you haven't mentioned."

"What's that?"

"A pole shift."

"Hey, I heard about that on TV recently. One of those 'how the world could end' shows."

"So what do you think, Mark?"

Mark took a breath and let it out in a huff. "I've read a lot about the possibility that the Earth occasionally does a tumble that shifts the rotational axis...you know, the place on a globe where the metal post pokes through...to somewhere else."

Jack frowned. "How could that be? Centrifugal force stabilizes the Earth. If the Earth rolled, the pole would, too."

Mark smiled. "There are theories. One is that something passing near the earth, a very large something, could exert enough magnetic force do it. Actually, the Earth as a globe wouldn't shift. Just the outer twenty to forty miles of crust would break loose and drift somewhere else."

"Why would it do that?"

"Well, the theory goes that the Mid-Atlantic Ridge is a large chunk of magnetic material and a major part of the Earth's crust. If something big enough passed by that could lock onto the Ridge magnetically, it might stop the crust from moving. The molten core would keep turning, and the crust would just break loose from the core. The crust would wrap in whatever direction it was pulled, until it stuck again to the core and came to a halt. The surface of the Earth would shift in relation to the poles. The poles wouldn't actually shift, but the surface or crust of the Earth would."

"Who dreamed that up?"

"Several sources discuss it. Some look at the evidence of such shifts."

"Really? What evidence?"

Mark continued, "Well, take the ice ages. You know the last ice age had ice down to the Nebraska-Kansas border. If you put the North Pole in the middle of Hudson Bay, the Arctic Circle comes down to the Nebraska-Kansas border. And the place where the mammoths lived was grassland in a moderate climate."

"The mammoths lived in icy areas."

"No, actually they didn't. Their bodies were found in icy areas, but the food in their mouths and stomachs came from a temperate grassland. They were flash frozen in mid-digestion."

"Flash frozen?"

"Yes. Transported from warm grassland to Arctic in the space of an hour, so the theory goes. The moist air hit cold air, formed snow that fell at a rate of feet per minute, and the mammoths suffocated where they stood upright in the snow falling over them."

"Suffocated? How do they know?"

"The males they've chipped out of the ice have erections, the classic evidence of suffocation."

"Jeeze. Where did you get all this?"

"In a book called *Worlds in Collision*, by a man named Immanuel Velikovsky. He was a very bright friend of Einstein's.

"So when did it happen?"

"One theory says pole shifts appear to happen roughly on a 3,600-year cycle. The last one happened at the time of the Exodus in Egypt and explains all the plagues, the parting of the Reed Sea, and the end of the Minoan civilization. About 7,200 years before that, Niagara Falls started cutting its way through the rock ledge it falls over. They've dated that. Assumed to be the end of the last ice age. And 3,600 years before that, a man named Noah was building his boat."

"So what's with the 3,600 years?"

"Doesn't matter. We're just talking about ways the world could end. If a pole shift were to happen on a 3,600-year cycle and explain the Exodus and Noah, then a coming pole shift might be the reason for TEOTWAKI."

"Well, how long ago was the Exodus?"

"About 3,600 years ago."

"Ah. So if shifts happen, we're due."

"Something like that."

"What would a pole shift do?"

"Before the shift, the magma in the Earth would start to roil. The Earth would get hotter. The weather would get weird, with snow in odd places, lots of rain here, drought there. Glaciers would melt. The polar ice caps would melt. Earthquakes would increase in number and severity. Volcanoes would belch and blow. Methane would leak from pockets below ground. Clouds of methane would mysteriously kill birds in the air and fish in the streams. Plates would be twisted and pulled. As plates jostled, some would dip under others, causing land to lose elevation. Land close to sea level would flood and not drain."

"Holy crap. That all sounds familiar. And then what?"

"The shift itself would be grim. If the crust moved, land would run into ocean, causing tsunamis of way more than Biblical proportions. Everyone on the coast of any continent would be drowned. Only those in the hills would avoid the deluge, and then they would have to dodge volcanoes, landslides, forest fires, earthquakes, and each other."

"Each other?"

"Yeah. The survivors wouldn't have much, and they'd be scrambling to make it to next week. Or tomorrow."

"So where do you get all this?"

"It's all over the Web, if you look for it. And I've read lots of books that talk about it. I guess, if you're looking for how the world would end, a pole shift is your ideal hypothesis."

"What do you mean by ideal?"

"Well, you have a vague feeling something bad is coming. Call it TEOTWAWKI. So you feel like preparing. If you prepare for a pole shift, you're ready for anything. That's what matters: being prepared. It's less important what the actual disaster is, if you've prepared for the Worst Imaginable Disaster Ever."

"A lot of what you've described fits what's going on now. Do you think we're headed for a pole shift?"

"I'll tell you when it happens. Here's the point. Let's say we're living right now on the edge of chaos, say 6 out of 10 on the disaster scale. So 7 would be land dropping, earthquakes worldwide, the plates tilting and jostling. Then 8 would be more of same, plus the chaos of collapsing infrastructure and agriculture. And 9 would be the last days just before the shift, when all you could do is crawl into your hole. Finally, 10 would be the pole shift. So the name of the game is *Surviving 10*."

A period of silence followed. None of the friends looked at each other. They all stared at Mark.

Abe finally spoke. "How would we do that?"

"Do everything any of the web sites talk about to prepare for an earthquake, hurricane, financial meltdown, or whatever. Plus a few more things."

"What would those few more things be?"

"Well, give me a few days to get my thoughts together. If you're really interested in Surviving 10, let's get together...say, next Saturday...to discuss it. Right now, I have a hamburger to finish."

"Where will we meet?"

He looked at Rachel, who nodded. "How about a potluck at five o'clock at our house, so we have Internet and our books handy."

With that agreed, the conversation hovered over the topic for a while, then drifted away.

Rachel leaned over to Mark and whispered, “That was smoothly done. I was worried.”

Mark smiled. Now, it begins.

TIME LEFT: FOURTEEN MONTHS, EVEN LESS

ASSEMBLING THE GROUP

Mark sent out an email during the week, giving his friends a list of web sites to look at. These highlighted the current thinking on preparedness from FEMA, the Red Cross, and the Mormons. He included a list of sites that offered supplies and equipment for emergency preparedness, hoping his friends would at least glance at the surface of the preparedness issues boiling on the Internet.

Mark and Rachel were retired. Mark had been a computer programmer and had owned his own business in the Midwest for the last 15 years of his working career. His passion all his adult life had been working wood with old tools. He'd had a big enough collection to stock a small museum, but they had sold it when they were getting ready to retire. Now he had just a small set of tools sufficient to handle the tasks of home repair and minor fabrication.

Rachel had done many things in her life, including writing and editing, and had been a senior manager for a book distributor and publisher. She and Mark had traveled a lot after retiring and ended up in Oregon. They lived in a mobile home in an over-55 retirement park on the edge of a small town at the south end of the Willamette Valley. Mark was a musician and had played fiddle in various bands. Fiddle music was an interest Mark and Rachel shared, and she was learning to play fiddle, too.

Mark and Rachel had four daughters, all grown. Jennifer lived in New York City. Jill lived in upstate New York. Cathy was going to graduate school in Georgia, and Carla lived in Austin, Texas.

Mark had once considered seminary, but now he and Rachel were not active in any church. Jill and Cathy occasionally attended church. Jennifer and Carla did not.

Mark was more idealistic, more emotional on the surface than Rachel. He cried at happy movies and often would decline to watch a sad one. And he made a hobby out of preparing for and surviving the end of the world.

Rachel had the practical mind of the CEO of some corporation. She could work through hassles that would give Mark indigestion and a headache. They were good foils for each other and good partners in a project. Rachel focused now on the preparing, without as much regard to why or for what.

She'd been in Seattle when Mount Saint Helens blew, and she'd dusted the ash off her car. She and Mark knew folks who'd been hit by hurricanes on the Gulf coast. Katrina was a call that would wake up any sensible person. Haiti and Chile fit into Mark's scenario of a run-up to pole shift.

Then there were civil and political issues. The economy. Rachel had lost her job when funding failed for a non-profit where she'd worked. Now they got by on Social Security. The country looked like it was sinking into a Second Depression.

At some deep level, she too felt something is coming.

All these thoughts swirled through Mark's mind as he and Rachel set out tables and chairs to accommodate the group that might show up to discuss Surviving 10. They hadn't asked for RSVP's and they were unsure how many might come.

They were surprised when all of their friends showed up.

The concern about preparedness seemed to be shared and fairly deep.

Donna was the first to arrive. She was the widowed owner of a small farm in the foothills of the Cascades, overlooking the south end of the Willamette Valley. Donna had a wealth of practical knowledge about livestock and farming. Her place was too small for much more than her flock of sheep and two relatively worthless dogs who made poor imitations of sheep dogs. She kept a big garden and grew a lot of what she ate during season.

The farm included the original house, which she used mostly for storage, her mobile home, a barn, a decaying cabin, another shed, and a pad with hookups for an RV. Walnut trees shaded the old house, with open ground and a vineyard to the west. To the east was timber-company forest that stretched for miles into the Cascades. The road past her place went on up and around the ridge to a half dozen homes on small plots of land.

Donna sang well and played keyboard. She was spiritual but not religious, a practical and hard-working woman.

Charlie and Paula arrived just after. Charlie was a semi-retired business executive whose hobby was woodworking. He had a phenomenal ability to make stuff quickly. He had done mission work in Central America and had a personal interest in things that would help people living in what was euphemistically called the "developing world." Among his achievements in this vein was to master the construction of the wood-saving, clean-burning "rocket stove."

Paula was a social worker and master gardener who made her own compost and sprouted her own seeds. They had a small flock of chickens, replenished irregularly when the neighborhood raccoons found new ways into the coop. Charlie attributed his good health to his daily diet of home-grown, free-range chicken eggs. The bounty from their organic garden certainly helped.

Charlie and Paula were active in their church, where Charlie was a worship leader and Paula was a lay minister.

Bill and Alice were semi-retired. Bill was a renaissance man with many skills, including woodworking and construction. His craftsmanship was meticulous, so his projects took way longer than Charlie's, but his results were as professional.

Alice was a secretary. She produced grand feasts in her kitchen, where friends gathered around to watch her perform. Their son, Rick, was nearly out of high school and well into applications to college. He did honors work in science and technology, had well-groomed friends, and actually liked his parents. It wasn't a total shock that he came with his parents to join the discussion.

Bill and Alice were not church goers. If Rick went, it was to be with friends.

Abe and Shelly were retired teachers. Abe enjoyed yard work. What he did to their place, others would call landscaping. He also exercised daily and was in remarkably good shape for his age. He could wield a skillful hammer, but he often preferred to have Charlie come over for the big construction projects. It wasn't always clear whether Charlie counted the compliment to his skill as a benefit to his back.

Shelly liked exercise as well and did yoga weekly. She and Abe traveled a bit and enjoyed going to movies and dinner out. Their daughter and her family lived in California, outside San Diego.

Abe was raised in a Jewish home. You couldn't get either Shelly or him inside any church now.

Jack and Bobbie were new to the group of friends through their friendship with Mark and Rachel. Jack worked for a timber company and had done everything from topping trees to working at the sawmill. He was a skilled musician, played guitar and had his own band, where Mark sometimes played fiddle and mandolin.

Bobbie worked for the city and supported Jack's band by making cookies for every rehearsal. Mark often said her cookies were the biggest reason he came to rehearsals. Jack, gentle soul that he was, probably believed him. Jack's daughter lived with her mother in Eugene. Their children at home were two large and goofy dogs, Roscoe and Trixie, who had changed their screen door into a screen curtain more than once.

Jack was part Native American and was active in a local tribe. He was a trained shaman and had led vision quests. His spirituality was deep and personal.

Greg and Sharon lived near Mark and Rachel in the retirement park, so their commute was short. Greg worked at the hardware store in town, and Sharon was a nurse. They had two grown sons, both married, who lived nearby. Greg was handy with tools and loved to fish. Sharon loved to cook, but her shifts at the hospital took most of her time and nearly all of her energy.

Last to come was Sara, who led the yoga class that Alice and Shelly attended. She was an office manager, sharp with numbers, and progressive with politics. Her daughter, Ashley, was ready to graduate from high school and start college. Sara said she'd invited Ashley to come with her to the potluck, but Ashley had had other plans.

Sara's spirituality focused on the Earth and mankind's responsibility to it. Her religiosity was ecumenical, enfolding what she considered to be the truths of Christianity, Buddhism, Hinduism and a little something else. A statue of Ganesh, which Wikipedia described as "the Hindu Remover of Obstacles, Lord of Beginnings, patron of arts and sciences, and deva of intellect and wisdom," sat on her desk. Her practice of yoga was more than exercise.

TIME LEFT: FOURTEEN MONTHS, EVEN LESS

MEETING OF MINDS

The conversation this evening was more focused than a week earlier. Everyone had comments on ways of preparing. And for what.

Mark and Rachel passed out various beverages, while Donna and Alice arranged the potluck offerings on a table. Then everyone grabbed plates and utensils and loaded up.

As they sat eating, Mark set the tone for the evening. “I could go on and on about a pole shift, but I'm afraid that would distract us from the really important issue of getting really well prepared for anything. The idea of a pole shift is useful to focus us on the preparation. It includes the best of every disaster: earthquake, flood, tsunami, volcanoes, forest fires, landslides, radiation, and all the economic and physical consequences of the collapse of agriculture, the destruction of our infrastructure, and the demise of our country as a political entity. Believe me, if you prepare for a pole shift, you're ready for anything.

Donna paused in mid-bite with a puzzled look. “Radiation? In a pole shift?”

“Sure. A shift would knock out all equipment, including cooling units at nuclear reactors, so the reactors and their pools full of spent fuel rods eventually would melt down, explode, and spew fallout on everyone downwind for a fair distance. The shift also does a number on facilities that store radioactive waste—oh, and I forgot to mention—facilities that store chemical agents like nerve gas.”

Several people laughed uneasily. Alice furrowed her brow. “Can anyone survive a pole shift?”

Mark was quick to answer. "Sure. If they have happened, our ancestors survived them. Several times."

Abe paused in mid-bite. "So, what we need is a big, lead box full of vegetables and water to ride it out?"

Mark laughed. "Well, not really. There are a number of things we can do. Starting with the most important one."

Everyone was silent. Mark waited. Bill took the bait. "And that would be?"

"Attitude."

"Attitude," Bill repeated. "This is beginning to sound like a sales meeting."

Mark laughed. "Well, really, attitude is key to surviving. Let me explain."

Mark picked up a book from the side table by his chair. He didn't pass it around, so the group would focus on his comments instead of reading the back of the book.

"This is *Deep Survival*, by Laurence Gonzales. Rachel and I have both read it. Now we're reading it again."

Mark continued, "Gonzales examines in scientific fashion who survives, and who dies, in all sorts of hairy situations. An experienced hunter might die while lost in the woods a single night, where a four-year-old might survive. Five people get cast adrift in the sea. Three die, but two survive. What makes the difference? Equipment, even training, didn't explain it. He started studying research into the psychology of risk taking and survival, as he puts it. In his prologue, he notes that supplies and gear don't seem to account for who survives. It's not even an issue of what's in the survivor's mind. It's the survivor's heart that matters.

"Gonzales uses a series of disasters where some die, others survive, pulling out of each a common thread. A snowmobile rider knows that there is a danger of an avalanche, but suddenly he takes off up a hill to try one more hammer-head. An avalanche starts, and he dies. Lots of experience. Good gear. Knowledge of snow. Why did he do it? Quite simply, he'd done lots of hammer-heads before, and it was fun to do them. The memory of the emotion fun was instantaneous and overrode the slower, more deliberate thinking about what to do or not to do. The emotional memory controlled the body more than the brain did.

"Lots of research shows that we operate a lot of the time at an emotional level. When we act instantaneously, we act at an emotional level, without thinking. The emotional reaction comes from a different part of the brain than calculated thought. Someone who is brain damaged might still be able to play the piano. If you've ever played a musical instrument, you remember when you first realized that your hands move to the right places in the right way without your thinking about it. That's because you've developed emotional benchmarks, burned into a different part of your brain.

"Or think about realizing you've just driven through town and don't remember stop signs or traffic...or am I the only one who ever did that?"

Everyone laughed. Bill was quick. "I was just following you."

Everyone laughed again.

Mark continued. "Gonzales describes an Army Ranger captain on a river raft trip. The raft hit a rock, and the captain went in the water. The guide tried to rescue him, but the captain laughed and pushed the guide away. He was tough and cool, strong and trained. Then he was sucked under, and he was dead, too. How could it be that a tough Army type could die like that, on his day off? Gonzales proposes that the captain's training had taught him to feel that self-sufficiency and pain were good, that having to be rescued was bad, so he had a good feeling about struggling on his own. Right up to the moment he died."

Mark continued. "So, the first point is that emotion is stronger than reason. That is important to remember, because when crisis hits, our first instinct is to react emotionally rather than think through options.

"The second point, I think, is that we keep a mental map of our environment, the way a blind person can navigate his house, or you can walk through your house in the dark. You're really walking through the map of your house in your mind. It's very subtle, and it's very helpful. Then you stay in a motel one night, wake up at 3 a.m., need to go to the bathroom, and realize your map is useless, or you go on autopilot and pee in the closet."

Everyone laughed. Donna said, "That can happen if you just rearrange your bedroom."

Lots of agreement to that.

Rachel added, "Mark and I go for lots of rides. We've noticed that the first time we go down a road, it seems to be longer and takes longer. The second trip seems to be over in maybe half the time. According to this book, we didn't have a mental map the first time, and there were lots of new images and landmarks to catalog, so our perception was that the length and time were longer. After that, the road was more familiar—and shorter."

Mark said, "Gonzales says that scientists have even found the part of the brain that creates the mental maps, and it's not the part where we do reasoning. As we navigate the world, we're either following our mental map for familiar territory, or we're drawing a new map for new territory. If we're under stress, it is much harder to draw new maps.

"There's another part of the brain that seems to drive the urge to get to a place or a goal. It's the part that says 'run' or 'get moving,' fight or flight. It's the part of our brain that responds instantly with a call to action. It also has nothing to do with reasoning."

Shelly added, "I don't see what this has to do with preparing for disaster."

Mark replied, "Well, think about it. Most of the time, we run on autopilot. We rely on mental maps. In a disaster, the maps are useless. The house you take for granted is rubble. The water faucet you depend on is dry. The electricity is off. It's raining, and you don't have a rain coat. So the mapping brain is confused and under stress, and it calls on the action brain to help out. The action brain says 'move' when logic would say 'stay put.' The action brain says 'run the snowmobile up the hill' when the reasoning brain would say 'an avalanche might happen.'

"I think the point is that we have to be aware of our mapping brain and our action brain and realize that a big part of dealing with disaster is how we respond mentally and emotionally. The emotional response to emergency is panic. And survivors seem eventually to get a grip on themselves and start reasoning a plan of action.

"Gonzales talks about a fellow who analyzed hundreds of search and rescue cases. The guy found that three-fourths of the ones who died did so in the first 48 hours. Those who die can die quickly, often of hypothermia. Some people just give up. Some get into trouble because they try to make reality conform to a mental map rather than see what's really there. Survival depends on a reasonable match of mental map to reality. It's about avoiding what's called 'woods shock,' where fear overwhelms a person who's completely lost his spatial orientation. Many who die in the woods die of confusion.

"Anybody here know Kubler-Ross's definition of the stages of grief?"

Some shook heads. Paula smiled. "Ministers and social workers know that: denial, anger, bargaining, depression, and acceptance."

Mark went on. "Right. Well, that's a pattern found in lots of contexts. It's the pattern of the brain trying to find itself after being lost. Death is a disaster, certainly, so it's no surprise that you go through the stages of grief when lost in the woods or following an earthquake.

"People in disaster are people in grief. People in grief are people in disaster. Same thing.

"Gonzales talks about a guy who made a wrong turn in Rocky Mountain National Park and got lost. He sat exposed in the rain one night with means of making shelter undisturbed in his pack. He sat in the cold, with matches in his pack. Then he got a grip. He finally made a shelter and built a fire, started to deal with his situation. He didn't give up. He accepted where he was and got about doing what he needed to do. Gonzales calls it the first rule of life: *Be here now.*

"The next thing Gonzales says reminds me of Lieutenant Spears in *Band of Brothers*, who told a soldier that the way to survive was to decide you're already dead. Gonzales says the same thing, that a survivor's toughest step is to give up hope of rescue and just move on in the present. That's the only way the brain can settle down and function.

"That is the whole point of *Deep Survival* and the lesson for us in preparing for disaster, whatever that disaster is. Get over mourning what you lost, and accept where you really are now.

"Gonzales pulled together all the steps survivors take to make it:

Look, see, and believe.Stay calm. Use humor and fear to focus.

Get organized and set up small, manageable tasks.

Be bold and cautious when carrying out tasks. Be meticulous about small steps.

Take joy in completing tasks.

Count your blessings. Be grateful you're alive.

Play, by singing, reciting poetry, anything to stimulate your mind.

See the beauty and treat the experience as a vision quest.

Develop a deep conviction that you will live.

Let go of your fear of dying.

Do whatever is necessary, have the will and the skill to use what you have.

Never give up.

"So preparing for disaster starts with understanding how the brain works during disaster, and preparing the brain to function during disaster. All the training and planning in the world is useless if the brain ignores it. So we have to be aware that we are in disaster, get a grip, and keep a grip to get beyond it."

Shelly said, "That sort of makes sense. I know grief. It's hard to go on, but you have to."

Paula added, "Well, some people don't go on. Saying 'you have to' is a personal choice, not a fact. You don't have to survive."

Mark nodded. "That really is the point. Do we choose to go on?"

Rachel said, "We've talked about taking lawn chairs to the beach if a pole shift happens, to watch the tsunami roll in. But then we get back to collecting camping equipment and reading books. In the end, it seems, we choose to survive."

Charlie said, "I did missionary work in Central America. Talk about culture shock. I can see that I had to do the remapping you talk about. After I accepted what was, it really was as normal as being here."

Mark replied, "I had the same experience in Vietnam and later working for a non-profit in India. I can see now that I pretty much accepted everything pretty quickly. I seemed to be asking *what's this* and *what's that*, living in the Now. I must have been deciding what the new 'normal' was."

Rachel asked, "So what's 'normal' in a disaster?"

Alice replied, "In Haiti, there was lots of dust, people running around, looting, no food, no water, injured people, no medical care, no direction. Then miserable camps, tarps and tents at best with the rainy season coming. And no help except from outside. What would happen if there hadn't been any help?"

"Look at New Orleans after Katrina," Rachel said. "People left on their own. No way to get out. The authorities just ran away, except for some police, and some of those stayed to loot, too. How do you get out of the way of a hurricane? The poor had no way out. You can't walk hundreds of miles."

Mark added, "And the few who tried to leave over that bridge afterwards were turned back by the deputies at the other end of the bridge. Probably a pretty common behavior."

"Nobody had food," Charlie said. "Or maybe if they did, it was under water. No water fit to drink. Nowhere to go pee or poop, and nasty water everywhere. Toilets quit and overflowed at the Superdome. Total chaos."

Mark asked, "So what lessons can we take from that?"

Abe chuckled. "Don't be in New Orleans during Katrina."

Everyone laughed.

Mark thumped his hand on the arm of his chair. "Exactly," he said. "That's the point! First of all, don't be somewhere obviously vulnerable to a disaster with a disaster heading your way. Rule Number One for disaster preparedness is *don't attend*."

Everyone laughed.

Mark prodded. "What else?"

Donna looked at Abe. "Don't plan on getting away after the disaster hits. Even if you can move, someone is likely to keep you from doing it."

Mark kept them moving. "Right. What else?"

"Don't count on being rescued. You've already said that," Abe added.

"Right. What else?"

Nobody said anything for a moment.

Mark gave a hint. "What about the ones who got away?"

Rachel responded. "They went to other cities. Many never came back. Where they went, how long they stayed, and what they lived in were largely out of their control."

"Good point," Mark said. "That's what happened when the authorities were marginally focused. Imagine what will happen when they're totally swamped by a worldwide disaster."

Mark paused and looked at the sky for a moment.

"So. Our vision of disaster is pretty accurate, thanks to Katrina, Haiti, Chile, television, and the web. Let's take Katrina. What would we do if we were in New Orleans and a hurricane was coming?"

Donna objected. "But we live in Oregon. We're more likely threatened by an earthquake than a hurricane. What good does it do to talk about hurricanes?"

Mark nodded. "Good question. Unless you have a dog like Jesse around, you have no warning of an earthquake. We're talking about preparation when you do have warning. You can see a hurricane coming. I'm assuming we'd also see a pole shift coming. So, if you have a large-scale cataclysm coming, what do you do?"

Abe was quick. "Don't attend."

Laughter all around.

"You're right," Mark added with a grin. "That's why Rachel and I are here in Oregon. We think Oregon is a relatively safe location. Moving to a safe location takes a lot of planning, a lot of time, and a major commitment of cash. Cash to move. Cash given up with jobs left behind. But being in a good place is absolutely critical. But say you're in New Orleans?"

Donna followed Mark's logic. "When the news says it's coming, leave. Then you can choose where you go. You have more control of where you'll be. You can take food with you, or plan to get it on the way."

Mark nodded. "I was on the Texas coast years ago when a hurricane approached. I was in a motel a block from the Gulf of Mexico. The mayor closed the motels, and we were ordered out of town. I took back roads to San Antonio and missed a bumper-to-bumper jam on the interstate. We got into a motel before they were all full. Taking the back roads bought us just enough time.

"Before we left, the grocery store was picked clean. I've never seen empty aisles like that before. The gas stations ran out of gas but ordered more in. The guy running the one I went to said he'd stay open as long as he could get gas and anybody needed it. He was out of regular, so I filled with premium. Everybody was in a good mood and cooperative. That was before the hurricane, so it was a fun adventure. It was easy to get away, but I had a Chevy Suburban at the time, and I could afford gas and motels."

Rachel asked, "But what if you don't own a car and can't get out?"

Charlie said, "If we're talking about planning ahead, you check around, find someone with a car, agree to pool money for fuel, fill up when the forecast says there might be a hurricane, and fill the trunk with food and water. Even have a destination in mind, a friend or relative to stay with. If the wind picks up, take off. If there's no hurricane, have a party."

"Many people don't think like that," Donna said. "They're tied to their place and family, so they don't want to go. Some may not have any money to do things like that. But it's the same for people who could afford to move. They just won't."

"And that mental map will kill them," Mark replied. "That's the point. That type of thinking, that nothing bad will happen or I have no choice, is not survivor thinking. But even people with few resources, if they spend just a moment talking about this, might be able to come up with a better plan. But they have to do it ahead of time. It's too late when the wind is blowing."

Alice asked, "What about earthquakes? If we're preparing for disaster and aren't ready to buy the idea of pole shift, but we still see the benefit of preparation, then not attending is not part of the plan. Boom. You're hit. Then what?"

Mark nodded. "I've asked myself the question. There's a lot you can do.

"What does a stewardess tell you to do about kids in case the airliner cabin loses pressure?"

Bill answered. "Put your own mask on, then help the kids."

Mark nodded. "Right. Make sure you're okay before responding to help others. So you're in an earthquake. Hopefully, we're not in any of the brick buildings around here. Say we're in our houses when it happens. What do we do?"

Bill said, "Probably the houses are a mess. So get out and look around. Worry about gas leaks. Turn off the gas. Deal with first aid issues."

Mark pushed like a school teacher. "Then what? What do we know about mental maps? What is reality after an earthquake?"

Alice responded. "Oh, the fridge is dead, along with everything in it. Grab the stuff that won't spoil, put it in the car, assuming a tree didn't fall on it."

"And?"

Abe was catching on. "Lock the car."

"Why?"

Abe shrugged. "What we know about disasters. Earthquake. Water mains broken. Gas leaking. Fires possible. No way to put them out. Food stores empty quickly. If the roads are screwed up, it may be a while before more food arrives. Convenience stores sell out of every bottled liquid. The car is your stash, your lifeboat."

Mark prodded again. "If you're hungry and thirsty, and you see food and water in a car, what do you do?"

Bill joined the dialog. "Smash a window, grab and run."

Mark came back. "If it's your car, what do you do?"

Abe's turn. "Shoot the sucker."

Laughter.

Donna spoke up. "That's what happened in Chile and Haiti."

Mark. "So what's a better plan?"

Blank looks.

Mark. "What's the first rule?"

Alice. "Get away. Don't attend."

Bill. "So, after an earthquake, relocate. Get away. Get the food and water out of sight. Avoid the fights over the dwindling supplies."

Mark. "In the event of an earthquake, what's the equivalent of putting your mask on before helping your kids?"

Bill. "Get away from the turmoil, set up a camp. Only then do you go help others."

Mark. "Right. So here in Taylorville, where do you go?"

Abe. "Almost any direction is out of town. More hills and forest south, east and west. North is pretty open."

Donna jumped in with what Mark hoped she'd say. "You could come to my place. It's out of the way. Several buildings. You could all camp out there."

Abe nodded. "That might work, if we could get there."

Mark kept the brainstorm going. "What is the biggest threat for the greatest destruction?"

Shelly. "Fire?"

Mark. "No. Think. What rivers run through town?"

Bill. "South Fork and East Fork. Oh. They both have dams just outside of town."

Mark elaborated. "Built before World War II, not up to earthquake standards. So if they go, we wish we had boats. But maybe they don't in the first jolt. But what happens after a big quake?"

Rachel. "Aftershocks."

Alice. "So if a dam didn't go with the first quake, it still could."

Mark. "So what do you do?"

Sara. "Find a hill out of the path of potential flooding in case one or both of the dams fail."

Alice. “Oh, I see your point about thinking about it ahead of time. I wouldn't have thought of that, and then I'd panic in the flood, totally unexpected. Not on my map.”

Mark. “So our earthquake plan is to get to a hill out of the way of the flood, even if there isn't one. Then what?”

Bill. “Uh, set up camp.”

Mark. “With what?”

Abe. “Well, if we go to Donna's, if we assume we'll go to Donna's, then we can plan ahead of time to have beds, cots, sleeping bags, whatever, for all of us to use.”

Alice. “What about food and water.”

Donna. “I have a well.”

Mark. “But you'd have no electricity.”

Bill. “Oh, so we stash water ahead of time. Or we bring it with us, with our food.”

Mark. “Assuming you have your own water stash. Assuming you can drive. How many bridges do you cross between your house and Donna's?”

Alice. “I don't know. Never noticed.”

Donna. “There aren't any bridges on my map.”

Mark. “How do you get to Donna's without a car?”

Abe. “Foot, bicycle.”

Mark. “If that's the case, what do you bring with you?”

Abe. “What you can fit in your pack.”

Mark. “What pack?”

Alice frowned. “This is getting pretty deep. But I can see the value in thinking through it. You certainly need to think about this stuff.”

Rachel. “And decide to do something about it.”

Donna. “And then do it.”

Alice. “It's easier to get started if you're not alone.”

Shelly. “Is the preparation for an earthquake the same as the prep for a hurricane?”

Mark. “Some of it. More in the way that earthquake prep would help in case of a hurricane. Maybe not so much the other way.”

Shelly. “So best to start with earthquake prep and go from there?”

Mark felt he'd finally gotten the point across. “That's a plan.”

Abe. “So, how do we do that?”

Mark. “There are lots of books. I've good a box full of them. There are three or four that have really influenced how I think about and prepare for TEOTWAWKI, The End of the World As We Know It. If you have time, I highly recommend that you read them. Being informed is the first step in preparation.”

"What are the books?"

"First is Les Stroud's book." Mark picked it off the table beside him. "The title is *Survive! Essential Skills and Tactics To Get You Out of Anywhere—Alive*. It's the best collection I've found that has in one place all the stuff I've gotten from other books and my own experience. Highly readable. Just enough information on lots of topics. I'll have my copy in my bug-out bag."

Bill. "What's a bug-out bag?"

Rachel jumped in. "Everything you really think you'll need if you have to bug out—run away—with little or no warning. On foot. Your survival kit."

"What are the other books?"

"The next three are fiction, actually science fiction of a sort, that can help get into mind the nature of people in disaster and how survivors survive. The first is *Dies the Fire* by S.M. Sterling. It's set right here in Oregon, just north of Eugene. The big punch line there is that only a strong group, ideally one with a service-to-other or STO orientation, survives. The second book is *One Second After*, by William Fortschen. The third is a story for teenagers called *Life as We Knew It*, by Susan Pfeffer, about a town hit by a totally unprecedented change in climate. Similar punch lines, and all pretty good descriptions of how society crumbles in the face of starvation. But again, those with a service-to-other orientation prevail."

Bill. "What's with this service-to-other bit?"

Mark. "Well, I ran into the idea on the Internet. Every human being has an orientation regarding self and others. Many—in my view, most—are oriented to service to self. They think of themselves, Number One, most of the time. They play to win, to gain, and don't mind if others lose in the process. They might even enjoy seeing others lose. They see winning and losing as the natural order. I'm sure you can think of many people like that.

"Service-to-other people think about others first most of the time. They'll tend to like the *Seven Habits* of Steven Covey, especially the win-win part. They help others, go out of their way. They believe in cooperation, mutual aid, paying it forward. They don't compete as well, so they rarely get into positions of authority.

"I think you folks are primarily service-to-other or STO types. And I consider that a compliment."

Rachel brought the discussion back to the books. "Another book would be *The Road*, by Cormac McCarthy, which could be another view of the same situation described in *One Second After*."

Mark smiled at her and continued. "There's a lot of stuff on the web. The Mormons have totally mastered the subject."

He picked up a pile of papers and began to pass them around. "Take one and pass 'em on. This is a compilation of stuff from several good sources.

"What we're talking about is earthquake preparation. The core of it is what everyone calls a 72-hour kit, a bug-out bag, if you will, enough to keep you going for 3 days. Food and water and anything else you really need. You can buy them or make them. Lots of places sell them. This document comes from the ground-zero experts on earthquakes, San Francisco. They call their site 72hours.org, no surprise. You can print the entire site to a PDF with one click. It's a good place to start."

Bill asked, "Why 72 hours?"

Charlie grinned. "That's how long it takes to recover from a major earthquake."

Everyone laughed.

"Tell Haiti that."

Many frowned. Nobody laughed.

Mark went on. "Everyone talks about 72-hour kits. The San Francisco folks say that's how long it would take to get major services going again. Uh-huh. Or you could say that's about all you can fit in a standard back pack, which is nearer the truth. Or it might be that authorities on the subject figure you'd freak out if they said 'you need a 3-month supply of stuff'.'It clearly took a lot longer than 72 hours to get things going in New Orleans after Katrina."

Alice asked, "I don't see the point of a 3-day kit when you're sitting in a house full of food. Maybe if you're on a hike, but why at home?"

Bill had an answer. "Well, if you look at the pictures from Haiti or Chile, you see a lot of folks not at home. Their homes collapsed. Everything was buried. Our house is wood, so we might get stuff out of it, if it didn't burn. But then, the 3-day kit would have been in the fire, too."

Donna had a idea and sort of lit up when it came to her. "Well, if I had a 3-day kit, I'd put it in the pickup. I'd still have it if I was at home. I'd sure need it if I weren't, and then I'd have my truck, because that's the only way I wouldn't be home."

Mark agreed. "Ours are in our van. Even if an earthquake knocked it over, hopefully we could still get in to the packs."

Rachel added, "This isn't about being absolutely prepared with precisely what you need to get by a foreseen disaster. This is about improving the odds. Make a plan. Have a month's supply—even a year's supply—at home, and a week's supply in the car, and 3 days supply in a pack you can run with."

Mark pointed to the east. "Look. We live on the river 3 miles downstream from a 70-year-old dam that wasn't built to withstand earthquakes. If we get a big one, we have to assume the dam went or is gonna go. So, no matter what happens initially, we're not going to stay in our house, if we have an earthquake. Maybe the dam holds for the first one, but it could go in an aftershock.

"So if the ground heaves, we're leaving. How much we take depends. Our van is loaded. Our bug-out kit is in it, handy if we're at the house. Maybe we load food, if we think we have time. But we're out of that house and up a hill. If the bridges are down, we have one way out. If they're still up, we have four ways, but two of those lead into the flood plain. Two roads lead to country. Two lead to a city full of desperate people. Don't think so. You need to be flexible."

Alice's eyebrows went up. "Wow, I hadn't thought of any of that. There are two rivers into town, with dams on both. We're downstream from both those dams. If either one went, we'd be surrounded by water."

Mark replied, "And you can't drive through flood water. If you decide you can't stay, you go, and you probably go on foot, with your 3-day kit—aren't you glad you have one—on your back. If you're not in flood water, do what we plan to do, load the car, and head in the direction of some high ground, ideally in the direction you prefer to go, as soon as you can. Know which way that is, expect streets to be messed up, and keep alternate routes in mind."

Rachel picked up the thread. "You can see why we say the first preparation is mental. Start by realizing it's a mistake, possibly a deadly mistake, to think nothing bad will happen, or things will be okay or the government will help us, or that it's silly to prepare."

Charlie said, "I'm on the river, too. But it's never flooded my land, and the barn is 3 feet higher than the house. I figure I'll be all right there."

Mark shook his head. "Charlie, the dam's always been up the river from you. Of course it hasn't flooded. If the dam goes, you're talking a wall of water. How high? Who knows. Supposed we're talking August, when the Corps has the lake full for all the water skiers. There wouldn't be anything left of your place but the foundations. The last place I'd be is at your place after an earthquake."

Charlie shrugged, but the look on his face admitted the truth.

Bill spoke. "So where do we get a bug-out bag?"

Mark replied. "You can buy them, but I recommend you make one. Look at the list of stuff, go find it, and learn to use each piece. If you buy a bag, you just throw it in the closet. If you make a bag, you consider each item, shop around, buy a good one—maybe better than the one in a commercial kit—and learn to use it. Everything in our kits was available right here in town.

"Here's what I think we should do: each of us goes out and gets a kit, bought or made, in the next week. Then we get back together for show and tell."

Abe nodded. "Good plan. When do we meet next?"

The group proposed various dates and times and decided on one. Everyone had a schedule conflict, and no time fit everyone's schedule. They picked a time that only one couldn't make. Okay, there are priorities. Preparing for disaster, even for a group seriously considering it, wasn't everyone's highest concern. Yet.

As he left, Charlie paused, smiled at Mark. "You don't look happy."

"Well, I think this is serious business. I think it should come first. I think it's a mistake not to take it very seriously."

"Well, it's easier to say when you're retired. Some of us have obligations. We don't have as much flexibility."

"But the schedule conflict this time was with another group. We're talking evening meetings."

"Life goes on. This is a 'maybe' thing. We all have obligations to other groups. And other interests."

"And other consequences. I just think it's unfair to others in a group not to be ready to carry your own weight. Suppose this comes down tonight. We all gather, and everyone has a kit but one. Now we're obligated to share, but someone has become an avoidable burden."

"True. But you assume a lot. First, maybe it won't happen. Or it does. Slim chance, but it does, but it's small, and nothing happens. Or it's really, really big, and we don't gather for three days, or a week, and all the stuff in our three-day bags is already gone. There's more than one type of burden, and more than one type of disaster. We're talking percentages. We're not talking 100%, so our participation doesn't have to be 100% either. Lighten up, Mark."

"Well, I agree with you, but I respond to the percentages differently. You say relax, we can prepare eventually. Over time. No rush. I'm just saying prepare first, then relax."

Mark continued. "Do you have a smoke alarm in your house?"

"Sure. Of course I do."

"When did you put it in?"

"Right after I moved in. I always have one."

"Why? Have you had a fire?"

"No. I see your point. But you're not talking about a smoke alarm. You want us to get a fire truck."

"Ah. So what would you consider to be a good smoke alarm for an earthquake?"

Charlie frowned, looked away.

Mark waited. "Look. The Red Cross. FEMA. The Mormons. Every expert on disaster. The news. Katrina. Haiti. Chile. Millions of folks all over the country that went without power for days last winter when snow fell on every damned state in the country. Even Florida, for gods' sake. Places in the South went four days. In the last year, there have been millions of people who could have used at least a little disaster prep. I don't think it is wise or mature to bury your head in sand. You carry chains. You have jumper cables. Why not an emergency kit?"

Charlie looked at him. Nodded. "Okay. You win. At least we're agreed to meet regularly and talk about this."

Mark smiled. "I'm just trying to share with friends what Rachel and I have already done. I think it's time. I think there's already smoke in the house, and it's time for alarms to go off."

Charlie nodded. "I'll see you next week. I'll have my kit. No. We'll have two kits. Paula, too."

"Thanks, Charlie. Glad you're part of our group."

TIME LEFT: THIRTEEN MONTHS

SESSION AT THE HOUSE

The group gathered. Some had backpacks. Some had bags full of stuff fresh from the store.

Mark and Rachel got out their kits and spread them out on the floor. The group gathered around.

Rachel picked up a compass. "I forget what's in the kit. I'm surprised every time I spread it out. Tell me why I have a compass."

Mark looked at it. "Suppose, over the long run, we decide that we need to get to the ocean to live off fish there. Which way is it?"

"That's easy. Down the river. Don't need a compass for that."

"No. The Willamette flows north. It's over 100 miles to Portland, through a valley that will be flooded. When we drive out to the coast now, we take the road that goes down the Umpqua, but we have 30 miles to Elkton before we reach it."

"But that's just south on the Interstate, then west through Drain. We would follow the road."

"Um, bad idea, I think. First off, there will be lots of reasons not to follow the road. Think about *The Road*, for one. Scary book. Scared people walking along the road. Scared people living along the road. Some taking from others. Everyone defending what they've got. And after an earthquake, some of the bridges will be down. Maybe all of them. And that road has landslides in good years. It may be totally gone in places. Following a road is not necessarily a good way to navigate.

"Think back to the Oregon trail. And the railroads. They followed rivers. What river goes from here to the coast?"

"If we don't include the Willamette, there isn't one."

"Not right here. But there is one not too far. The Smith River. It runs about as straight as anything that isn't a road. You catch it in the next valley west, south of Loraine. Say you roughly follow the road to Loraine. Moving slowly. Up hill. Down. Come to a road, which winds all over. Which way do you go? A compass can confirm that you're going in roughly the right direction to find the valley and the river."

Alice was quick. "But if there was a pole shift, which way does the compass point then? How can you depend on it?"

Mark was pleased she'd asked. "There will still be a north pole. The compass will still point to it. Only the surface of the Earth moved. The magnetic core still pulls the compass needle the same direction. Only the land is oriented differently. Say something that is north of us now measures to be roughly west of us after the shift. I figure we need to take some bearings on prominent landmarks now, make a diagram that shows where they are now. If we had a shift, then we'd take new bearings on the same landmarks. Those should confirm how much the map has twisted. We have a book of topographical maps for the entire state in our bag. We twist the maps to match the shift and set off on a new bearing that aims us at the Smith River.

"At least, having a compass gives us that option."

Alice shook her head. "Sorry I asked. Navigation will be your job. But this is our three-day kit. We don't need a compass in the first three days."

Mark replied. "But this may be our only kit. Three days is just a name, not a prediction. I think we need to have in it the most critical things we'll really need if we have a major disaster and this is all we save. You know: TEOTWAWKI. The End of the World As We Know It. SHTF. Shit Hits the Fan.

"In fact, I'm beginning to think about what to have in my pocket in case I can't even get to the three-day bag. Call it a hip pocket survival kit."

Shelly looked through the stuff laid out on the floor. "Why all this stuff?"

Mark said, "Three reasons: survive, keep up, keep going."

"Some of the stuff is what you'd need to survive in the moments after a major disaster. Your first response kit. This includes a small first aid kit, dust mask for volcanic dust, goggles for wind-blown debris, hatchet, flashlight, whistle so we can signal each other, crowbar, good shoes. Stuff that equips you to be a rescuer.

"Some of the stuff is to allow you to keep up with what's happening. The portable radio, rechargeable batteries, solar battery charger, map of the area, and the compass, so you can continue to know where you are if you have to move.

"The rest of the stuff is to keep you going on with life: water, food, sanitation, clothing, and shelter.

"Let's face it. Your kit is only enough for a few days. After that, you need to be rescued, or you need to start improvising. If you're lucky, your pre-disaster home is still there in some fashion, and you can draw on your stash of food and supplies. Or maybe not. We'll get to the 'not' later. For now, we're talking the first few days.

"Water is the big problem. You can go for days without food, but you need water soon and often to keep going. But you have to assume that any water you can find is tainted. So you either filter, treat, or boil all the water you end of drinking.

"Our kit contains as small filter straw for a single bottle, a batch water filter for larger volume, some water treatment tablets, and a water boiling kit: a pot and some matches. All the options you have any reason to expect. Forget carrying all the water you'll need—a gallon weighs eight pounds. You'll be lucky to have a canteen-full. You need to stay hydrated, drinking often, so you need to be able to make drinkable water in large quantities over time.

"The Army says fill your canteen and drop in some tablets. They assume you have a continuous supply of the little suckers. One bottle will last maybe a week. Then what? How many bottles do you have? No matter, you'll run out. Besides, the pills go out of date, and the water tastes bad.

"Then there's filtering. Filters give out after a while. They'll likely last you longer than a bottle of pills.

"Then you're down to boiling, which isn't hard if you make a habit of it. But boiling is tough if you're on the move or for some reason can't or don't want to light a fire.

"So, I'd say use pills or your filter if you're mobile, boil water when you're 'in camp.' That way, the stuff you can't replace lasts as long as possible."

Everyone nodded. A few scribbled notes. Donna and Alice knelt down to examine the kit on the floor.

Bill decided to share recent news with the group. "I saw a newscast about a city in Massachusetts that had a problem with their water supply during a flood. The mayor said 'boil water,' but the people in town went nuts instead, ransacking the stores for bottled water. Like they didn't know how to boil water. Give me a break."

Charlie leaned forward. "I'm really up on boiling water. Their problem was they didn't trust the process, and they *really* didn't know how to do it. How long do you boil? A minute? Fifteen minutes? Three minutes? Nobody told them how long, so they didn't trust boiling."

Donna said, “Okay, so how long? Just how do you do it?”

Charlie said, “You only need to pasteurize water to kill the intestinal bugs in it. That means raising the temperature of water to roughly 150 degrees Fahrenheit. You don't have to boil it, which is 212 degrees.”

Donna frowned. “Oh, come on. How do I know when water is 150 degrees?”

Charlie looked smug. “Simple. Just heat water until it starts to boil. When you see the bubbles start, you're done. By the time the water is cool enough to use, it's been at 150 degrees or more long enough to make it safe to drink.”

Mark had discussed this with Charlie. “There's also a cute device called a WAPI, or water pasteurization indicator, which will tell you when the water is pasteurized. It has wax in it that melts at the right temperature. When the wax melts, you're done. Only problem I see with that is you could easily lose your WAPI.”

Everyone howled.

Mark went on, “You can't lose seeing water start to boil. So I agree with Charlie that just bringing water to boil is the way to go.

“Then there's the problem of public health. Sanitation. You boil a pot of water, and some kid sticks a dirty cup in it and wastes all of it. You need to treat boiled water like gold. Pour it into containers with lids, and pour out to serve. Never dip. The whole process becomes something of a Japanese Tea Ceremony. If you don't, you might as well drink dirty water and learn to deal with the shits.

“Here are some other points about sanitation. You need to boil the water you wash dishes with. The water you brush your teeth with. The water you wash your hands with. You'll run out of antiseptic wipes and gels. But there's no reason you should run out of boiled water.”

Abe looked at the stuff on the floor and asked, “What about a tent? I don't see a tent.”

Mark replied, “Tents are heavy, and they're never big enough. Our approach is like the Army's. Each person carries a tarp, just like the shelter-halves soldiers use, and some light cord. The tarps vary in size but are at least six feet by eight feet, large enough to cover several people. Some could carry even larger ones. With a big enough team's collection of tarps, you can practically stitch together a house, using sticks, boards, poles, trees, whatever you find, for support. You can use a tarp to catch rain water or reflect the heat of a fire. If you have to move your camp, fold up the tarps, wind up the cord, and leave the sticks behind.”

Abe said, “You think maybe we should try all this maybe once.”

With a little discussion, they agreed on a field day to try their kits.

TIME LEFT: LESS THAN THIRTEEN MONTHS

PRACTICE AT THE LAKE

The group gathered in a small grove of trees around a fire ring at the lake. Everyone had a pack of some sort with a version of the kit. Several joked that they'd met in the camping aisle at Wal-Mart.

"Hey, everybody," Mark called. "Name of the game is 'shelter, fire, water.' Let's build a camp."

Each person brought out a tarp and their package of clothes line. Then they just stood and looked around.

"What do we do?" someone asked.

"Wrap yourself in your tarp," someone replied. Laughter echoed in the trees.

"Build a house," Mark replied. "We need a kitchen, a bathroom, a place to hang out, and a place to sleep."

"Why not just sleep in the hangout?" Shelly asked.

"In chaos, you need to work in shifts. Someone needs to be awake and on guard 24-7, so the night guards need relatively undisturbed sleep during the daytime. So the bedroom needs to be away from the hangout and the kitchen, the smells and noise, with shade from the sun and wind."

They discussed the options and got started. The kitchen would be where the fire ring was. The wind was out of the north, so they decide the hangout and bedroom would be north of the fire ring to avoid the smoke.

For the hangout, they strung a large tarp between three trees and a rock, with the low flap upwind. They stashed all their packs in the hangout, then went to work on the bedroom.

They selected a space roughly 30 feet from the hangout, rigged a roof and walls on the east, north and south for shade.

The bathroom was just for discussion, since the park management would frown on their digging a hole. Using the National Outdoor Living School (NOLS) guidelines for cat holes, the most primitive type of latrine, they selected a site about 200 feet away, downwind from the camp, and away from the lake. For security, the site was visible from the main camp. They didn't dig the hole, but they set up an enclosure, using one tarp for a roof and one for privacy.

Then the kitchen.

Abe asked, “Should we put the tarp over the fire pit? Then we could cook even in the rain.”

Mark nodded. “Good idea. Cook under cover, but with plenty of ventilation. If we were just preparing for an earthquake, it might not be as important. But say we're preparing for a pole shift. There would be rain. Lots of it. For a long time. So we need to be able to cook in the rain.”

There were only two trees near the fire ring, not enough for a real structure. So the group looked for some branches. The options were slim, since the park staff had policed the campground. Mark explained that in a real emergency, they could go ahead and cut some poles. Bill came back with two branches, big smile on his face. All he said was, “Don't ask.”

With the poles and two rocks, the crew rigged the tarp over the fire pit.

Now, fire and water.

Both Mark and Charlie had studied the cook stove research available on the Web, especially the work done at Aprovecho Research Center in Cottage Grove, Oregon. So they knew about the advantages of the rocket stove. The rocket stove uses far less wood and burns cleaner —virtually smokeless—than a wood fire usually built in the fire rings. Mark had bought a factory-built rocket stove designed by Aprovecho and sold in the US by StoveTec and EcoZoom, just to see how it worked.

Mark explained, “After a pole shift, there will be lots of rain, and dry wood will be hard to find. So you want the wood you have to go as far as possible. There's no better way to do that than a rocket stove.

"Over time, we'd have to be able to build rocket stoves. For now, we'll work with this factory-built model. It's as good as it gets for a wood-burning rocket stove. This one is a good example, but it's too heavy to haul very far."

Mark set the green stove on the fire ring grill and inserted the fuel shelf into the stove's fuel door. He pointed to the mass of ceramic inside the stove.

"The first thing about a rocket stove is the combustion chamber. This one looks like brick, but it actually is lighter than water. It would float if you dropped just the chamber in water. That means it insulates. Insulating the fire means it lights easier, gets hotter with less wood, and more of the heat goes into the pot on top. I saw a stove made the same shape, but out of cast iron. The iron absorbed all the heat, and you couldn't keep the fire lit. So watch this."

Mark put five small sticks side by side on the fuel shelf with just their tips touching in the center of the stove. Then he took some small twigs, dry grass, and a pine cone and dropped them into the stove from above.

"The second thing about a rocket stove is the fuel shelf. It allows air to come in below the fire, be pre-heated and make the fire hotter. No ashes and coals to choke the air flow."

One match, and the grass caught with a brief puff of smoke. The twigs followed, and the pine cone lit. In less than 20 seconds, the five fuel sticks were burning, and a jet of smokeless fire rose from the top of the stove.

Abe said, "I see why they call it a rocket. It looks like a propane stove."

Mark smiled. "And you can make it hotter by adding a stick, or cooler by pulling a stick out. Five sticks are as much as I've ever needed. You can boil water with five sticks. Three will keep a pot simmering. It's really as easy to control as a propane stove, and in our experience, actually hotter. When we're camping and need hot water, we use this baby instead of our propane stove. And you can bake bread in a dutch oven set on top—no coals required."

As the wood burned, Mark pushed the fuel sticks in. By the time a stick was totally burned up, he'd replaced it with a new one.

"No smoke means you won't breathe smoke, have red eyes, runny nose, or get pneumonia. Smoke kills over a million people a year worldwide. Cooking without smoke is healthy. And it means nobody across the lake knows we're cooking here.

"Small sticks for fuel mean we can cook with stuff that falls out of trees every night. Dead limbs and such. You don't have to cut down a tree and split it up to cook. No trees falling mean less effort to cook food. It also means one less thing to give you away to folks you don't want to find you.

"All benefits of a rocket stove."

Charlie added, "You can make big ones and boil lots of water. You can make one with a wok or a griddle. The idea's the same. Insulate the fire. Fuel shelf. Air from below. Small sticks burning at their tips."

Bill said, "Let me try."

Mark pulled out each of the sticks and ground out its flames. The fire was out in a few seconds.

"Notice how little ash remains," Mark said.

Abe said, "Wow. That was quick and easy. No smoke even when you put out the fire. To put out a typical fire, you'd have to douse it with water or dirt, and it would smoke like a...well...chimney."

Everyone laughed. A few nodded.

Over the next two hours, everyone had a chance to light the rocket stove, tend the fire, and put it out.

They filled small pots with water and noted how long it took to bring it to boil, and they decided that a rocket stove could boil drinking water quickly with very little fuel. They tossed around ideas about how they might organize the day around lighting the fire, pasteurizing drinking water and wash water, and cooking.

"I can see that we really should try all of this for several days," Alice said. "Wish we had the time."

"We usually make time for the urgent, rather than the important," Bill replied. "Is this important?"

"I suppose so," Alice sighed. "But not today. We have to go."

The group packed up the tarps and stove, cleaned the site, and agreed to meet again soon to try it all for several days.

TIME LEFT: TWELVE MONTHS

MARK'S QUANDARY

Mark stewed on Bill's comment. For him, preparing a group for disaster was highly important. But it was hard even for him to say it was urgent on a given day.

Mark believed a pole shift really was coming. And soon.

Maybe poles don't shift, and there really were ice ages. Maybe poles do shift, but the next shift won't happen for a thousand years. The idea was not mainstream science. But there were enough examples of science distorted by vanity, money, ego and hubris, that Mark didn't any longer consider science flawless on the subject. Scientists were, after all, human, even if they sometimes thought themselves gods.

He'd watched several shows on TV that explicitly mentioned pole shift as a possible disaster approaching mankind. If the idea had made it to TV, at least a few others took the idea very seriously.

Mark was even taking a chance with his own group of friends. Pole shift wasn't exactly conventional wisdom. He'd managed to get the idea on the table without alienating his friends. Preparing for a pole shift was perhaps the best way to focus preparation for any disaster.

The proposition: people on Earth fall into three groups. Those who are oriented to service to self, those who are oriented to service to others, and the undecided who could go either way, depending on events. That idea was for Mark almost as great a revelation as the idea of pole shifts itself. It explained much that had happened in his own life, and it explained better than any other theory what was going right or wrong, mostly wrong, in the world.

Surviving 10

There was no question in Mark's mind that it was good to be service-to-other and bad to be service-to-self. The people in the group Mark had pulled together were generally unselfish. That's why he'd selected them. Or perhaps, why they were his friends in the first place. Mark would call them thoughtful, even though they all had stuff they worried about.

Mark had read about pole shifts for ten years or more but had not told more than one or two about the idea.

He was deeply influenced by several sources on the subject.

First, there was the body of evidence presented by Immanuel Velikovsky, his first encounter with the idea of a pole shift.

Then there was the work of Zecharia Sitchin, scholar of the libraries from Sumer, the world's first great civilization. Mark had read all but two of his books about what he found there.

And there were other books, like White's study, *Pole Shift*, and Hapgood's *Path of the Pole*. Mark had read them all.

There was evidence all around.

But what had brought it all into focus was ZetaTalk, a site on the Internet that was too big, too detailed, to be a fabrication, and it had been on line for over ten years, updated daily, with a steady thump of predictions and evidence. ZetaTalk was specific, authoritative on the certainty of a pole shift to happen very soon. It's drumbeat of evidence matched the daily headlines.

ZetaTalk's premise was, on its face, absurd: aliens from Zeta Reticuli were warning a woman in Wisconsin of an impending pole shift, urging mankind to get ready. But the more he studied the material, the more Mark believed it.

The Zeta message was unequivocal. A large planet five times the size of Earth was approaching. Its mass disturbed the Earth's magma, causing it to roil, heating the Earth, melting the polar cap, calving bergs off Greenland, collapsing the ice shelves of Antarctica. Far more damage than carbon dioxide could cause by itself. The planet was getting closer daily, and the Earth's crustal plates flexed in its pull. Plates in the Pacific were tipping, causing floods that never drained in Pakistan and unprecedented floods in Australia. The Philippine islands were slowly sinking, along with Indonesia. The press blamed rain, but there wasn't enough rain to explain the flooding. And some of the flood water was salty, suggesting the sea was invading the land. You could see that in some satellite photographs.

According to ZetaTalk, when the as-yet-unannounced Planet X was close enough, it would lock the Mid-Atlantic Ridge, temporarily halting the Earth's rotation, just as it had 3,600 years earlier for Joshua at the battle of Gibeon. Planet X caused all the plagues in Egypt and triggered the explosion of Thera that wiped out the Minoan civilization. The tsunami from that blast pulled away the sea for Moses and sent it back to drown the Pharaoh's army.

Planet X explained the deviations in the orbits of the planets that had driven astronomers a century ago to search for a cause. The search had ended when they found Pluto, only to be resumed when a probe got to Pluto and found it wasn't large enough to cause the mischief in the planets. There still had to be something else.

NASA knew about Planet X. Both Sitchin and ZetaTalk said so. They'd found it in 1983. One news article announced it, the only news article, before the news disappeared from sight, buried by authorities. Too scary, to dangerous to share with the populace. But there had been that article. Sitchin had found it, and Mark had a copy. NASA's entire space program was focused on watching Planet X so the Powers That Be, the PTB, would know what to do, and when. The PTB were building bunkers and stashing supplies they weren't planning to share with the public. Deep Impact for real. That made the Zetas mad. ZetaTalk claimed that Planet X now appeared on photos from several satellites, including SOHO and Stereo. Mark had seen the photos.

Now Mark had finally decided there was enough evidence, historical and geologic, from floods to earthquakes and turmoil around Indonesia, viewed through the lens of ZetaTalk, to persuade him to speak out. If he cared for others, he had to say something, to get his friends ready. And so he had. And they had listened. He was a bit surprised and a bit wary.

He'd told them about pole shifts. But mostly as a theoretical exercise.

Would he tell them about Sitchin and especially about ZetaTalk? Would that help or hurt?

And did it matter, if they did prepare as he proposed?

And what would they do in a disaster? Or worse, the ultimate disaster, a pole shift?

If ZetaTalk was right, he'd find out soon enough.

TIME LEFT: TWELVE MONTHS

LETTER TO THE KIDS

"What's the matter?" Rachel probed.

Mark looked at nothing across the room. "Was it that obvious?"

"You've been chewing on something since we got back."

"Well, we've told our friends, but..."

"The kids."

"Yeah."

"I figured you'd tell them sooner or later. Why haven't you?"

"It was easy for us to pick up and move. Nothing left to lose. Close to retirement. They're so totally wrapped up with starting lives. They're all in towns they chose deliberately. Carla is in Austin by choice. Kids, school, career. Living her life. Jennifer in New York City, for gods' sake, a very bad place to be during the shift. Jill in upstate New York, at the end of one of the Finger Lakes. You can see the rip in aerial photos. Cathy in Georgia with millions of potential refugees."

"Well, do you really believe in pole shifts?"

"Do you?"

"I asked you. You're the one who brought it up. You're the one who told me. Why me and not the girls?"

"I guess I'm afraid of what they might think. I've wanted them to think well of me."

"Why would telling them change that? It didn't change how I thought of you. You didn't just say 'ZetaTalk told me there would be a pole shift.' You took your time and laid out the case, and you were clear you weren't one-hundred percent convinced. We weighed the evidence. And we made our own choices. We moved here because of that. Oregon looked good in the safe locations list. Why can't you do the same for our kids?"

"Harder to do. We were together. We had time. They're spread out all over."

"Well, if you believe, you should tell them. Why don't you write a letter to them?"

"A letter? You mean a small book."

"Whatever. You could send them links to all the stuff on the internet. But what would be best if you told them what you yourself believe, why you believe it, and why, most of all, you're telling them. Leave it open that if they want to know more, they need to ask. Then you've done what you can."

"You think I should do that now?"

"What do you think?"

"Why haven't you told them? Why is my job to do it?"

"You know why. You have the details. You have the years of study and conversation. And mostly, you have the integrity. I'd mess up the details. All I know is I'm with you, and we're doing what you think we should do. I'm a follower in this. You are the leader. It's clear when we're with the group. You owe the same to your kids."

"Okay. You're right. I'll write a letter."

Mark drafted an email to his daughters and sent it to Rachel for her blessing. He trusted her wisdom and her skill with words.

Rachel looked up from her laptop. She'd just finished reading the draft of Mark's letter to the kids.

She sighed.

"Well, I like the way you make it okay to prepare without having to buy the pole shift idea. I think they should all be prepared. I'd like to give each of them a 72-hour bag."

Mark knew that Rachel was not necessarily as convinced about pole shifts, but she was most definitely convinced about the need to prepare.

The news was increasingly full of reasons, the most recent the severe flooding in Australia. Wild weather.

Mark smiled. "The problem with giving a bag is the lack of buy-in. Put it in the closet and forget it. I suppose that's better than nothing, but I'd rather they'd each think about it and put their own together."

Rachel continued. "I also like the way you built up to the idea of pole shifts. That's pretty kooky for most. But to a great extent, you're really laying your own integrity and common sense on the line."

"Like planting a seed. Can't make the growth happen. I just think this is something I finally have to reveal, to say, to go on the record. I've been into this stuff for 10 years, and my trust in it has only grown. There's finally enough going on with earthquakes and weather and stuff that I have decided to say something."

"I also think it was a good idea to just make them aware and tell them to watch the news. Let events decide. You planted the idea, and preparing in general is a good idea. They'll each have to decide on their own how much to believe and what to do."

That night, Mark copied the text into a fresh email, addressed it to the kids, hesitated...and clicked "Send".

Then nothing. For a week.

Rachel began to think the lack of response was more rude than foreboding. "They should at least say 'Thank you'." Mark was inclined to suppose that the apparent length of the email might delay their even reading it.

He was right. One by one, the kids responded.

Jill lived in upstate New York near Ithaca. She called, and they discussed what ZetaTalk had to say about the area. According to Mark's sources, that area was better off than many. They talked about preparing. Jill agreed that it would help get through a snow-related power failure, if nothing else. The parting was cordial.

Next to check in was Carla in Austin, via email. She intended to hang with her city. Mark wrote back that flooding at the coast would drive survivors into Austin, that the result would make the Mexico drug wars look like a minor skirmish. Mark advised moving away from Texas well before moving was impossible. Still, he knew that she had just gotten life and family together there and likely would still be there whenever whatever happened. He also knew that she thought he was crazy as a loon. But he'd done what he felt he had to do.

Jennifer in New York City called Mark. In answer to her first question, Mark assured her that he was dead serious. She'd looked at ZetaTalk and was astounded by the amount of information on the site. It would be intimidating to someone who was seeing it for the first time. For her, the proposition was a real challenge. She'd invested so much for so long in a career in New York City. She didn't own a car, and she had no idea how she'd get out of the city without public transportation.

Mark suggested that she just keep an eye on the news. If a tsunami hit Europe or Indonesia sank—two pretty momentous events that would be hard to deny—then she might consider going to see her sister in Ithaca and just never come back. Go while the U.S. was still mostly functioning, before folks were forced to walk out of a shattered city. Their conversation was low key. It was clear Jennifer was trying to get her head around the whole thing.

Mark was more sure after their talk that pinning action to major events around the world was a good way to proceed. Let events trigger action. He just hoped action would be possible following those events.

When Cathy called from Georgia, all she said was that if the major events started happening, she'd just go home to Missouri. Mark told her that Missouri would be as bad as Georgia, and he read her what the ZetaTalk site had to say. In fact, their dire prediction for Missouri had a lot to do with Mark and Rachel's decision to move from there. Mark suggested instead a visit to her sister in Ithaca, but Cathy was concerned about her dad and step mom in Missouri.

Ah, Mark thought, and so it goes. Her dad was deeply religious. A lot of the ZetaTalk story would conflict, perhaps violently, with much of what he believed from the Old Testament. Mark knew the texts, but he read them in a totally unorthodox way, to say the least. A lifetime of assumptions and stories is hard to disassemble. And it was now for Cathy, in her own way, to decide whom to tell and what to say as well about all of this. Like passing a rumor.

Mark wondered what the other kids were saying, if anything, to their friends.

He hoped they'd just forward what he'd written, to keep as much intact as possible, to keep the context the same. But then, it was only Mark's own understanding of all the stuff, and he knew the Zetas weren't talking to him every week.

Not that he remembered, anyway.

TIME LEFT: ELEVEN MONTHS

STARTING AT THE FARM

The group met regularly to review their preparing.

Donna's offer to have the group come to her farm made sense. The farm was well above the valley, clear of any floods from any dams, and it appeared to be far enough from higher hills to be safe from landslides. They agreed to use Donna's farm as a rallying point and possible survival site. That decision simplified planning.

Donna's farm lay in the Cascade foothills east of the Willamette Valley. The road up to it was paved, so access was easy, but it had not always been so. In Oregon Trail days, the Willamette Valley was a wetland in the winter. Mark had heard tales of pioneers living in the south end of the valley, wanting to go 20 miles north to Eugene, who would have to cross the mountains to the west into the next valley, go up that valley, and cross back to Eugene from the west. Nearly three times the distance.

Over the years, local roads had developed along the hillsides east and west of the valley floor to provide all-weather access north and south. The road east of the valley was a roller coaster and crossed many streams that flowed into the Willamette. Like many roads in Oregon, it showed the tell-tale lengthwise cracks of roadbed slowly giving way and sliding downhill. Interstate 5 went straight up the middle of the wetland, in most places raised on a roadbed of dirt hauled in for that purpose. Mark figured that all these roads would collapse during the coming quakes. The rainy times after the shift would make travel very far in Oregon extremely difficult.

Donna's farm was old, the remnant of a much larger pioneer farm. Her house perched on high ground, with several barns and sheds nearby. The farm also had a parking pad with sewer, water and electrical connections for a recreational vehicle. Between the barns and the house, Donna maintained a large garden surrounded by high deer fence.

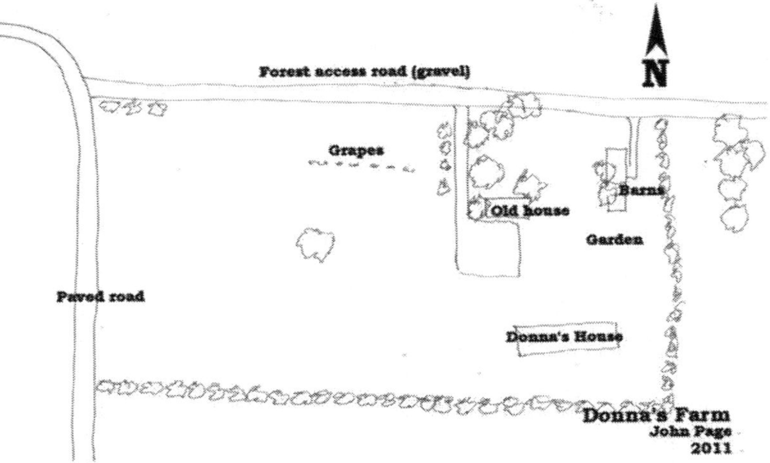

So Donna's farm was an excellent place to be for Surviving 10.

Each family started to purchase large quantities of food at stores in Eugene: dry milk, flour, rice, beans, even raw wheat, and other commodities. They used several food calculators to decide how much food to acquire, but in all cases the need was beyond their ability to buy, right away anyway. They did what they could, adding regularly to the growing stockpile in the old house at Donna's.

Storing all the food was a matter of some discussion. Most sealed their various commodities in plastic bags sealed in five-gallon plastic pails. Some of what they bought came that way.

Some used oxygen absorber packets. Others had read on the Internet that wheat, for example, stored well without the packets. One site said the reason for eliminating the oxygen was not to prolong the storage life, but to kill any insects in the container. That site suggested diatomaceous earth for that purpose. In the end, the group did some of each. Time would tell what worked and if it mattered.

Every family bought a CB radio, a deep-cycle 12 volt battery, and a battery charger. They met to rig and test the radios and the batteries. Once all the radios were working, they agreed on a channel to use to reach each other, and on a set of messages to use for critical events that would not attract attention or arouse suspicion.

"Donna's basement is flooded. Can you give me a hand?" would be the alert that it was time, and everyone was headed for Donna's.

"X's basement is flooded." meant that whoever X was needed assistance.

"X is having car trouble." meant that X needed help, preferably armed.

Firearms were a topic of some discussion. There was no disagreement that they would need firearms for hunting and for protection from four- and two-legged predators. Every family had at least one gun of some sort. The rugged survivalist web sites recommended certain types and sizes of hand guns, rifles and shotguns.

The group decided that standardizing would simplify ammunition purchases, so they agreed on .22 rifles for hunting small game and .410 shotguns for birds. Since they already had a number of them, they selected .30-06 rifles with scopes for big game and 20 gauge shotguns for varmints of all types. They chose 20 gauge over 12 gauge only because the group was generally older, and the smaller shotgun would be easier for everyone to handle. Once the decision of types and sizes was made, each family added to the ammunition stock as they could, buying from stores all over the area.

Donna selected a hill at the edge of her farm where they could safely shoot, and they all met several times to master shooting. The early sessions focused on safe operation, aiming, breathing, and squeezing the trigger. They also sighted in all the rifles so they could reliably hit a six-inch target at 75 yards. That accuracy was no big deal for real marksmen, but 75 yards was as far as they could see around Donna's place, with all the hills and trees.

A number of good shooters emerged from the group, and Mark sorted away the idea of more training for them, and soon.

Charlie built a chicken coop at Donna's so he'd have a place to move his chickens if the need arose. Donna liked the idea and went ahead and got a few of her own. The coop included a space to store feed. Charlie and Donna loaded the feed into five-gallon pails.

Charlie, Paula, Abe and Shelly helped Donna lay out an expanded garden that would support them if the need arose. It was too late to plant, so all they could do was plan and prepare the soil. Paula started a compost pile and brought some of the compost from her garden stock to work into the soil. Abe trimmed some of the fruit trees to promote better yields next year. The group laid in a large stock of heirloom, non-hybrid seeds from Territorial Seed in Cottage Grove, so they could count on seed saving if it came to that. There would be no more they could do until early spring.

All the men got together to make wood-burning stoves, using instructions and photos from several web sites. They called themselves the Stove Wizards.

One of the stoves they made was a VITA stove, simple sheet metal that worked almost as well as a true rocket stove. It would be a real benefit in a true disaster situation.

Then they all made rocket stoves out of salvaged tin cans, using wood ash as the insulation.

This project gave the newbies a chance to learn how to use metal shears and cope with sharp edges. And it introduced everybody to the principles of rocket stoves. Such stoves would disintegrate quickly under regular use, but they were useful for learning how to use the tools and master rocket stove principles.

Next was a larger stove used with large pots, called an institutional stove because a lot of institutions such as orphanages and schools in the developing world used them. The pots held as much as 15 gallons of water, enough for a bath or a fair amount of laundry. Charlie made the first one out of scrounged 55-gallon steel drums, then helped each of the others to make one of their own. Abe wondered if they'd need that many stoves, but the ensuing discussion revealed the need for many stoves for a group of two dozen doing everything from making tea to bathing.

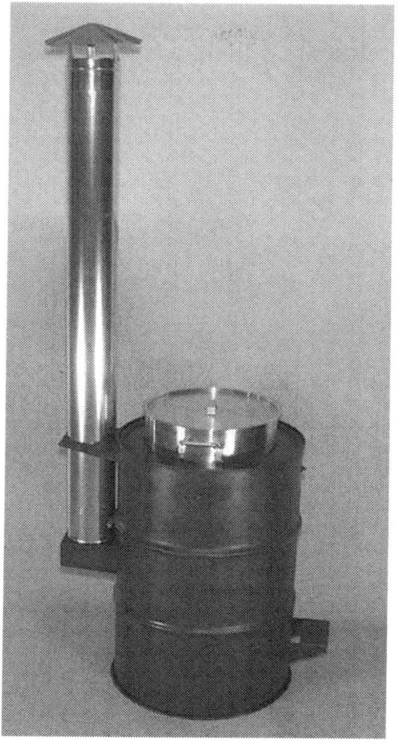

A major feature of the institutional stove was that it had a chimney, so it could be used indoors. Charlie located a supply of sheet metal, and with it they made chimneys for each stove.

Then, the group made a Justa stove, a large cook stove with a steel griddle on top. It also had a chimney and would work nicely in an enclosed kitchen. They used vermiculite for the insulation and fire brick for the combustion chamber. The outside body was brick salvaged from the farm. It worked amazingly well. They could see why the Justa stove was popular in Central and South America, as it used little wood and produced no smoke.

Finally, they fussed with several designs for heating stoves, looking for a simple stove with a chimney that would heat a tent. Again, the goal was to use small sticks of wood in a metal stove with a chimney that removed the smoke from the living area. They studied the plans for rocket mass heaters made of clay or rock, but they decided that such a stove would not likely be practical in a disaster setting.

But occasionally, they built an open fire, just to have one. It was fun to quaff wine around an open fire, but then the wind would shift, and they would remember why they were working so hard to eliminate smoky fires from their lives.

TIME LEFT: NINE MONTHS
7 OF 10

The cell phone vibrated. Mark pulled it out of its holster and looked at the display: Charlie.

Mark answered.

Charlie spoke slowly. “Paula and I have been talking about all this. She has a lot of respect for you, but she thinks you're crazy. You really buy ZetaTalk?”

Mark had taken the chance of telling Charlie more than he'd told others. Charlie read a lot of science fiction, so the idea of ZetaTalk should not have been as much of a shock.

“That's why we're in Oregon.”

“100%?”

“Maybe 80%. I don't trust any source 100%.”

“Sooner or later it is or it isn't. Do you go on forever believing it, or sooner or later you give it up?”

“Well, ZetaTalk is very clear on a few things. The shift happens before 2012, and a very specific set of events happen before the shift, and Nibiru —Planet X—is clearly visible to all before the shift. So, I figure if the events start happening, I start collecting cans of food and boxes of ammunition. If nothing happens by the end of 2012, I get on with life. In the meantime, hey, we're in Oregon, and I met you. Nothing lost.”

“Thanks. So tell me again what the tell-tale events are.”

“Lemme think. ZetaTalk says there's a scale of disaster from 1 to 10, with the pole shift being 10. We're at 6 now. What's coming next is a bunch of mega disasters that take us to 7. It's all about the plates finally unlocking and starting to jostle. Not just earthquakes on faults. Whole plate movements. Africa twists, so the floor of the Mediterranean drops off Algeria. That's sorta noticeable.

"The plates in the Pacific begin to slide, the Indonesian plate starts to slide under India, India tilts up in the east, down in the west, Pakistan sinks, and Indonesia drops significantly. Islands sink. South America unlocks and builds more of the Andes. The Caribbean plate crunches in the process, and more islands sink. So then the two plates that make up North America finally have room to more and start to slide past each other.

"The New Madrid fault breaks loose. The Mississippi widens, taking out the bridges and roads across it. Land to the west of the Mississippi drops. All this jolts the Atlantic, which rips open, sending a devastating tsunami toward Europe. Massive disasters one after another, all very noticeable. Oh, yeah, and Japan gets hit with massive earthquakes. It's all about the plates coming loose, with hell breaking out wherever the plates touch or slide."

"Hmm. I'd say those are pretty specific. Does ZetaTalk say when?"

"Well, they hint that the move to 7 starts before the end of 2010. They won't say more, because they don't want to give the Powers That Be any advantage, so they say. There are some clues that the major events happen around the end of magnetic trimesters, which come in April, August and December."

"Magnetic trimesters?"

"Yeah. There is a large magnetic field that surrounds the Solar System and exerts a strong influence on the Sun and all the planets. It pulses three times a year, and all the planets feel the pulse. NASA just discovered it, but ZetaTalk mentioned it some time ago."

"Uh, okay. So when do you think?"

"I say let's see what this December is like. If 7 starts then, all this will be clear in 2011. Big stuff will happen, or it's all hooey."

"What are you telling your daughters?"

"Watch the signs. If the major precursor events happen, cancel life as you knew it and take to the hills. Until then, keep your day job and assume there will be a tomorrow."

"But you didn't."

"True. But I could retire at 62, and we could see that our jobs would die in the depression that was going to hit the country. So we decided to move early while we could still find a buyer for our house. We leveraged house and credit cards and sales of belongings and all to get here in a position to make a stand. And we were right, because the company we'd worked for has had major layoffs. Wouldn't have been able to give away our house had we stayed. Besides, we wanted to try the Northwest life anyway, so we'd have come here shift or no. Maybe only not so soon."

"Well, that's all reasonable. Mind if I share that with Paula?"

"Please do. But remember, the issue is not if there will be a pole shift, it is still about preparing for disaster. The '10' we have to face may not be the '10' ZetaTalk predicts. So focus on preparing, not ZetaTalk. Just use them as the target."

"Makes sense. I admire your objectivity. Thanks, Friend. Be well."

Mark and Rachel made a round of calls to check in with daughters and cover again the need to have a plan and watch events. She thought that the best thing that could happen was that the kids would think they were crazy when the need to survive 10 never happened, or that they would be somewhat prepared when surviving 10 became a reality.

Carla in Austin was on the north edge of the area predicted to be washed by a surge from the gulf during the shift. Refugees would overwhelm those who survived in Austin and even further north. Starvation and disease would decimate those not killed outright. Mark pressed her to consider leaving such a big city. Even with the big quakes happening around the world that seemed to fit the predicted precursor pattern, Carla did not believe the ZetaTalk message and was firm in her intention to ignore the whole warning and stay where she was. She thought Mark was a senile fool. Their parting was cool.

Jennifer lived in New York City, so she was clearly the most vulnerable of all. ZetaTalk was clear that the quakes prior and the shift itself would destroy the city, along with every other city on either coast of the U.S. Those who didn't die in the tsunamis would face starvation and lawless mobs hunting food and rapine. Mark felt it was time for Jennifer to leave the city, perhaps to join her sister in Ithaca. They discussed the uncertainty of the situation. Maybe there wouldn't be a shift, and Jennifer would be giving up for nothing a well-earned job and future in her work. Or maybe she had a bit more time.

Mark asked if she had a plan for getting out of the city. She assumed she'd take some sort of bus or train. Mark pressed the idea that if she waited, there wouldn't be any bus or train running. She didn't own a car, and the fellow she was dating didn't either. Like most Americans, they lived like there was a tomorrow. Mark didn't think that walking out of New York would be possible once walking was the only option.

Jennifer said she'd think about it.

Jill in Ithaca was in better shape. ZetaTalk said that the St. Lawrence Seaway was going to split open as the two pieces of the North American plate slid past each other. The land there would rise and not experience either the quakes or the flooding to be seen elsewhere. Beyond that, Jill would have to hope that there were enough service-to-other people in the Ithaca area to put a post-shift community together.

Cathy was like Jennifer. She lived in Georgia, and ZetaTalk said all of Georgia was doomed. The land along the coast would drop during the shift as the Atlantic widened, and the slosh would wash away everything . Her best option appeared to be to join her sisters in Ithaca. Going home to Missouri would not likely be an option, given the chaos predicted along the Mississippi. Besides, Missouri itself was not predicted to fare well before, during, or after the shift.

If she did not move toward Ithaca, her only option would be to get into the Appalachian Mountains to the northwest. But in the chaos, she would have to be very lucky to find a service-to-other community there that would welcome her.

Cathy promised to think about going to Ithaca.

In all their conversations, Mark and Rachel stressed their belief that events would clearly show if a pole shift was coming, that those who prepared and moved to safe places could survive, but after the shift, they would need to form or find a relatively small survival community of primarily service-to-other people to get beyond a few months. Again, the focus was on preparing.

And watching.

It was getting harder to tell what was really going on. There were days when the ZetaTalk site was just not there. ZetaTalk had set up mirror sites and had published a list of links. Mark tried the mirror sites. Usually, one of them was up. He wondered if the government was jamming, or if the chaos of the quakes was at fault. He supposed it would not suit The Powers That Be if their help hit the road for Ithaca. And the big message of ZetaTalk was move to a safe location.

Mark and Rachel also talked a lot with their friends. Less doubt. More certainty. More serious planning and preparation. Behavior changed. They all expected bigger quakes nearby, ones that would cause real damage. Taylorville was a quaint town of wood houses and brick buildings in the business district. They joked about how their favorite coffee houses could become brickyards in a moment, so they found themselves avoiding old brick buildings. They topped their gas tanks and kept them full. They increased purchases of canned goods, dry milk, flour, beans, and wheat.

Mark had a grain mill he'd bought before Y2K, so he bought a small pail full of raw wheat. He and Rachel tried to use their mill to make flour and learned all they needed to know about grain mills but hadn't known to ask. The mill had been cheap. It was crude, had no fine adjustments, and included tiny grains of metal in the flour. It might work to grind corn for chicken feed, but it couldn't grind wheat into flour fine enough for practical use. So they made a survey of grain mills available at Lehman's and Amazon, finally narrowing the choice down to one they could afford that could make flour.

Rachel commented that it was a good thing they'd tried their mill. She wondered how many people might have stockpiled but not practiced. It they were counting on the mill Mark had bought ten years earlier, which was still available, they would have to settle for cream of wheat and shards cereal instead of bread.

In December, there were more earthquakes, close together, and events all over the world unfolded as listed in the ZetaTalk script.

Terrible floods hit Australia. ZetaTalk said the plate was tipping, raising the east coast of Australia enough that water couldn't drain, forming a vast inland sea that sloshed around as the plate tilted one way, then another.

Mark sent emails to his daughters, advising that they pay attention to events.

The new year came, and disasters continued.

Earthquakes shook Africa, and giant rogue waves smashed boats in the Mediterranean. News reports did not report the floor of the Mediterranean dropping, but the waves suggested to readers of ZetaTalk that it had, as predicted.

By February, it was clear that Indonesia was sinking, suffering massive floods on the other side of the plate from Australia. News reports finally admitted that land was being covered by salt water, indicating that the sea was encroaching as the land sank. Some officials talked of 'king tides' but did not, could not explain why such a tide only affected land in certain places. There were multiple jolts and several tsunamis, two large ones. Coastal towns went under sea water in Indonesia and western India. Flood waters spread in Pakistan. Nobody commented on land rising in eastern India. Some officials guessed at casualties, but reports from the area were scant. Mark suspected the news was suppressed.

A few islands sank from sight. Not just in Indonesia. The Caribbean as well. Towns in Columbia reported sinkholes, crumbling buildings, constant shaking.

And new land appeared in the seas where the plates were buckling or rising.

Sinkholes along the Mississippi suggested land was becoming unstable there, perhaps dropping. Mark noted especially the sinkholes in upstate New York and southern Canada, warning that the seaway was stretching. Volcanoes all over the world were smoking or puffing. No one could argue that the rash of earth adjustments was normal. Talking heads on TV wagged about adjustments, historic patterns, speculated about supervolcanoes.

The news remained calm and dismissive. ZetaTalk explained that the press was largely owned by corporate interests that intended to keep the public calm and at their jobs.

Then a massive underwater earthquake in the Atlantic sent a tsunami up the coast of Europe, just as ZetaTalk had predicted. News of damage and casualties was spotty. Mark thought the news sounded controlled. The Internet was more reliable, but it always had included details that the official news sources left out.

It was odd. Mark felt that the whole planet was convulsing, shaking, rattling, but locally, around him in Oregon, there were few signs.

Until the New Madrid Fault went.

That one, he felt. A rumble under foot, like a train going by, but no train. Birds flews from trees.

Mark checked the satellite TV. Some reports of network problems. Some channels were gone. No signal. The radio had nothing. Then confusion. Not like Katrina, where the slow approach of the hurricane had given news people time to position and prepare. With a massive earthquake, those at the scene were instantly deprived of their tools and links. Those outside could not immediately see how large the affected area was. All communications seemed shaken. Networks weren't there.

Web sites all over were off line. Mark knew the Web depended on Domain Name Servers, or DNS, to translate web site names into the 12-digit IP addresses the Internet really used to connect browsers to sites. Every web user's computer depended on a name server, usually assigned by the internet service provider for that connection, which shared links with all the other servers on the planet to connect users to web sites worldwide.

So Mark checked some sites he knew were on the west coast. They worked. He tried one in New York. Not found. So his own DNS somewhere in Oregon was up, but maybe the internet links that far east were gone.

Mark tried some Google queries. Still working. But Google had servers all over the world, including a big center up the road in Oregon.

He ran queries for sites in Iowa. Not found. Illinois. Not found. Missouri. A few worked. Others not found. Arkansas. Not found. Tennessee. Not found.

He tried LiveIreland.com, which he knew came from Dublin, Ireland. Not found.

No clear picture. Mark thought about the day he was born, during World War II. He'd checked newspapers published that day—a common birthday present to history buffs—and found they were just reporting events that had happened days or weeks earlier in Europe.

You might guess or feel that big events were happening elsewhere, but locally, there was not a clue.

He called friends. Nobody knew, but nobody argued that a major, major disaster had hit the middle of the country.

He called daughters. Nobody answered, and for the first time, he had no option to leave messages.

None of this was a surprise. In a way, it was a relief. Mark had stuck his neck out telling Charlie about ZetaTalk and Nibiru, the approaching 12th Planet. ZetaTalk had predicted the quakes and sinkholes and volcanoes, explaining in detail how the approaching planet would shake loose the plates that join to make up the Earth's surface.

His friends were more confident in their acceptance of the scenario Mark had told them about. They all agreed that it was time to get extremely serious about preparation for the predicted pole shift.

Mark was relieved, too, that he had written his letter to their daughters. They had his view and his advice. They should be on alert and making more informed decisions about what to do.

Where he and Rachel were in Oregon, they could not do more.

TIME LEFT: EIGHT MONTHS

PLANNING DEFENSE

Mark stopped by Charlie's to see how he was doing.

Charlie brought up a book he'd just read.

"I just finished *Patriots*, that novel by Rawles. I recall you've read it?"

"Yeah. Small group flees the cities as the U.S. collapses into anarchy driven by financial collapse. Have a nice day."

"What did you think of it?"

"He's really into weapons, guns, ambushes. There's also the business of armed resistance to a rogue government. A political disaster, not a natural one, triggered by economics."

"What do you think about the redoubt, the weapons? Do we need more than we've got? The guys in *Patriots* were armed like the Marines. Should we do more?"

"Well, I see a couple of differences. For one thing, the disaster in the book is economic, so the roads and bridges are still intact, and they can take motor vehicles across several states. And bad guys move in convoys. In our case, we're facing a worldwide physical disaster that will take out every bridge and shred every road. Nobody will be driving anywhere for a long time. A few plutocrats might have a private army and air force, but I don't think there will be any near us, and besides, the troops might decide their boss is disposable after the food runs out. So I don't see anybody from Kentucky trying to assert control in Oregon for the rest of our lives.

"So that brings to mind the sort of need we'll have for weapons. I think the road and bridge destruction will tend to make conflict more local. Looters rather than armies. I plan to hide from them, go to ground, and stay invisible. I certainly don't think it's wise to set up a fortress with wire around the perimeter. All that does is say 'we did all this because we have lots of food.' Invite the desperate and vicious to come after us. Ideally, nobody alive will know we're wherever we are unless we want 'em to. If someone does find us, at most, I would use the *Lucifer's Hammer* approach —negotiate while a hidden sniper covers the threat.

"So I'm thinking we go to Donna's and wait. If we're threatened there, we can fight or fly. So we'd need to think about a hideout. The .30-06's are for last-resort situations, the occasional bear or mountain lion. I'm betting on the .22's for hunting. Very quietly. Wild meat to supplement vegetables. Hunter-gatherer living. Totally different situation and plot than *Patriots*."

Charlie nodded. Then he frowned. "Have you thought about this hideout?"

"Yeah. A lot."

"Where?"

"Back in the hills above Donna's place."

"Why there?"

"It's handy to Donna's. Donna's farm is ideal. The road is pretty winding going up there and may not survive the big quakes, which is even better, because that will deter scavengers looking for easy pickings. The land is not clear, which might be a problem seeing anybody coming. But once we get there, we can see about how to deal with that."

"You mean clear the land?"

"Maybe just the opposite. Cleared land is an advertisement. 'Here we are.' I'd like it to look like nobody survived there. We just need to figure ways to detect if anybody's coming toward us. Maybe dogs. Don't know yet."

"But what's the deal then with the forest above Donna's place?"

"If Donna's place is threatened, we can retire uphill into the forest above it. It's tree plantation, mostly. We find a stand of Douglas fir along a clear-cut, which gives us a clear field of vision as need be. Going that way is a last resort if Donna's place doesn't work out."

Charlie hadn't been in the military, but he'd watched lots of war movies. "How would you defend the place?"

Mark could have been a history teacher. He had read countless books about battle, especially those in the Civil War. He'd also watched the same movies Charlie had, and he'd read a lot about small unit tactics. "I would follow Longstreet's advice to Lee: go on the defensive. In that, I agree with Rawles's approach in *Patriots*. Set up prepared positions at Donna's that cover all the approaches, from which sniper teams can deal with what comes. Work out ranges, put up range markers so the snipers know exactly the distance to a target. Have charts showing all the ranges in all the positions. Then train the teams."

Charlie was impressed. "You seem to have thought out everything. Who are the snipers?"

"There are seven of us that could do it, judging from the shooting I've seen."

"How would you train?"

"Form sniper-spotter teams. The spotter can keep an eye out while the sniper is focused on his scope. The spotter calls the shot and the range. The sniper fires. The spotter observes the result, calls corrections for the next shot, as needed."

"Who would you pick for this?"

"You, me, Bill, Abe, Jack, Donna, and Greg."

"Donna?"

"Sure. It's her place, and she knows how to deal with varmints. Plus she's a good shot."

"Who spots?"

"Each sniper chooses. I'd have Rachel. But she and I would be a last-resort sniper team. If we follow the *Lucifer's Hammer* approach, I'd be out front negotiating while the snipers covered the threat, and the spotters watched for my signal to fire."

"Where would the positions be?"

"Suppose we go do some recon and see?"

They called Bill, Abe, Jack, and Greg. All were available, so Mark and Charlie picked them up, then headed to Donna's.

Mark slowed as he approached a steep stretch of the road to Donna's and looked carefully at the terrain.

Why was the road there? The road literally hung from the side of a steep ridge, land that ran along the edge of a large cattle ranch. The ranch land rolled steeply, easily passable on foot but a challenge to wheeled vehicles. The good land was pasture. The road was built on what was left —steep, rocky—to give access to landholders and the tree plantation above the ranch and Donna's farm, deeper into the Cascades.

The road past Donna's farm continued uphill to the gate that marked the boundary of the tree plantation. Often the gate was open, but a sign warned that it might be closed at any time. Hunters went into the plantation regularly on the logging roads that threaded the hills.

The plantation beyond the gate looked to the uneducated like Douglas fir forest. Those more aware could see that all the trees in a stand were exactly the same size, the same age, planted together all at once. A crop. The company harvested the crop roughly every 30 years, clear-cutting every tree in a stand, then replanting a new crop. So the hills above Taylorville were a patchwork of stands of trees of different heights, interspersed by recently cut open ground. The clear-cuts were a tangle of slash—trimmed-off branches—stumps, and chewed up ground.

The plantation was a monoculture. Nothing grew there except Douglas fir. Nothing else of use. No nut-bearing trees, no herbs, no medicinal plants.

Not exactly an ideal place to try surviving, Mark thought.

He turned into Donna's driveway and parked in one of two available spaces.

They all got out, and Mark led them on a tour. He'd read about the British general, Wellington, who knew how to spot "dead ground"—ground "out of play"—where troops could shelter from a fight. So Mark had developed his own mental game, looking for places easy to defend, places that could not be defended, and ways to get at either.

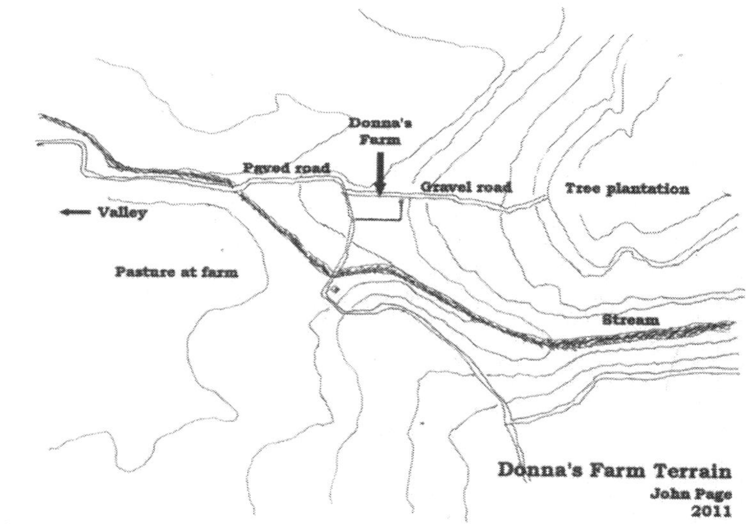

Mark pointed to the west. "Donna's farm is a big rectangle of hedges, laid out east-west along this ridge. The road from the valley comes up to the northeast corner of the farm, there, and splits. A gravel road runs along the north side of the farm, past where we stand, and continues into tree plantation." He swung around and pointed to the plantation to the east.

Then he turned back to the west. "The paved road turns south along the west side of Donna's farm, drops into that ravine and up the other side, to those houses to the south."

The group followed where Mark pointed, getting their bearings.

Mark pointed to the northwest corner again. "The likely approach to us is up the road from the valley. Unless you know the area, that's the only way up here. So travelers would hit the northeast corner, there. If someone was really sneaky, he'd come over that mountain south of us, cross the road above us, and come down on us from behind. Those appear to me to be the two threats. So let's see if we can find some places that cover the valley road, the trees, and fields around us, especially to the south."

Mark pulled out two sheets of paper. They were prints of a Google Earth view of the farm, one looking north, the other looking east. He'd made them some time ago, figuring they might be helpful. Everyone laughed, and Charlie slapped Mark on the back.

"Cool move, Dude."

Mark grinned.

They looked at the view to the north for a while, pointing at various features, looking at it from all angles, comparing it with the land where they stood.

After a while, Bill suggested a solution. "Suppose we focus on the northwest corner? That's well away from Donna's house and garden. We ought to confront anybody coming well away from the farm compound, here." He pointed to the houses on the printout.

"The brush along the gravel road blocks our view of people on foot, so I'd remove it."

Charlie frowned. "But the hedge also hides us."

Bill shook his head. "Well, if they're standing there where the gravel road splits off, they're already too close. Probably coming up here because they know we're here. No point in trying to hide while giving up being able to see what's on the road."

Charlie looked over at Donna's house. "Wonder what Donna would think about our tearing out the hedge?"

Bill looked as well. "Only one way to find out. But if we take it out, what do we do then?"

Bill looked at the sheet, then looked at the ground, then back at the sheet. He pointed to the middle of the rectangle of the farm. "This is high ground. I'd build a little fort here, well disguised, where a sniper team or two could cover all the ground from here to here." His hand waved over all the land on the map to the west, south and north of the farm.

Mark was enjoying Bill's analysis. "What about the east? There are lots of trees there. We'd be blind until someone was on top of us."

Bill looked to the east, then back at the map. "Well, if somebody goes to the trouble to snake up this draw, sneak through those trees, just to get at us, we're probably toast. They'd be far more skilled than we are. We could put a little fort here," he pointed to where the line of trees came to the gravel road, "but there aren't enough of us to man a full perimeter. No, I'd just focus on the northwest, build a fort in the middle of the farm, and hope we're right."

"Well," Mark paused, "suppose we put a bunker on the southeast corner, here, where the windbreak turns. It would give us a place to cover a lot of the ground to the east, and it might flank someone coming down through the trees east of us. Have it there, but not manned. Focus what we have on the central fort."

Charlie nodded, recalling a confrontation between U.S. Army troops and Sioux Indians in the late 1860's. "Like the Wagon Box Fight, where all the defenders clustered together and defeated a much larger force coming from all directions."

"Right."

Mark summarized. "Well, guys, what do you think?"

The guys agreed.

"Fine. Let's go see if Donna is fond of that hedge."

She wasn't. She'd have taken it out years before had it not been for the work involved. Now she had both motive and means. "I'll buy the gas for your saws!"

The next day, the crew got to work. It took two days, but finally, they had the fence clear from the northwest corner to the driveway.

The next task was the fort. There was a clump of bushes roughly where they thought the fort should go. Ideal. They dug into the ground clear around the south, west, and north sides of the bushes to make a trench roughly 4-feet deep, 3-feet wide, with a ramp into the trench on the east side. They piled the dirt to the outside and sloped it away in all directions, trusting that the bare dirt would fade into the background before there was any need for the fort. They built a cover of plywood over the trench a foot above the ground and covered it with brown tarps. Then they piled the brush from the destroyed hedge on top of the tarp. When they were done, it looked like your average farmyard brush pile, waiting to be burned.

Bill and Charlie found a pile of metal fence posts near Donna's barn. They painted the tops of the posts white, then scuffed the paint so it looked old. They drove a post at the northwest corner, another at the southwest corner, another further down the road where it first appeared coming up the hill, and one in the middle of each side of the farm boundary. They paced off the distance from each post to the fort and added the ranges to the map. The longest distance was just 75 yards, well within the skill of the team.

Mark asked each sniper to pick a spotter. The spotters needed binoculars, so they had to take care of that detail. Mark asked everyone to read some material he'd downloaded, sections of the Army Field Manual 23-10, *Sniper Training*, and a book in the library, *Sniper*, by Adrian Gilbert.

He explained what to focus on. “Don't worry about the fancy suits, the missions and such. We're talking mostly about the shooting skills. Pay attention to that. The range estimation, the effect of wind. That sort of stuff. Then we'll do some training, and that's it. Hope we never need it.”

That was all they could do. Due diligence, Charlie called it.

TIME LEFT: SEVEN MONTHS

GETTING THEIR ACT TOGETHER

Mark parked in one of the two spaces by Donna's driveway. Others arrived and wedged their vehicles between trees and sheds. The last parked on the road and walked in.

Donna served tea to the group in her living room, then stood to one side, put her hands on her hips, grinned, and said, "Well, when are you all moving in?"

Everyone laughed.

Charlie spoke. "I think we're all decided that something big is coming, maybe already started. It might well be a pole shift. So what do we do?"

Everyone looked at Mark.

He pursed his lips, took a breath and exhaled. "Any plan is better than no plan. So here's one to chew on."

He wrote on a flip chart pad.

Assumptions:
Quakes: dams go, valley floods
Roads, bridges go
Landslides
Donna's farm-
above valley
no higher ground to slide
available
Forest above to hide in if needed

He tore the sheet off, handed it to Bill to tape to the wall, and continued on a new sheet.

Plan:
Prepare ASAP while roads open
Retreat site at Donna's
Food for team for ~6 months
Clothing for winter, wet weather
Seeds, garden stuff to go beyond
Canning stuff
Tools
Cases of tarps
Weapons and ammunition

Bill asked, "What clothes?"

Mark turned, paused, tore the sheet off the pad, and started a new one as Bill taped.

Clothing
Parka
motorcycle helmet
goggles
respirator
gloves
boots
wool socks
ponchos
wet suit

"Uh, could you maybe explain all that?"

Mark went down the list.

"Parka is partly for possible cold weather, but mainly for padding. A shift would be a rough ride.

"Motorcycle helmet is head and face protection during the shift.

"Goggles are eye protection. We may deal with dust, debris and wind for some time.

"Respirator is lung protection against dust, especially volcanic ash."

Charlie nodded and said, "Oh, the three Sisters."

Mark replied. "Let's assume only the volcanoes that have erupted during the last 10,000 years. That would be only South Sister. North and Middle have been dormant for a much longer time. The wind pattern after a shift would carry much of the ash out to sea, which would be the new south from us. So yes, we should assume the South Sister plume would go over us, so we should prepare for ash. The hardware store in town has respirators that would work.

"Gloves of various sorts, for cold weather, rock handling, tree cutting, handling hot things. All of that.

"Boots to last a lifetime walking on rocks, in mud, across streams. Can't have too many, 'though we'll probably be making Indian-style foot wear before too many years after.

"Ponchos to work in the rain without getting soaked. Oh, rain hats, too."

He added *hats* to the list.

"By wet suit, I mean rain coat and rain pants. We'd have wet weather a lot after the shift."

He didn't make a point of the ZetaTalk prediction that gloom and mist might last the rest of all their lives, with few exceptions. Oregonians were depressed enough by the normal weather. Maybe they'd get lucky, be one of the exceptions, and see sun again.

Someone asked, "What's with the tarps?"

Mark walked over to the flip-chart sheet and pointed to the word. "That's for tents, walls, canopies, any sort of roofing. Folks in Florida after a hurricane call it 'FEMA roofing.' I was in Miami after a hurricane, and there were blue tarps all over the roofs of houses. After the shift, the ground would be shaking occasionally for a long time. We'd need light structures that don't care about earthquakes. A simple pole frame covered by tarps will do quite well. We should have several cases of tarps in various sizes.

"As you can see," Mark continued as he pointed to the lists, "this all goes beyond our 72-hour kits a whole bunch. Think of it as preparing to sail to the New World in the 1600's. What do you choose to have with you to start a new life?"

Bill spoke. "Okay, so we're establishing New Jamestown or New Plymouth. Who do we need in our crew to make a go of it?"

Mark knew Bill had been in the Navy, and he appreciated both Bill's logical approach and his military experience. He smiled at the reference to crew.

So he asked, "Anybody know anything about either colony?"

Rachel laughed. "Look out, class, it's a trap. Mark should have been a history teacher."

They all laughed with her.

Shelly said, "Okay, Mark, tell us."

"Well, our situation has some similarities to both Jamestown and Plymouth, but more, I think, to Plymouth. We're on our own, trying to survive. Our goal is not to make a lot of money for folks back in the home country. There is no company back home to send help and supplies. We're likely up against natives who dislike us and don't maybe want to share food with us. There is no larger government to rule us, so we need to make our own compact. We'll try to get along with natives. It's likely that newcomers will join us, probably providing more burden than support. So in all that, we're going to be a lot like Plymouth.

"But we've built a fort, so in that way, we're going to be like Jamestown. Plymouth dropped into land occupied by relatively civilized natives under chiefs the Pilgrims could negotiate with. We won't, so we need some defenses, from wild animals, too, as well as crazed natives. From a military point of view, this farm isn't defensible, with woods and higher ground above it. But there is a possibility that the shift will knock out most of the natives, so we may not have much of a threat to deal with. If we start getting approached by organized gangs of freeloaders, we'll have to find a better place. But we can prepare for the shift here and plan to farm here to start with."

Alice spoke. "This is all a bit mind boggling. Setting up Plymouth. My God, isn't that a bit extreme. We are a civilized country. Maybe the government pulls together. Do we have to go into the wild?"

Mark replied. "Assume the worst. Imagine New Orleans after Katrina with no outside world to come in and help. No FEMA. No Corps of Engineers. No news. No food. No restraint on police shootings. I'm not counting on towns pulling together.

"Something big has just happened in the middle of the country. Nobody's saying how big. The government is totally swamped with trouble, and it's just starting. They'll be exhausted and incapable of helping well before the shift. Nonexistent after.

"Beside all that, starvation will start almost immediately. Three days of food in the stores. Maybe a week or two in most houses. Then panic. Cities and towns will be death traps. Not only from lack of food. Most folks take clean water for granted. During and after the shift, if you want clean water, you'll have to make it. Most folks won't, so we'll see dysentery and cholera all around us, with no officials or doctors to act or respond. I think it's better to be in our own little colony and find we didn't need to be, than the other way around."

Jack waved his hand. "Speaking as the only Indian chief in the neighborhood, I'd like to welcome all you pilgrims."

The group howled. A knee-slapping howl.

When they'd recovered, Bill asked, "How do we look for skill sets? Do we need to recruit some people who have skills we don't have?"

Mark grinned. Bill was a great shill. "Well, speaking of that, I have a little chart here."

Laughter again. A few clapped.

"I've listed everyone we have, who has what skills and interests. Please take a look at it and amend as needed."

"What are the choices? Or did we have a choice?"

Laughter.

"Well, how about these: *hunt, garden, cook, fish, fabricate, heal, and snipe*."

Nods around. Mark waited.

"Any others?"

The group was silent.

"What does *fabricate* cover?"

"You choose. Wood, metal, brick. Everything from stoves to houses. Electricity. Electronics? What?"

"That's pretty broad."

"Well, it happens that you folks can do all that. You're really very talented."

Rachel, the practical one, raised a point that had been on her mind. "What about new skills we'll need? Like *soap making, weaving, trapping, canning, seed saving*. Those things?"

Mark knew she would bring that up. Her timing was excellent. "Very good point. Let's make a list of those, and everybody take a look at the list. Sign up for the one you want to learn. If there are any not taken, we'll assign volunteers."

Donna started a list.

"How about *healers*?"

"Well, we are really fortunate to have Sharon. Others can help. Sharon will also work to prevent the need for healing: *public health, sanitation*, that sort of stuff. The only thing better would be a doctor, but they're probably going to be needed somewhere else. She'll need help, so add *medic* to the list and sign up if you're interested."

"Looks good. A place to start."

"Well, I do have one thought. Greg and Sharon have two sons, Brad and Doug. They're both good hunters, mechanically gifted. Both married. Two kids each. I'd nominate them to join us."

"If you think they're okay, they're just fine with me."

Everyone agreed. Greg and Sharon grinned.

"Have we included everyone you want to go to our new colony with? Now's the time to say."

Silence for a moment, then Donna spoke for the group. "We're done."

Mark was relieved. They were out of time.

"Well, do we do this?"

Everyone nodded. Abe summed it up: "Nothing to lose."

Mark looked at Donna. "Can we do this at your place?"

Donna grinned. "Come ahead!"

TIME LEFT: SEVEN MONTHS
ZETATALK REVEALED

Mark was insistent. "We have to move quickly. We need to nail down how much of what to gather in the next few days. We're running out of time. Finish up food stocks, medical supplies, ammunition, absolutely anything else we're going to take to a new colony."

Alice frowned. "How do we look for food?"

Mark was quick. "The food we've bought just gets us to the first harvest. After that, we need to be able to feed ourselves. We'll need to grow, gather, fish and hunt."

Paula asked, "What do you plan to grow?"

Mark thought for a moment. After the shift, they would be a lot further south, wind blowing, rain falling for some time—at least the first few years. Crops that grow in Oregon might not do well at a latitude closer to the equator.

He'd checked on crops in Central America. He emphasized those. "Well, potatoes are a pretty good survival crop if we can keep them from rotting. When a starving native comes by to steal food, he'll look for tomatoes, corn, stuff he knows what it looks like. He won't know a potato plant from a weed, especially if they're planted all over to look like weeds. After the plants die back, they look even more like weeds. You don't have to harvest all of them at once, as long as you harvest the last before frost, which we might not have again, and harvested potatoes can keep 6 months. If we have enough varieties, we might survive the stray blight in the process.

"Other crops would be corn, squash, sweet potatoes, radishes, carrots, and such. Oh, and dandelions."

Donna added, "You can do a lot with dandelions. Wine, salad, the whole plant is edible."

Mark smiled, "And they're high in vitamin C, as are potatoes, so no scurvy to worry about. Can't imagine dandelions not flourishing almost anywhere in whatever climate we end up with."

"What about coffee. Could we grow coffee trees?"

"I don't know. We'll have to see. We'd need seeds to plant, and I have no idea where we'd get 'em."

Charlie stood, stretched, and said, "Well, I'm sure gonna lay in a stash of coffee."

"Well, then, make it coffee beans," Mark added.

"Beans," Charlie replied.

"Un-roasted."

"Uh, why un-roasted?"

"They last longer."

"Oh. Right. Un-roasted."

Donna laughed. "Speaking of which, I suppose it's time for coffee. Who wants some?"

As Mark stirred his coffee, Charlie stood up, faced Mark, and smiled. "Mark, you've talked a lot about pole shifts. You've given way more detail than you could make up, and it's all proven true. Old Friend, you're good, but you're not that good. Do you suppose it's time to tell everybody where you're getting your info?"

Mark was surprised. Charlie knew. Evidently he now believed. No point in dragging this out, Mark thought.

"Okay, folks. Charlie's right. I've given you lots of details about natural disasters, and they're happening as predicted. I've shared a lot of ideas and predictions, and I didn't think them all up on my own.

"I have a source. A web site called *ZetaTalk*. It's been going in various forms for over 15 years, predicting all the stuff that's happening now. I can show you page after page of specifics that have panned out. I consider this site to be reliable and authoritative."

"Who does it? Where is it coming from?"

John took a breath. "Well, a woman named Nancy writes the stuff, which she gets from aliens from Zeta Reticuli. Not channeling. Communicating telepathically."

"You're kidding." Lots of laughter. A few moans. Rachel rolled her eyes.

"No, I'm dead serious. Anybody here that doesn't believe in UFO's?"

No response.

"Well, there you are. You believe in the possibility. There is life out there. There are aliens. They're here, and the Zetas, at least, care about us."

"How do you know you're not being had?"

"Well, think about it. If they have the ability to come here from another star system, and they haven't bothered us, they're not going to. Think about Star Trek. The Prime Directive. Don't mess with primitive populations on backward planets. Well, where do you suppose that idea came from? That's the way aliens work. Communicate on the sly, in dreams, with crop circles, anything but an obvious, physical appearance in broad daylight. They won't do that. If they were out to get us, or eat us, or whatever, they'd just go ahead and do it. Nothing we could do could stop them. That they haven't is the clear evidence that they don't, and they won't."

"Why do they care?"

"Why do you care about dogs at the pound? You just do. The Zetas are pretty clear that they care, roughly the same way."

"Are we going to be adopted?"

Laughter. This was going better than Mark had feared.

"Cute. Make sure you have your shots." That comment, coming from nowhere, hit him as almost spooky. He'd forgotten immunizations. Now or later? Now.

"Oh, funny that should come out that way. We all need to go get our immunizations updated. Tell the shot people you're planning to travel through Central America. That should cover the threats. Especially be sure you get a tetanus booster and something for yellow fever, if they'll give it. You ought to get a dental check-up, too. And lay in a huge supply of any medications you need. As much as your doctor will allow."

Everyone stared at him. Charlie was grinning.

"Now, where was I? Oh yes. All I can say is go to the site, www.zetatalk.com, and see for yourself what they have to say. Read the biography section about Nancy. Then browse the site. It's all about a pole shift that is about to hit. They are clear on events: shift before December, 2012, that's 10 on a disaster scale of 10, with levels 8 and 9 in the months before that. We're already in 7 with the land sinking in Indonesia, chaos in Australia, the New Madrid in the U.S., mega quake in Japan, and tsunami hitting Europe. It's all there, and they said it years ago. They won't say for sure, but I'm assuming we're looking at maybe six months of wall-to-wall quakes and then the shift. Ideally, we should have a year's supply of food for everyone. I figure we collect what we can and start planting potatoes and a garden as soon as we can. We may be subsistence farming through the shift itself. Assume major disruptions of food supplies well before the shift."

"Holy shit," Abe said. "So you're saying we're really going to have a pole shift? This isn't just an assumption for planning?"

"Right. We are going to have a pole shift in roughly six to twelve months."

Abe stared. "Mark, you truly believe this?"

Mark nodded. "Rachel and I believe this. Well, I probably do more than Rachel. We're here in Oregon because of ZetaTalk. Go see what they say about Oregon. Then check anywhere else you like. They discuss the fate of every place on the planet. I've pressed you all to prepare because ZetaTalk says we're running out of time. Figure six months and plan accordingly."

Mark stopped, looked around.

Donna laughed as she looked at Charlie. "Charlie, did you know about this?"

Charlie bowed. "Yes, I did. Mark told me a while back. I've been all over the site. I have to say it looks weird, but it's all strangely believable. I have to say I believe Mark, and I think ZetaTalk is enough to get me started preparing."

Donna broke the tension. "Well hell, people. Look around. Mark's been right. If this is the reason, let's run with it. Let's just assume the worst case and get moving."

And that was how it went.

TIME LEFT: SEVEN MONTHS

DELEGATING TASKS

The group discussed food and supplies for some time.

Mark sat down with Bill and Charlie.

Bill said, "We're talking about heat and water."

"And?"

"We've been talking about what to do about water up here when the power goes out and Donna's well is useless. It's too deep for a hand pump. Time for plan B. Charlie's thinking we need maybe 2 liters of water per person per day. Twenty people. That's 40, maybe 50 liters of water, so let's say 15 gallons per day. We can boil that easy, if boiling is all we need to do, using an institutional-size rocket stove."

Bill continued. "But we're thinking about what to do if distilling is needed."

Mark nodded. "And it will be, safe to assume."

"So we're working up a material list for a water still to fit the same institutional stove."

"Excellent. You've got a week," Mark said as he grinned, got up, and went to join Greg and Sharon.

"So, what do you think?"

"Stunned but ready to help. You're sure about this?" Greg asked.

"Sure enough to prepare. Worst case is we miss a quake in the valley."

"What about food? Hunting and fishing?"

"Lots of folks hunt in this area. I think it'll be safe to assume the game will vanish. There are fish in the river, but the water is tainted with mercury, so we have to limit what we eat. Rather, we used to have to limit what we eat. Long-term mercury poisoning is probably less bad than short-term starvation. You fish, I know."

"Every chance I get."

"Well, get your gear together. You're the designated fisherman."

"Will do. My sons are good, too. Will be fun to catch and eat."

Sharon smiled and said, "What about a medical kit?"

Mark thought about the bag in the van. "I have a small surgical kit, a few spare sutures, and a fairly standard first aid kit. Not what you'd call EMT-ready. Can you help?"

Sharon was on her home ground. "Sure. I'm familiar with emergency medicine. Can't do the drugs, though. Without equipment and facilities, we can't do surgery or intensive care."

Mark had thought about that. "Wouldn't expect you to. Most we can do is handle minor injuries and recoverable illnesses. Same medical insurance Thomas Jefferson had. Stay healthy. Bind minor wounds. Pay attention to sanitation. If someone gets badly hurt, be prepared to say goodbye. Can you be the medic, vet, and public health officer?"

"You bet. That's what I do."

"Great. You're it. Can you figure up what we ought to have in the way of bandages, ointments, and such?"

"Sure. I'd aim for an EMT kit. We'll never be able to do much more than an EMT can do at the scene."

Mark thought of the material he'd downloaded from Hesperion.org. "You might check Hesperion's *When There Is No Doctor* for other things we should get. How about infectious diseases, quarantines, and such?"

Sharon thought a moment. "Have a place where you can isolate, and scare everybody into learning how to sneeze right."

Mark grinned. "Into your armpit?"

"No, silly. Your elbow."

"Right. I knew that. Very glad you're on the crew."

Sharon smiled. "Thanks. We really thank you for including us."

Mark stood and walked to the center of the crowd.

"Hokay, folks. We have a medic and a fisherman, and some moonshiners. How about gardening?"

Alice raised her hand.

Mark looked at Charlie. "How about Paula? She does great gardens."

Charlie shrugged. "She'll help at the time, but it's gonna take an earthquake or two to get her on board."

"We need people now to plan what the garden will look like to support two dozen people."

Sara raised her hand and said, "I can help with that."

"Okay, let's get it planned. We need to order seed pronto, in case shipments halt before spring. In fact, they may already be interrupted. Donna's the honcho."

Alice said, "Maybe we need to look at the garden space?"

Alice, Sara, Shelly and Donna got up, put on their coats, and headed for the door.

Abe said, "I'll go with them and look at the fences. We're going to need more."

Jack motioned to Mark, so he went and sat down beside him.

He said, "You know the medicine men have been talking about this for a long time."

"Yeah. And not just the Hopi."

"How can we help?"

"Well, after the shift, all the houses will be rubble, so we'll need to focus on hogan or wikiup-style housing. How about taking on the project to develop the methods for Aftertime houses, techniques and designs, using stuff that's available around here?"

"I've built a few lodges. Northwest style. I've got a chain saw or two, axes, wedges and a sledge hammer."

"Well, forget the chain saws. We'll run out of gas pretty quick. Can we figure out a way to do without?"

"Well, it's really hard to bring down a tree with an axe."

"I know. But we need light dwellings, not log cabins. Many native tribes didn't cut down a lot of trees. Hard to do with stone axes. They worked with saplings, small stuff. We may need to move often to avoid things that go bump day and night. We'll need light structures we can build quickly, then abandon, that still offer good shelter. Also, a light structure won't fall on you in an earthquake, or if it does, you can just get up and lift it off. How about building something with the slash in the clear-cuts?"

"Hmm. That would be a challenge. What do you have in mind?"

"I have a book written by one of the founders of the Boy Scouts, Dan Beard, called *Shelters, Shacks and Shanties*. It's got good designs for all sorts of structures that would work for us."

"Where do I get a copy?"

"I already have it. Here." Mark went over to his pack, opened it, and pulled out a small paperback. He brought it back and handed it to Jack.

"My brother has a copy of the original edition. Bought it at a church book fair when we were kids. We both read it cover to cover. I found it was still in print on Amazon, so I ordered a fresh copy. Then I found a copy on the net, so I have a PDF of it as well. A while back, I took the original members of the crew out to the lake and had them practice making structures with tarps. Problem there was we couldn't cut saplings, so we couldn't build the kind of houses you see in this book. I think we'll need places more sturdy than just tarps between trees. So I'd like you to pioneer this stuff."

Jack leafed through the book, examining the structures in the front of the book that most closely resembled Native American prototypes.

"This looks very interesting. Now that I see what you want. Does it have to be totally primitive, pre-Columbus?" Jack asked with a grin.

"Uh, no. I thought we might use tarps for waterproofing, roofs and such. At least to start. If we need to bug out, we take the tarps, leave the poles, and do it again. So tarps are authorized. Just not blue ones," Mark grinned back. "Use the green or brown kind that, ya know, blend in."

"What size?"

"Let's try 10 foot by 12 foot. A standard size with lots of uses, and easy to handle."

"I'm on it. How many?"

"How about two cases, at least? We can't have enough."

"Why's that?"

"Well, after the shift, it will rain a lot for a long time. We may have to grow under cover...you know, roofs over the garden beds, so we may need tarps just for the garden as well as anywhere else we want to be dry."

"Okay. I'm on it."

Mark turned to Bobbie and smiled. " Bobbie?"

She smiled. "Who's cooking?"

"We all will, but a head cook would be good. You ever cooked with a rocket stove?"

"No, but I'd like to."

Mark explained, then called to Charlie. "Charlie, do we have an institutional rocket stove up here for education?"

"Sure. We have several. I'll go set one up."

"That'll do." He turned to Bobbie. "It's one thing to know how to cook in a modern kitchen, another thing to run a rocket stove, and a whole new world to combine the two for two dozen people."

"You're not kidding. I'm looking forward to that."

Charlie set an institutional rocket stove, one the Stove Wizards had just built, on Donna's front porch. They filled the pot with several gallons of water, loaded the pot in the stove, and lit the fire. Charlie and Bobbie worked with the stove for some time. Bobbie was excited. “I've never seen so little wood make something so hot!”

She said the trick would be finding recipes that worked with hot water. She had lots of ideas for pasta, rice, beans. She said the big stove was really a very large, wood-fired crock pot.

Mark thought about cooking beans a moment, looked at Charlie and said, “We need a hay box.”

“Oh, right. We do.”

Bobbie looked puzzled. “What's a hay box?”

Charlie smiled. “It's a *retained heat cooker.* Isn't that a lovely term? You boil water on the rocket stove, dump in the food to cook, but you don't leave the pot on the stove. Instead, you put the pot with the hot water and the food in an insulated box—the original insulation was hay, which is why it's called a hay box—which retains enough heat to cook the food without using any more firewood.”

“Oh, that's cool!”

“No, actually, it's hot.”

They laughed.

Mark had experimented on a camping trip once. “Actually, you can do almost as well with a quilt, even a towel, over the pot. The idea is to retain as much heat as possible.”

Bobbie lit up. “Oh, like a tea cozy.”

“Exactly. A pot cozy, but with a bottom as well.”

“So we need a cozy for each pot.”

“Right. That's a great idea. Easier to carry and store cozies than big boxes full of insulation.”

“I'll make some up. That's a really neat idea. You can do more with a stove if you don't have to commit it to just one pot full of food. Or, if that's all you need, you use a lot less wood.”

Mark grinned. “Charlie, I think we have a great head chef.”

They joked about bathing in the pot, but Charlie said they'd likely fill a tub with cold water and mix in hot water from the pot.

That brought to mind a new question. It must have occurred to several people at the same time, since someone asked just then where the bathroom would be.

Donna laughed and said, “Bathroom? Haw! You mean the outhouse!”

Charlie laughed. “No, Donna. They're called *composting toilets* now.”

“Not around here, they're not!”

Stunned looks, gradually replaced by new realization of the type of life that was coming.

TIME LEFT: SEVEN MONTHS

COMPOSTING TOILET

Mark thought: nothing like confronting an outhouse to take their minds off aliens from Zeta Reticuli. He chuckled to himself. *Wait until they confront the last toilet paper.*

Clearly, they'd need an outhouse. The farm once had one, but it was long gone. The quakes would take the septic systems—there were two. So they'd need a new outhouse. The question was where to put it.

They'd set aside a place for the group campsite in a field to the south of the farm. The field sloped to a stream that ran through the farm. They would need the stream for water, so they needed to keep waste away from it. An outhouse simply could not be near the campsite.

The farm lay on a ridge that ran east and west, rising to the east into the tree plantation above it. The gravel road ran just to the north of the farm along the crest of the ridge, continuing on into the plantation. The stream they chose as their water source ran out of the hills and along the south side of the ridge. Nobody lived along it, so it was the least likely to be polluted. Except for runoff from the plantation, which might contain herbicides and pesticides.

To the north of the road, the land sloped downward over land long used as a sheep pasture, with a small stream at the bottom. Runoff there had long polluted the stream, so they needn't feel guilty about adding anything new to its load. The slope down to the north began on the farm. So they selected a site on the farm where the land sloped to the north, away from their water, for the bathroom.

Mark asked, "Donna, where's your well?"

Donna pointed to a spot about 25 yards from the site they had selected for the outhouse.

"Bummer."

Donna shrugged. "No problem. If we have water and the septic system still works, we'll use the toilets. If we have a quake that takes out the well, won't matter where it was. We'll use the outhouse then."

Sharon made a big deal of the need to protect the water source stream from human pollution. They would have to make it a matter of constant devotion to keep the water reasonably safe. Mark was pleased that Sharon had picked up the reins on public health.

The next question was what sort of outhouse, and more critically, who would build it, and when. Donna said they could do it any time. Passers by would think someone was working on a septic system, even though it was no where near the spot.

Mark had a copy of a UN document called *The Design of Ventilated Improved Pit Latrines* that he'd pulled off the Internet. It had been hard to find information from U.S. sources, but the subject was current in the third world. He assembled what one wag called the "pit crew" to look over the document and plan what they would build. They finally decided not to over-build, since it was not clear how long they would remain at the farm. The plans called for a lined pit with a tight cover, a seat with a tight lid, a vent pipe, water-tight roof, fly and mosquito screening, and a tight door. With a chuckle, Abe added a Sears catalog he had in his basement.

The pit would be four feet square, six feet deep. They thought they could hand-dig a hole that size in two days. For lining, they decided to use plastic sheeting. The eight-foot-square covering floor would be wood, set over the pit, with a hole in the middle of the pit. Like a deck with 2x6 frame and 2x6 decking. Over the hole, they would build a box of plywood with an oval hole in it, over which they would screw a toilet seat, sealing the gaps with foam insulation. No urinal, so no pointers. Just setters.

For a covering structure, they decided to make four 2x4 and plywood panels for walls. One wall would have a door, the ones on either side would slope to the back and have salvaged windows with full screening, and the shorter back wall would be solid. The walls would screw or bolt together, so they could be disassembled and moved as needed. For a roof, they would make a 2x4 grid covered by translucent fiberglass roof panels. In a corner, they would add a 6" PVC pipe extending from below the floor in the pit up through the roof, to ventilate the pit. They would paint the

PVC above the roof black, fasten screen over it, and add a spark arresting cap. From a distance, the shed would look like a small storage building with a wood stove inside. To add to the look, they decided to add a small wood pile.

TIME LEFT: SEVEN MONTHS

SHELTER

While the pit crew made their plans, Charlie and Bill laid out a kitchen space beside the old house, open to the air, and they estimated the material to build a metal roof over it. Here, Charlie would set up two 60-liter institutional rocket stoves that they would use for cooking and water purification.

Mark suggested screening the structure, so they made it into a screened porch, which still provided plenty of air circulation for the wood fires.

Over the next week, crews came and went, hauling, storing, digging and building. They were careful to coordinate visits so there were not so many people at the farm at the same time.

Charlie moved his chickens to the farm, adding them to Donna's flock. Now they had thirteen hens and two roosters.

To keep construction noise down, Charlie and Bill pre-cut all the material for the privy at Charlie's place and hauled it to the farm to assemble. Being the inventive sort, Charlie devised ways to simplify set-up, take-down, and relocation of the privy structure if the need should arise. One of these was to substitute plywood for 2x4s for the floor of the deck. His changes made setting up a half-hour project.

As work proceeded at the farm, Jack called Mark, suggesting they get together to discuss the wikiup project. They met the next day and went through Beard's book. After some discussion, they selected the "Pontiac" style structure for their first attempt. It was basically an A-frame structure of poles that could be made tall enough to stand in and could be covered by tarps or more permanent material. The one in the picture required 24 poles of various lengths, tied together by cord or wire. Adding a chimney or even a fireplace was possible.

The Pontiac of birch bark.

They went up into the tree plantation to a recent clear-cut. In ten minutes they had selected 24 poles from slash on the ground. They put these in Jack's truck and hauled them back to Donna's. In an hour, using rope and nothing for tools but an axe and a pocket knife, they had the structure ready for covering. With roof poles 2 feet apart, they decided that two 10x12 tarps or their equivalent would serve as a roof. They'd need to experiment to see how best to cover the ends, but it was clear that the basic structure was workable and offered more space than a tent. Standardizing on one design with standard sizes of tarps would simplify setting up and allow larger structures to be made by joining several units together.

They took the structure apart and piled the poles on the ground. The next meeting of the whole crew would include “pontiac” practice.

Progress was so rapid, that some were getting a bit smug.

Bad idea.

TIME LEFT: FIVE MONTHS
QUAKE

After the thundering quakes and Earth upheavals around the world, life did not get back to normal.

For one thing, the news was odd. So little comment when the ground was shaking, the volcanoes were smoking, and the weather was wild.

You could tell it was happening, but news was focused on everything but, even for events in the U.S. Could have been from the breakdowns in communications. But to those who were familiar with ZetaTalk, it looked a lot more like cover-up.

The grand drama described in ZetaTalk gave the reader the view of the events from somewhere in space. On the ground, it was much harder to tell what was going on, whether the big events had happened, whether it was time to bug out. The frames of reference became local events and rumor. The dams were still in place, but heavy rain had the lakes full. Mark didn't like living below the dam, but he didn't like the idea of moving to primitive space too soon.

Then early one morning, an earthquake hit the south end of the Willamette Valley. Mark and Rachel were still in bed in their mobile home in the over-55 park.

A big quake. Half a minute or more. Books and china cascaded from book shelves. Something crashed in the kitchen. Figurines from the shelf over the bed landed around them. One dog went wild. The other was frozen with dilated eyes. Big help. The whole house shook, jumped with a force that threw them to the floor, then tilted as the place slid off its blocks. When it hit the ground, furniture all over the house tumbled and windows crashed. Then the shaking stopped.

Mark yelled. "Grab clothes and dogs. It's time to run."

They struggled in the dark to find clothes jumbled with belongings. It was raining outside, and rain was coming through the broken window in a wall that tilted toward the sky. The house was twisted, and cracks had opened in the walls and roof as well.

He tried the door in the hall just outside the bedroom, but it was jammed and would not open. The house had settled toward the west, so the west door out of the kitchen was probably blocked. Mark climbed over stuff in the hall and went through the kitchen to see. The refrigerator had fallen over and blocked the path to the west door. He could hear water from a broken pipe spraying against the underside of the floor. Mark was glad they didn't have a natural gas connection, because it would have taken a long time to get to the shutoff as jumbled as everything was.

He continued into the living room, headed for the front door, which opened east. He'd converted the front porch into a sun room several years earlier, so the living room door was usually open. When the house rolled off its blocks, it pulled loose from the sun room. The sill of the front door was now a foot low and a foot away from the floor of the sun room. The sun room roof was shredded, and water from the mangled roof dripped down over the front door.

Mark lunged into the sun room and saw that the door to the outside was smashed and open. So they had a way out. He ran out into the dawn to check on the van, their lifeboat and way out. The van was still in the driveway. He looked around the park. He could see the glow of several fires. He could hear screaming and shouting on other streets, but his street was silent and lifeless.

He ran back inside and met Rachel at the door between the living room and the sun room. She had a dog under each arm.

"You take these. I'll find the cat."

Mark took the dogs out to the van and came back. He located the laptops, threw them in their cases, grabbed the backup drive, and hauled them to the van.

As he ran back to the door, Rachel was there with the cat. Mark took him to the van. As he opened the van door the second time, he noticed the broken window. No way the cat could be unrestrained in the van. Mark grabbed the cat carrier they kept in the van for this purpose under the second seat, stuffed the howling beast inside, zipped it up, and slammed the door.

Rachel met him at the door again with a canvas bag full of what she could grab from the kitchen.

Mark said, "This is it. Let's get out of here."

He helped her up into the sun room, and together they moved to the van.

Their next door neighbor was standing in her driveway. She looked confused. Her manufactured home had fared better than their mobile home, but many of its windows were broken.

Mark yelled, “You need to get in your car and drive up to the intersection by the interstate.”

She looked at him oddly and said, “My windows broke. My new windows.”

“You need to get up to the intersection. We've got an old dam up the river that might have already gone.”

“What? Oh. Okay.”

“You've got to move. Can you do that?”

“Yes. I think so.”

“Do you want to come with us? That's where we're going.”

“No. I'll get some things and drive myself.”

“You're sure?”

“Yes. I'll be fine.”

Their neighbor on the other side came out of his house.

“Quite the shaker, eh? Where are you going?”

“Up to the interstate intersection. High ground. The dam is three miles above us. May already be gone.”

“Oh, it won't be a problem.”

“Yes it will. It was designed before World War II. Not earthquake resistant. I wouldn't trust it or stay below it until it's been checked.”

“You think? Well, can't hurt to drive up there and see. Thanks.”

It troubled Mark that those around him had no clue and were totally unprepared. The decision to form his group was a hard one, since it was mostly about those they would not include. Now his focus had to be his group, and their safety depended on privacy—even secrecy. A new low on Maslow's hierarchy.

Mark backed the van into the street and headed down the street toward the exit to the park. The headlights caught large cracks in the pavement. He drove slowly around and over. Water was pouring out of several of the cracks. In one place he drove up on the sidewalk rather than risk finding out there was no bottom to one large puddle. It took longer than he liked to get to the exit, which sloped up to the highway that skirted the park on the east. The highway was torn up but passable. In a series of slow jumps and rumbles, he got the van to the high ground where the road went across the bridge over the interstate. He did not cross the bridge.

He stopped the van and got out. There was no one else there. He walked over to the bridge, which was relatively new. Oregon had been replacing a lot of bridges on the interstate. The road leading up to the bridge was crumbled, and there was a deep crack where the road met the bridge. He could see both directions on I-5 from where he stood. No traffic moved. He could see headlights pointing down the lanes, in the ditches, up embankments. He could see tail lights in the wrong lanes where cars had spun around. He counted three vehicles on fire.

The oddest part of the scene was the silence. There was no traffic, and the lack of road noise was deafening. The new silence was eerie background to muffled shouts, a yelling here, someone crying out on the interstate. The bridge over the interstate, now impassible, led into town. He could see fires all over the valley, a siren somewhere, flashing lights of a police car. Help needed everywhere. No help anywhere.

Then he noticed that there were no street lights. All the lights he saw were fires, which also glowed orange like the sodium vapor lights that usually lit the streets.

Fires glowed through gathering smoke. The town looked like hell.

Down in the middle of town, something suddenly blew up like a bomb. Flaming debris rose and fell. Farther north, Mark could see a huge fire billowing, flames clear above the trees between. He knew there was a huge natural gas line somewhere in the valley. Maybe it was there. Or ended there now.

Mark pondered the quandary. Offer help. Where. Here? There? Everywhere? Everybody? Take care of his family first? Rachel. His friends in the crew. *If we lose pressurization at altitude, put your own mask on first, before helping others.* It seemed the next thing to do.

Mark got back in the van and thought out loud for Rachel's benefit.

"The bridge is blocked. The ramp to the interstate is open. Behind us is a low road to the dam. To our right is the road to Donna's, if it's still usable. But it goes through town. We could get involved that way. Or we can take the interstate to the exit by Donna's. The interstate is the newest road, built to the best standards. We could go into town, see if we can collect or check on our friends. Or we could head for Donna's. If Donna's, by the interstate. I vote for the interstate."

"You're repeating yourself. What about our friends? The crew?"

"Try the cell phone."

"You're kidding."

"No. They can be surprising in disasters."

Rachel looked at her phone.

"Three bars."

"Any that serve drinks at this hour?"

"Not funny. I'll try Abe's cell."

They were startled when Abe answered.

"You guys okay?"

Mark could hear Abe faintly on Rachel's phone.

Okay. What you going to do?

"We're ending up at Donna's, but how we get there is open yet."

Go there now? Is this the shift?

Rachel handed the phone to Mark.

"No, Abe, this isn't the shift. This is just your normal magnitude 7 earthquake. I'm betting the dams will go, if they aren't gone already. I think we need to get up the hill for a while and see what happens."

"Okay. I think we can get there."

"Best hurry. See you there. Can you check on Charlie and Bill?"

"Sure."

"Tell them the dams might be going. Let's gather at Donna's until we know what's happening."

"Will do. Good luck. Take care."

"You too."

Mark handed the phone to Rachel.

"Call Jack. I'll see how the interstate looks."

Jack was at the sawmill when the quake hit. The day shift had started at dawn. He answered his phone, which wasn't normal. Jack was involved in quake recovery. He didn't know where Bobbie was, said he would try to reach her. He was thinking of deserting the mill to go check on her. He said they'd get to Donna's when they could.

Mark headed down the ramp and onto the interstate, headed north toward Donna's exit.

Rachel called Donna. No answer. Donna didn't have a cell phone, so maybe the lines were down. No. Donna used a cordless phone. With the power out, her phone's base station would be dead. Note to self: get old fashioned phone for Donna.

Better yet, have everyone turn on their CB radios. So why not? Mark slowed to a stop, pulled out his hand-held CB, slapped the magnetic antenna on the roof, plugged the power cable, and clicked it on.

Nothing. Yet.

The interstate was a mess of cars and trucks. Mark wove through the stationary traffic to the next exit, one closer to Donna. A police car with flashing lights blocked the lanes, giving Mark only the option of the exit. A police officer stood by his car, so Mark stopped to ask why the interstate was closed.

A gasoline tanker had rolled and spilled but not burned. Nobody was going near it.

Mark thought out loud again.

"Get off here and go east, we go straight toward the dam on the other lake. Go west, we go over the old overpass over the tracks, down to Highway 99 and out past Charlie's. Let's go west."

The overpass was blocked by a police car. More flashing lights.

Another WPA relic that didn't make the cut.

Mark threaded back streets to the road that went under the overpass and over the tracks. Torn up but passable, though several houses were burning as they drove by. He finally turned onto Highway 99 and headed north. The pavement was crumbled, but his van could roll over the breaks. To his surprise, the short bridge just south of Charlie's was still there. At Charlie's place, he parked on the road and walked in. Charlie was in his driveway. Mark said it was time, and Charlie agreed. Mark walked back to the van, got in, and said, "Next stop, Donna's."

He headed north to the road that went east across the interstate and up into the hills to Donna's. The road was mostly flat except for a stretch that had been cut into the edge of a hill, high above an older cut made for the railroad. There was no shoulder, and the drop from the edge of the road to the tracks below was straight down. That was the stretch that worried him next.

As he approached, he could see a hole in the northbound lane, his lane, where the outside edge of the cut had just fallen away, burying the tracks below. Figures. The southbound lane looked intact. For the moment.

He stopped the van and walked up to the hole. The gap did not undercut the southbound lane, and it looked fairly solid.

Choices. Beyond here, the road flattens out. No place to turn around. Use the southbound lane and hope the traffic is light.

Mark pulled the van into the opposite lane and sped past the hole. Rachel remained silent, clutched her door handle.

As they rounded the curve, both lanes appeared intact. Except for the rock.

Mark slammed on the brakes and swerved to miss the rock, which sat on the line in the middle of the road. It was big. Big enough to damage. He ran over several smaller ones and hoped that the tires survived.

Earthquakes. Spilled gasoline tankers. Landslides.

And working cell phones. Go figure.

Mark told Rachel to call Abe and Charlie to tell them about the collapsed lane and slide on 99, and to turn on their CB radios. As she did, he came to the road that turned east.

Hope the bridge over the interstate is passable, or we're on foot.

It was, and they headed into the hills up the road to Donna's. Mark was surprised that the road was still there, since it hung on the side of a hill. But there it was.

In a little over three hours, they were all at Donna's, except Jack, still involved at work, and Bobbie. Jack had reached her, and she was okay.

Donna's mobile home had slid off its blocks and sat at an angle on the side of the hill. She was uncommonly cheery about it. It would become salvage. The old house still stood where it was built. A small blessing.

Surviving 10

TIME LEFT: FIVE MONTHS
AFTER THE QUAKE

They gathered at the old house. Mark kindled a small rocket stove on the cement porch and heated water for coffee. They talked about options.

Mark summarized. “This isn't an isolated earthquake. There will certainly be more. This isn't the shift. I'm guessing, based on hints from ZetaTalk, that we're headed into months of shaking and rattling. More of what we had today. The shift will happen at or just after the end of a magnetic trimester.

That's either December, April, or August. Well, this last December brought us the precursor 7 of 10 events we haven't heard much about lately. But they're happening. No surprise. April is too soon for the shift after that. Then there's August, which is good, actually, because we have half a chance of getting in a crop before it hits. So I assume we have until August to get ready.”

“Do we stay here, or go home?”

“The dams haven't gone yet, but I think we should assume they will. So we should live like they're gonna go. If either one of them goes, the town is toast, what's left of it. We shouldn't be there.”

“For the next seven months?”

“Here's the thing. The planet that will trigger the shift is still coming, and the Earth is shuddering under the impact of its magnetic pull. It hasn't passed yet. We've accumulated a lot of food, and we may need all of it just to get to the shift. It will probably be gone before we get there. We may or may not have a shot at more food, because this rattling is worldwide. No more trucks up from California. Ever. Starvation may be starting already. The folks who haven't done their grocery shopping this week don't know it yet. We're already in the Aftertime. It's best we recognize that and get on with our program.

"We do need to be a bit better prepared. We were lucky that the cell towers still worked. Trust me. That will end. That's why we all got CB radios. Need to keep them on and pay attention.

"We'll need all the food we can find. Suppose we go back one at a time and clean out our houses?"

"How long do we have?"

"Until the next earthquake. Who's good at predicting them?"

Everyone laughed. Someone passed around snacks.

The mindset of a survival community with a plan was taking hold. The mindset was key. *Draw a new mental map.* Then come the details. Details they could handle. But mindset first.

Over the next two days, they all returned to their homes to retrieve what was useful. The interstate was open, which helped.

Mark and Rachel pulled up to the remains of their house. His neighbor came out, wondering where they'd been. *Staying with friends. Back for a few things.* Mark could read in his eyes something between puzzlement and resignation. He and his wife had no family near. He talked about going to live near them in Missouri. Mark wished him luck.

No water leaked now. The house smelled of mold. They pulled the quilt off the bed and made a sack of it, like Santa. Or a burglar. They filled it with whatever might be of use, especially any food that would keep. The refrigerator lay door down in the kitchen. The smell was awful. Mark climbed over it to get to stuff in the cupboards beyond it, handing things back to Rachel. When the quilt was full, Mark hauled it to the van.

Rachel found a blanket and started loading clothes, bedding. Another load.

Mark grabbed his tools, the deep cycle battery, and the battery charger from the carport shed, rakes and shovels, and a roll of plastic sheeting from the garden shed. Rachel loaded a few keepsakes and all the books they could grab.

Mark packed and loaded the tower computer, the printer, the remains of a case of printer paper and their spare toner cartridge. Rachel asked him why. He said he had a lot of stuff on his hard drive that was worth knowing "Aftertime" and that he needed to print it. She asked what he planned to use for electricity. He reminded her about the battery and the inverter they kept in the van.

And so it went. In an hour, they abandoned the house in the park by the river.

When they got back to the farm, Jack and Bobbie were there. Jack said the sawmill was closed for lack of logs. Nobody could haul over the broken back roads.

Good. Now they had Jack.

Charlie made repeated trips between his place and Donna's farm. Paula, finally convinced, was helping him now. Over the years, he'd acquired a huge stock of wood, plumbing supplies, pipes, sheet metal, metal roofing, hardware, nails, bolts, screws, tools of every sort. His barn had been better equipped than some hardware stores. He brought it all and stacked it in Donna's barn and sheds. With his usual methodical approach, it was well organized, and he was immediately retrieving various items for one project or another.

Abe, Jack and Bill collected a wad of cash from the group and made a circuit of the town for PVC pipe, fittings and cement. Then they checked two discount stores and the grocery store for a list of critical items: first aid supplies, gas stabilizer, vinegar, alcohol, hydrogen peroxide, liquid soap, bar soap, laundry soap, bleach, salt, pepper, sugar, honey, and canned food. Especially salt. They were not alone in their search, as people in town appeared to be stocking up or working to repair quake damage. They found lots of PVC pipe and some of the goods on their list. Store shelves were getting bare. They came back without any cash, but they had two pickup trucks full of goods.

Under Jack's direction, the group built Pontiac-style sheds for each family in a field just south of the fence around Donna's farm, and life began on the mountain.

Mark and Rachel let their dogs, Jesse and Emma roam. Jesse, a cocker mix, stayed close. Emma, a terrier, ranged wide with energy and abandon. They also decided, after long soul-searching, to let their poor cat out of his cage and let him roam. He'd been a house cat all his life, only escaping twice in the twelve years since his adoption. He really wanted to roam, and there was no longer a house for him to be the cat in. He would likely not last long, given his age and the fact that he had been declawed. But that was nature's way.

Mark knew it might have been kinder to put him down while vets were still available, but he just couldn't do it. So now, the Universe would settle the matter, as it had for millennia.

Altogether, the group had ten dogs and three cats. They all commenced to get acquainted with the farm and each other.

Two days later, Jesse ran to Mark, clung close and shook, eyes dilated. The chickens were riled up, and Mark suspected what was coming. Then all the birds in the valley took to the air, and a strong quake shook the valley. A huge roar from south of town told them the dam at the lake there had finally gone. They could hear the crashing three miles away.

Mark could imagine a wall of water coursing toward the retirement park where he and Rachel had lived. It would grind the homes in the park into mush and stuff the mush under the bridge on the interstate. There might be a momentary dam at the bridge to give the town a half hour of extra time, but with the communications so badly shattered, nobody in the town would know it.

The rising lake behind the jumble of wreckage would finally break through and blast under the bridge into the sawmill, scouring it flat. The engorged tangle of wreckage, water and logs would surge down the river into town.

They stood quietly, discussing what must be happening. Mark shared his scenario. As if to confirm it, they heard a growing roar from the south. Over the roar, they heard a louder crash nearer them, just over the hill to the south. The other dam had likewise failed. Its wall of water met the flood from the south to pulverize and bury in mud the shattered remains of the town.

The continuous roar and crash after crash told the crew at the farm what had happened. They could see the sheet of water spreading in the valley at the foot of their hill, loaded with trees, lumber, whole roofs, mobile homes and other remains of civilization.

They were too far north to see what had been the town.

They knew there was no reason to go back there now.

Surviving 10

TIME LEFT: FIVE MONTHS, A LITTLE LESS

AT THE FARM

The crew had settled in to life on the farm. Given the devastation in the valley below them, no one in the vicinity seemed to care what they were up to. It was obvious that many of the houses in the hills north and south of the farm were abandoned. Many were damaged, and occupants had drifted elsewhere for something less damaged. People living in tents or huddled in old farm houses were nothing unusual anymore.

When their food ran out, people tended to drift back to places that used to have food. Some went right by Donna's farm on their way to the valley, heading north toward the cities. They said they were hoping to find food distribution somewhere north. Surly this would be handled like Katrina. Mark told them he might be right behind them.

There were more quakes. The power was on and off. When it was on, Mark printed documents from his hard drive, a trove of material on survival technology. The sort you'd need in an Aftertime. They went through the case of paper and two toner cartridges Mark and Rachel brought from their house. Mark asked his friends to find all the printer paper they could. On a hunch, they found a shelf full of cases at a small store and some offices up the hill from town. The store and offices were abandoned and fairly well looted—but evidently, nobody had seen any use for printer paper. They took it all.

The well still worked when the power was on, so they ran water into tanks, buckets, drums, bath tubs (there were three on the farm) and the stock tank whenever they could. The call "power!" would bring the water team to the spigots with vessels to fill.

They had all become expert users of the rocket stove. They had a whole fleet of them, all but one home-built. The group had collected almost a dozen cast iron frying pans, several dutch ovens, and a large number of stainless steel and aluminum pots and pans. Each institutional stove was custom made to fit its own pot. Many of the pots came from the same source, so they were all the same size and interchangeable, and Charlie had acquired a number of extras. There would be no more, unless they found them later, or Charlie could figure out how to make them.

They used so much water to stay clean that heating water conflicted with other activities such as cooking. So Jack built a Pontiac-style structure to house a laundry. Inside, they dedicated one institutional rocket stove to heating water for washing. Charlie and Bill permanently mounted it on a platform that allowed easy feeding of wood to the fire. He rigged a tank beside the stove and plumbed a pipe from it to a valve at a sink below. Then he insulated the tank with some sheets of foam held by twisted electrical wire. Doing laundry then involved filling the pot in the stove and heating the water.They could dip the hot water into a basin, using a small pot with a handle, or they could dump it into the insulated tank, and enjoy hot, running water at the sink. After some days, they began to see other uses for the hot water tank, including a shower.

Charlie and Mark discussed better plumbing, but they decided to defer such constructions until after the shift they were now entirely convinced was coming. Now they regularly considered *before* things and *after* things. Everything they were now doing would have to be dismantled and stored to survive the shift.

Jack constructed another Pontiac-style structure to be the bath house. A claw-foot bathtub sat in the center, with its own institutional stove for hot water beside. A portion of the crew bathed each day.

The kitchen contained a small, 30-liter institutional stove and four single-pot stoves. These allowed cooking a wide variety of foods. They used two dutch ovens on the single pot stoves to bake cornbread, and they had some similar success with wheat breads. They had a dwindling supply of flour and corn meal, and they wished they had stockpiled unground wheat and corn while they had the opportunity.

In the long run, they would largely be limited to the corn they could grow, or finding something similar to replace it.

Looking toward the day the well would die, they worked on ways to use creek water and rain water.

Given the likelihood that the runoff from the plantation contained poisonous chemicals, they decided to distill water, rather than try to filter it. Mark found designs for several types of stills in his archive. One used copper tubing cooled in a water bath, pretty much like what a moonshiner would use. They had some copper tubing, and Charlie had a butane torch and solder, but they decided to wait on using any of it until after the shift.

Instead, they went for a lower-tech plan based on a design for a solar still, but using a rocket stove for heat, since the sunlight was faint at best. After a few tries, Charlie had it working. With so much rain and so much water in the creek, Charlie said that, given enough rocket stoves, he could brew water for any number of people.

They'd divided the crew into teams. Water. Food. Wood. Sanitation. Everyone worked on the garden. Four trained with Sharon as the medical team.

Mark argued that security needed to be ingrained before the pole shift made the world totally desperate. They decided to have two guards at night, with staggered shifts, so there would be no "changing of the guard" gap. The guard going off duty would wake his or her replacement, so no alarm clocks would disturb the rest of the crew. With more people about during the day, they chose to have just one guard on alert then, provided that there would always be at least two people in the settlement at all times. They kept a scope-mounted .30-06 rifle in the guard tower.

There were twenty in the clan who could guard reliably. Working down through twenty names meant the night-shift duty eventually came to everyone on the list. The late night guards slept late. They kept a wind-up clock in the guard tower, so the guard changes became a sort of pulse for the clan.

Guard duty during the day was mostly looking, watching for movement or any change in the landscape. The nights were dark without the glow from lights in town and along the roads. At night, vision was next to useless. Guards counted on the dogs to notice the out-of-place sound or movement.

They also decided to develop a crude system of hand signals, assuming it might be helpful to convey meaning without making noise, either during hunts or worse, during attacks. Nobody knew American Sign Language. They had the U.S. Army hand signals, which were closer to need, so they learned and practiced those. They improvised additional signs as they decided they needed them. Practicing in the woods became a bit of a game as they worked out ways to deploy effectively as a group without making any sound. Donna called it "charades in the woods," which was a fairly honest description. Abe said it was more like "panting mime." By either description, learning hand signals helped to glue the group together.

As the days warmed, the sky remained overcast. It rained constantly, but hey, this was Oregon, and that's what it did in Oregon. But the mud spots left by the rain told them that volcanoes were smoking. The rain included ash. Mark's white van turned brownish gray.

They learned to prepare the garden and gather wood in the rain. They rigged a shed to stack wood to dry. If the rain didn't slacken, they might have trouble getting the garden in. The even discussed building sheds to cover the garden. They would certainly need sheds over the garden in the Aftertime. They might also need them before.

The wood team scoured the hills for wood. The rocket stoves used small sticks, so the wood team focused on slash—leftovers of the timber harvest—and windfall, rather than cutting, sawing and splitting trees. They did not use the chain saws because of the noise they made. The group did not want to attract any attention, and they blessed the rocket stoves for that.

They set aside a place down one side of the ridge to use as a dump.

Mark chuckled as he thought about what archaeologists might think years hence, digging through their dump. In colonial America, dumps were full of broken pots, silently explaining who had been there and how they had lived. Here, not even broken pots made it to the dump, because they saved all type of ceramics—broken plates, cups without handles and the like—to grind up to make grog, which they planned to add to clay to make new ceramics. Grog would make a stronger ceramic more suited to combustion chambers for rocket stoves, which they planned to make from local clay. All the garbage went to compost, the fat to soap, worn clothes for rags, rags for paper—when they got around to making it. After recycling and composting, not much was left for the dump.

For a while, they kept one truck fueled for expeditions, but there wasn't much of any place to go after the dams went. The road south went nowhere. The road north was shattered. They didn't know if the interstate was still open north, and without much reason to try, they chose not to risk an expedition into what might be an increasingly desperate urban area.

Eventually, they decided to siphon gas from the vehicles as they needed it for the chain saws.

Mark began to suspect that they would not ever be besieged by mobs looking for food and rapine. The many quakes and the steady rain appeared to have emptied the south end of the Willamette Valley. They had fewer and fewer neighbors. The crumbled roads and the mess left by the tsunami from the ruptured dams pretty well ended wandering in their end of the valley.

He had wondered if they were remote enough from the big cities to the north. In the days of interstates, Eugene was only half an hour away. As days passed, those cities seemed to move farther and farther away. Only the very hardy could get to a farm in the south end of the valley, and why would they try?

Still, the group kept up their guard, scanning the road and fields around. They kept an eye on homes and farms nearby, staying aware of who was still there. They weren't very much like survivalists, patrolling with rifles and such. But they did pay attention, and they did talk about what was going on around them.

The weather grew less gloomy. There was an occasional hint of sun in the clouds, but no blue sky. Mark really wanted to see open sky. If ZetaTalk was right, Nibiru might be visible to mere mortals. But the sky was too cloudy. He asked guards to watch for a view of the sun and let him know if it could be seen.

Paula and Shelly worked on the garden. Paula needed to start sprouting seed. Charlie and Jack rigged a Pontiac shed with clear plastic siding to serve as her greenhouse. They built it over a live pile of compost, and the heat the pile generated helped moderate the temperature. The sun was dim through the clouds, but it added noticeable warmth to the greenhouse as well, especially once they had the sides and ends closed in.

Abe worked on fences around the area that would be the garden.

Donna and Charlie watched over the sheep and the chickens. Abe and Jack beefed up the fences around them. With fewer humans up the road, yips of coyotes in the hills sounded much closer.

It might as well have been the eighteenth century. None of the drama discussed in ZetaTalk was evident to them where they were. They heard and felt rumbles in the ground nearly every day. What the rumbles meant was out of sight. If plates were crashing and islands sinking, they couldn't tell there on the farm. Mark could imagine the chaos in sinking lands, the panic and mayhem in cities out of food. But there was no sign of it where they were.

Maybe that was the real punch line of SafeLocs. SafeLocs was the section of the ZetaTalk web site that detailed most locations on the planet and whether they were safe or not during and after the shift. Mark had studied SafeLocs in detail for several years. He and Rachel were in Oregon because SafeLocs said it was a good place before and after the shift. During the shift, the valleys would be hot, so survivors needed to be in the hills. Following that advice, his crew had moved to such a location.

They'd followed the simplest advice about disasters: don't attend.

But they were still early in the end game. Mark knew from ZetaTalk that the rough ride was still ahead.

TIME LEFT: FOUR MONTHS

GETTING ON

The rains came and went, but it was drier than winter. Still cool. Most days were cloudy. There was some volcanic ash, but not enough to worry about. With less rain, they had gotten the garden in, and there were signs of growth all around. The sky was light, and they could feel real warmth in the greenhouse, but there still was no blue sky or sun they could see.

Life had a rhythm of its own, now. Few disagreements. Some were depressed, but the daily cycle of activity helped them cope. Simple tasks, work and rest, work and rest, eat, work, eat, gather in the evenings.

Mark had not expected that they would have this much time together before the shift, which had allowed them to form a sort of family. The upheavals of ZetaTalk's 7 of 10 scenario were more destructive, the chaos more total, enough to end life as they had known it, but not as cataclysmic as the shift would be. So they had time to get ready.

Maybe the world was already at 8 of 10. Who knew?

They were adept at living without electricity. Use the light of day, and sleep at night. Save candles and batteries for real need. They avoided open fires that might advertise they were there. The night guard depended on the dogs to alert for anything strange beyond the fence. Donna’s Great Pyrenees dog stayed in the pen with the sheep, more as alarm than for defense. The coyotes stayed away.

They'd put aside food, which they had intended would carry them after the shift. They were consuming it much earlier than Mark had expected. What the garden would produce he didn't know. They had focused on crops that they could harvest before the end of August. Mark suspected they would be down to food they grew to get them beyond the shift. Given that there was no telling when the first harvest after the shift would happen.

Various families had brought different sorts of food. They had canned vegetables and fruits, canned tuna and chicken, canned and dried soups, a dwindling supply of flour and corn meal, powdered milk, rice, and beans. Some had stocked up at Sam's Club, which had begun stocking dehydrated food and raw wheat favored by those preparing for emergencies.

The daily diet was almost southern, with lots of rice and beans, spiked with meat and veggies. The chickens were laying, so they had eggs—not nearly enough for everyone every day, but some. Charlie and Donna focused on hatching to increase the flock, knowing that not all would make it through the shift.

The garden had lots of squash, beans, peas, and potatoes coming along. They planned to harvest what they could up to the last minute and leave the potatoes in the ground through the shift. They also tried growing potatoes in barrels, reputed to be a way to achieve a phenomenal quantity of potatoes in a small space.

Assuming the shift happened at the end of summer, that gave them several months yet. Even better if it didn't happen until later. They would have food, and they had the other skills. And the mindset.

Greg had shot a number of rabbits, which gave the cooks a chance to make rabbit stew. The meat yielded a little fat. The soap makers had their first batch from the fat, wood ash and water. They needed more batches, but results were promising. They knew they would succeed, as long as they could get fat.

Everyone poured through the archive of appropriate technology that Mark and Rachel had saved on their computers and printed to paper. Handwritten sheets were posted everywhere with formulas and brief instructions gleaned from the archive.

The learning and doing contributed to a weird sense of optimism as doom approached. Few had time to focus on depression. The terror of the shift was imagined, not yet real. So morale was high.

Mindset was most important. In the evenings, after dinner, they would talk about their old life, ZetaTalk, what was coming, and the Aftertime. Mark kept his comments upbeat, focusing on the work ahead of them. They talked a lot about *service to self* and *service to others*. The crew was pretty much service-to-other oriented. Nobody wanted to be a burden. Nobody tried to take advantage. There was certainly no profit to be made in this sort of community. But the profit motive had never been a part of the lives of these people, even when times were good. To a certain extent, lack of commercial interest was a defining aspect of their character, maybe why they were in Oregon in the first place.

But if the shift happened in August, it would cut months off the growing season, so the harvest might be meager. They all knew that, so they focused on the garden, hunting, and learning to trap.

Maybe they would be hunter-gatherers rather than farmers Aftertime.

They had no contact with the outside world. The cell phones were dead. There was no mail. They had no news of friends or family away from their lifeboat on the hill.

On the other hand, nobody came up the hill to see if they were all right.

They decided that was good news.

TIME LEFT: THREE MONTHS

BECOMING NEW PLYMOUTH

The group was there at Donna's farm, saved from the catastrophes in the valley below them, because of Mark and Rachel, so the group deferred to the two of them for guidance and planning. In the back of his mind, Mark kept thinking about how the world had fallen apart, even before the earthquakes and all. The corruption of government and commerce would have ended the world as they had known it even if there had been no Nibiru. No. Had ended the life they'd known. Every one of them had experienced unemployment, tight money. At least three had gone through bankruptcy.

So what was next? The Aftertime. How would they cope? Survive? Prosper?

As he chewed on the question, he thought about the Plymouth colony.

Mark and Rachel had been preparing for the shift for all of the 10 years they'd been married. Skills. Knowledge. Location. Mindset. They had accumulated a library of books they thought were helpful, if not essential, to homesteading the new Earth of the Aftertime. One of the books in the library was a National Geographic book called *The Wild Shores-America's Beginnings*. It gave an summary of the events and perils of two colonies: Jamestown and Plymouth.

Mark liked the idea of Jamestown—the wilderness, the fort, the early industry, and the growth of the colony leading to the development of Williamsburg, whose reconstruction in Virginia he had loved to visit. He'd been to Jamestown and had stood in front of the church, right on the spot where archaeologists later found remains of the fort.

He'd also been to Plymouth, which was harder to grasp, given how twentieth-century the area was, not as charming or revealing as Colonial Williamsburg.

His study of the two colonies brought into focus a few major differences between them.

Jamestown was a commercial enterprise, launched by capitalists expecting a return. The earliest settlers were focused on finding gold and goods to ship back to England. They neglected basic skills like farming and fared so poorly that they were in the act of abandoning the colony when a relief ship arrived just as they were sailing away.

Not a useful model.

Plymouth, on the other hand, was a labor of faith by a group of people trying to get away from England. Financiers were still involved, but not to the extent with Jamestown. The Puritans hoped to make a place for themselves, to which they could summon more like themselves back in Europe. They tried to get along with the natives. But repeatedly in the early years, newcomers arrived who had not borne the trials but wished to eat the harvest, nearly sundering the colony by famine. On one occasion, a totally unrelated group of colonists arrived looking for somewhere else, stayed the winter, and disputed everything.

Probably a more realistic model of their future.

And there was that bit about the Mayflower Compact—worth considering as they contemplated how to avoid corruption and selfishness in the Aftertime.

In many ways, the crew at Donna's farm more resembled Plymouth. So New Plymouth, maybe?

One evening, as conversation flagged, Mark raised the subject.

"We're like the Plymouth colony."

That naturally brought looks, questions, and the usual eye roll from Rachel. Silence for a moment.

Then Bill rose to the bait, with a grin. "Oh? In what way or ways, Mark? Pleeease tell us."

Donna said, "Hey, this is cool. I like turkey."

Everyone laughed. Mark grinned and told them about Jamestown and Plymouth.

"It seems to me that we're headed for Plymouth. Lots of ways. We're dedicated to each other. There are no bankers in the group. We don't owe any money we're likely to be paying back now. We're headed for a fresh start on a new shore. Then we're likely to encounter the new natives. Some will be friendly. Others not. We don't want to fight, but we probably will. We won't have enough to share, but we probably will.

"But what is interesting to me about Plymouth is that they knew up front they needed to do something about handling formally how they were going to rule themselves. Leaving out the stuff about the name of God and King, here's what it said."

He pulled out a piece of paper and read from it.

> *We whose names are underwritten, Having undertaken...a Voyage to plant the First Colony in the Northern Parts of Virginia, do by these presents solemnly and mutually in the presence of God and one of another, Covenant and Combine ourselves together into a Civil Body Politic, for our better ordering and preservation and furtherance of the ends aforesaid; and by virtue hereof to enact, constitute and frame such just and equal Laws, Ordinances, Acts, Constitutions and Offices, from time to time, as shall be thought most meet and convenient for the general good of the Colony, unto which we promise all due submission and obedience.*

Bill said, "That's it? I expected more. Can't say I ever read it, though."

Mark nodded. "Right. The compact wasn't a constitution, or even Robert's rules. There are no details about government. All it does is say they agreed to be a committee of the whole to make decisions and abide by those decisions."

Abe laughed and said, "So you think we need a compact of our own?"

Charlie leaned forward. "Aren't we already doing that. Do we need to sign something?"

Mark looked around. "Well, when the Mayflower arrived in Massachusetts, they had been expecting to land in Virginia. If they'd arrived in Virginia, they'd have been subject to rule by the Virginia colony. But out in the wild, some of the folks on the boat saw the opportunity to do what they damned well pleased without any restraints. That spelled trouble, so the guys who wrote and signed the compact did so to establish some sort of restraints. Turns out, the signers weren't even the majority of those present, and not all of them were pilgrims. Some were ship's crew. But they said, if you want to stay with us, you abide by our rules. Our way or the highway. In time, they did actually have to evict people who refused to abide.

"I think we ought to think about this, maybe have something in place before we encounter natives. There's some value in having a formal recognition of group sovereignty. Otherwise, we have to re-negotiate with every newcomer. And I believe there will be newcomers eventually."

Charlie shook his head. "I'm an old hippie, and I don't like lots of rules. But I see the reason of it."

Donna laughed. "Can we reword it slightly. No kings here."

Someone mumbled, "Hey. I was going to apply for that job."

Someone else replied, "Not until after me."

Laughter all around.

Mark said, "Well, it appears that they agreed first how to agree, then agreed on details like what officials they would need, and who those officials would be. Given their English heritage, they decided to have a governor and elected one. Our heritage is a bit broader, so we could choose otherwise."

Someone asked, "We're Americans. Don't we have a Constitution we could use?"

Mark shook his head. "Well, the U.S. Constitution was a document developed by representatives of sovereign states. It was about how sovereign states would join to form a nation. The big issues were how to pay the war debts so financiers in Europe would loan Americans more money to speculate in land, and how to pay for an army to deal with a long and troublesome frontier. The state legislatures under the Articles of Confederation were very subject to demands of their citizens, forgiving taxes, leaving debts unpaid, ignoring requests for funds to pay for the national army.

"The guys who wrote the Constitution were looking for a way to limit the influence of private citizens. The Constitution was actually anti-democratic. The guys who wrote it, many of them, feared democracy. So they included a house of lords, called the senate, to put the brakes on democratic motives in the house of representatives. They left so little for the little people, that they had to concede ten amendments just to get it accepted.

"I could go on. But we don't have any of the issues the writers of the constitution faced, or, I trust, any fear of democracy."

Nods all around.

Rachel said, "For heavens sake, just agree with him, or we'll get a longer lecture."

Abe laughed and said, "And a test."

Jack spoke up. "I'm Native American, belong to a tribe, and have that heritage. I really appreciate the idea that we can decide for ourselves about the things that matter to us."

Donna said, "We could be a tribe or a clan. You want to live with us, join the clan."

Charlie replied, "I'd like to think about this. I have some strong feelings about government. My hippie heritage is as strong as Jack's. Can we table this? I'll bring some ideas back shortly."

Everyone agreed happily.

The next day, Mark walked over to the wash house, where Charlie was fussing with plumbing.

Mark watched what he was doing for a bit. Charlie stopped and said, "You want to help, or talk?"

Mark grinned. "You're good. Just wanted to thank you for your comment last night. I'm looking forward to hearing what you're thinking."

Charlie tilted his head. "It's not a big thing. I'm sort of excited. Like starting creation over."

"Would you be ready to discuss tonight?"

"Are we in a hurry?"

"Sort of. We are running out of time. I think we'll be better going into the shift with this behind us."

"Okay. Yes, I can be ready. Can I take some time off to get ready?"

"Hell, yes. There's nobody in charge yet to stop you."

"Hokay, Amigo."

That evening, everyone knew Charlie was going to offer his ideas.

Charlie stood, looked around, and started.

"As you know, I'm a tree-hugging, banker-hating, beer-lovin' libertarian, who came to Oregon to be with all of you, who are just like me. I've been upset all my life about what the U.S. government lets big people do to little people, and what they let big people do to the land. And I've lost a lot because of lawyers. So I have a couple of big issues I'd like to address.

"First, I hope we don't have money, or if we do, it's without bankers. No money lending at interest."

Cheers all around.

Abe said, "Hell, that's even in the Bible. My half, anyway."

"Second, I hope we keep electioneering short and make bribery in all its forms illegal."

Cheers again.

"Third, I hope we keep life simple and uncomplicated, close to the land, close to those next to us. So that means, as far as I can see, that we accept that we are stewards of the land, but we don't own the land, so nobody can abuse the land for their own personal profit."

Cheers once more.

Jack said, "You're sounding like Chief Seattle. This is really interesting. I had to do some research on a speech Chief Seattle gave. There are many versions. I carry a copy of the most authentic version. May I read it?"

Everyone called out for him to read.

Jack took out the paper from his wallet, put on his glasses, and held the paper so he could see the words in the fire light. He looked at the paper for a moment. Then he read.

> *...why should I mourn at the untimely fate of my people? Tribe follows tribe, and nation follows nation, like the waves of the sea. It is the order of nature, and regret is useless. Your time of decay may be distant, but it will surely come, for even the White Man whose God walked and talked with him as friend to friend, cannot be exempt from the common destiny. We may be brothers after all. We will see.*
>
> *Every part of this soil is sacred in the estimation of my people. Every hillside, every valley, every plain and grove, has been hallowed by some sad or happy event in days long vanished. Even the rocks, which seem to be dumb and dead as they swelter in the sun along the silent shore, thrill with memories of stirring events connected with the lives of my people, and the very dust upon which you now stand responds more lovingly to their footsteps than yours, because it is rich with the blood of our ancestors, and our bare feet are conscious of the sympathetic touch. Our departed braves, fond mothers, glad, happy hearted maidens, and even the little children who lived here and rejoiced here for a brief season, will love these somber solitudes and at eventide they greet shadowy returning spirits.*

Jack dropped the paper to his side, tried to speak, pursed his lips.

Shelly spoke. "God. Makes me think about all the people recently here, now gone."

Donna added, "Well, you all can have my land. You may have a fight on your hands about farms around us, but not mine."

Charlie said, “It is sad what we've allowed greedy and selfish people to do to the land. I say, at least, let's try to do better. Stewards, not owners. Ownership of land has brought such misery and ruin.”

Rachel had a unique viewpoint for this group. “We've lived quite a while in RVs and mobile homes without owning the land. No big deal for us.”

Mark looked at Charlie. “Anything else?”

Charlie nodded. “Yeah. A few things.

“You all can believe anything you want. I don't care what any book says, because in the end, it's really always about what you think it says. Just tell me what you think, we'll discuss it, and vote. Take responsibility for your opinions. Don't blame a god or hide behind him. If you want to form a theocracy with tinhorn ayatollahs and all, go form your own group.”

Donna added, “On a different mountain.”

There was no apparent disagreement with anything Charlie said.

Mark stood and thanked Charlie. Several added their own comments. Then Mark wrapped up the discussion.

“I'm glad Charlie brought up these issues. They are a part of who he is, and he is a part of who we are becoming. I invite any of you who has a concern or belief to share it this way, to jump in at any time. I don't think we made any formal decision on Charlie's points just now, but we probably should at some time in the future. That's why we probably need to decide first how to decide such things, and agree to abide by those decisions. It won't always be unanimous. So we need to agree on whether everything needs to be unanimous, or majority rule, or whatever. I guess that's my point about where I think we need to start.”

Bill asked, “How would you have us go about it?”

Mark replied, “Well, Mayflower style, we'd all sign a document that says we agree to be a governing body and to abide by our decisions. Then that body would address the issues Charlie has raised, and a lot more, probably. I think we're going to have to wing this. And we're likely to have to deal with folks who try to impose some other law, before or after the shift. We'll need a way to decide as a group what to do.”

Sara saw the drift. “It appears to me that we're about to give our highest loyalty to this group, rather than the country we grew up in. Is that what we're doing?”

Everyone sat quietly for a moment. Then Abe spoke for the group. “Pretty much. That's what we're doing. Fine with me. There was a lot I didn't care for in that one, and I'm not sure it's there anymore, anyway.”

Mark surveyed the group. All agreed with Abe.

Alice moved things along. “Let's go ahead with this. We need something right now. If the U.S. ever shows up again, we'll go with that. Until then, we're on our own. Why don't you guys get together and compose a compact, we'll sign it, and then we can get back to work?”

Donna chuckled and replied, “Oh, you think they're going to let women sign it?”

Charlie laughed and shouted back, “Damn right, we will!”

Everyone laughed then.

And so it was done.

In the next few days, they met, signed their compact, and settled matters of officers, duties, roles and authority. The organization was loose. Out of respect for Jack, and because they all felt the need for a fresh start from the nasty last days of the U.S., the head guy became the chief, the group a clan, and the committee of all those over 14 years of age, the clan council. They chose clan instead of tribe to avoid setting off strangers who might have issues with Native Americans. Charlie, Jack and Mark were also musicians with a taste for Irish music, so being a clan was a plus.

Mark privately kept Ireland in his thoughts. ZetaTalk said nobody there would survive the shift. He wasn't even part Irish, but his soul stirred to the music, and he was determined to keep it alive as best he could.

The group immediately chose Mark to be chief. They were all there in one piece because of Mark, and he was more aware of the things they needed to do in final preparation for the shift.

The council accepted Charlie's list of concerns. A written copy went into a box with the compact, forming as it were, the beginnings of a body of law for the clan. They all hoped, as they signed, that their new body of law would never require lawyers to keep track of it.

TIME LEFT: TWO MONTHS
SECOND SUN

Then the day came that the sun shone. Not just the sun. They all looked up and saw it. It. Nibiru. The second sun. The *winged globe*—a large glowing planet with a fleet of moons. Just as the Sumerians, Sitchin and ZetaTalk had described. Then clouds covered it. They were committed. Certain.

They rushed to get in crops, do the canning, prepare the jars. It turned out that the institutional rocket stoves were ideal for water bath canning. They had several pressure cookers—the old kind that worked on a stove top—which worked beautifully on the smaller rocket stoves. Donna had an enormous collection of jars, so they canned everything in sight. They packed the jars in boxes padded with straw, hoping they would survive the coming shock. The potatoes grew well all over the farm. They left them in the ground.

The earth shook. Wind blew. Night. Dawn. But the lightest part of the sky was not east. They had reached 8 of 10. Mark knew the shift was close. Time to prepare.

Mark called a meeting to discuss the final preparations.

"The shift will be the longest earthquake you'll ever know, accompanied by hot ground and a very long hurricane. We need to prepare for all three. Once the plate we're on begins to move, it will be a bumpy ride until the plate stops moving. The worst jolt will likely come then, when it stops. Really, really bad hit, with all sorts of things flying.

"So we need to secure anything we want in the Aftertime. The houses will be gone. The road will be gone. Our best hope is to be in shallow trenches in the open, where trees and hillsides won't come down on us, and what we're on won't slide somewhere else. To me, our best option appears to be over there."

He pointed to a part of the garden down the ridge from the house.

"We need to dig a trench—gee, I sound like God talking to Noah—or trenches, two feet wide and three feet deep, as long as they need to be to hold all of us. When the shift starts, we get in the trenches and hang on. We're well up from the valley, so I'm hoping we don't have to deal with hot ground. The trench is our best defense against stuff flying around. In the trench, even though it's August, we'll wear long pants, boots, parkas, rain suits, motor cycle or bike helmets, goggles and gloves. Padding.

"Oh, the trenches should run parallel to the coast."

"Why that way?" Charlie asked.

"When the shift is over, according to ZetaTalk, Oregon will be on the south coast of what's left of the continent, closer to the equator. I figure if we're going to move to the south, we'll be passing under a lot of air to get there. I figure that will make the wind from the coast. Really, really big wind. That's just a guess, but it's all we have to go on.

"And we need to bury anything we want to have with us after the shift. Tools, stoves, pots, buckets, food, clothes, you name it. In a trench or hole, well covered to keep the stuff from blowing away. We need to bury poles for Pontiac structures, tarps, plastic sheeting, rope, wire, the works. Take down all the Pontiacs and store them. Everything above ground will be shattered and blown away.

"I understand the shift itself will take about an hour. I don't know how long it will take for things to settle down enough after that that we can get up out of our trenches and move around. Might be a while. So I'd suggest each person pack and have with them in their trench a bug out bag, a 72-hour kit, with all the stuff a 72-hour kit contains, especially 3 days worth of food."

"What about the dogs and cats?"

"Wish we had a good answer. I'd say use or make a harness for each dog—a collar won't be enough—and plan to have your dog with you in your trench. Dogs will panic and probably try to run away, wherever way *away* is. Don't hurt yourself trying to stop them. If they go, they go. Cats—we'll put ours in his cat carrier, if we can find him and corral him. I'll put our dogs on leashes. We do the best we can."

"How about guns?"

"Well...I doubt we have much need of them for the moment. Any predators will be wild with fear, I think, and not much interested in stopping to eat. So...let's put the pistols we have in our bug-out bags, just in case, and secure the rifles and shotguns in the caches. Well wrapped and oiled. This is going to be very wild and very wet.

"Oh, and let's have trench shovels and axes handy."

They got to digging, hauling, taking down. Many of the families had moved out of tents into Pontiacs, so they dismantled and stowed them in secure caches. They dug a trench for the rocket stoves, filled the stoves with rocks, and tipped them into the ditch. They dug five trenches parallel to each other in the west garden for the clan, with caches around for all the Aftertime kit.

They herded the chickens into a coop Charlie had made. It was an A-frame structure—Charlie had hoped the triangular design would survive better than a square one. One side hinged so they could open it completely. The interior was divided into compartments, each big enough to hold four chickens. Charlie had padded everything with old quilts and blankets. Once the chickens were all inside, they would fix a cargo net over them to hold them closely in their compartments, to keep them from being shaken around inside the structure and likely killed. Mark said the Earth would tell them when it was time to stow the chickens.

All they could do for the sheep was pen them closely and hope the herd instinct would keep them from hurting each other in panic. The pen was strong fence wire over braced poles on all sides, floor and the roof. Once the sheep were crowded in, they would wire the gate shut and spread a tarp over the roof.

Musical instruments and laptops, all in their cases, went into padded boxes wrapped in tarps.

They packed all the tools in tool boxes and wrapped the boxes in plastic sheeting secured with duct tape.

Charlie had accumulated 6 clean 55-gallon drums with lids. Into these, they packed food and supplies—everything not already packed somewhere else—with all their clothes for padding. They clamped the lids on and wrapped each drum in layers of heavy plastic, fastened with duct tape. They dug holes for the drums and tipped them in.

They wrapped small bundles of books from their library in plastic and taped all the seams. They laid the bundles in heavy plastic tubs, wrapped these in tarps, and sealed all the seams with duct tape.

In all, they used nearly a dozen rolls of duct tape and 300 feet of plastic sheeting to secure everything they hoped to have intact after the shift.

Nothing of use was left loose.

How do you pack for a new world?

They were about to find out if they'd guessed well.

NO TIME LEFT
TEOTWAWKI

The Earth did tell them it was time. A shuddering moan, deep and everywhere. They did the last things: the hysterical chickens in their coop, the sheep in their pen, the dogs in harness, the cats in carriers. Then the clan headed for the trenches.

Mark and Rachel laid a tarp in their trench. They lay down on the tarp and pulled the end of it over them.

The moan in the Earth grew to a roar. Roar? No. No word could describe it. All the earthquakes and volcanoes of the Earth at once. Jet engines at takeoff. Times an inexpressible number. All pitches. All sounds.

Ears hurt. The air shook.

Ground vibrated. Lurched. Sideways. Up. Sideways. Many times. Wind gusts poured over.

Arms around each other now. Backs to the sides of the trench. Dogs between them. Shaking. Cat meowing continuously in his carrier, barely audible in the roar.

Lurch. Wind. Endless sound. Gusts. Steady blast. Debris. Like hail on tarp. Mark wanted to look but froze. Ground exploded. Now beside the trench. Rachel flailing. A dog thrashing at leash tied to wrist. Other dog flat on ground. Soaked. Like rats. Debris. Branches. Sand against helmet. Dirt. Push Rachel to ditch. Grab dog. Roll to ditch. Tarp gone. Grope for cat. Pull. Roll. Ditch just a depression. Hold on. Clutch. Crawl. Gale wind. Hurricane. Trash sailing. Earth shake. Forever. Then a lull. Over? Gale.

Rain. No. Fire hose. How long? Minutes? Hours? Trash. Torrents. Shaking. Mud. Rocks. Wind. Trash. Roar. Again. Still. Forever.

The ground leapt, and they rose, flew out of the ditch, what was left of it. They'd have gone farther if they hadn't been holding each other. The ground leapt again. And again. They had let go, and they rolled separately to the next ditch. It was empty. Rain and debris pelted as before. Mark tried to see where Rachel was. Mud on his helmet blocked view of everything. He wiped the visor and looked, saw Rachel, crawled to her. She grabbed him. He looked for the dogs. Couldn't see either one. Leash still on his wrist, but no dog at the end of it. He became instantly concerned about his cat, somewhere in his carrier. He crawled back to their ditch to look for the carrier. He felt guilty and worried about the poor beast.

The ground was warm. ZetaTalk had said the Oregon coast would be heated by the subducting Pacific plates, that survivors had to avoid the valleys where the crust was thinner. Mark wondered if they were high enough. How much hotter would the ground become? It was tolerable, but he was sweating in his heavy clothes.

A slamming body blow knocked the air from his lungs. His head hit the visor of his helmet, pressed into the side of the trench. Dirt and debris landed on him, thrown by some malevolent hand. A rock in the side of the ditch punched him in the side as he pressed into it. He felt heavy. Breathless.

Mark hoped that was the moment the crust stopped and the shift was over. ZetaTalk had said that the worst crunch would come at the end, when the drifting plates ground to a halt. Mark had told his clan to expect something big, with no way of knowing what that would be. Body surfing in a churned up farm field.

He ached. His head throbbed. His ears roared like jet engines. He couldn't tell whether the sound was in the air around him or inside his head. Slowly, breath returned. He could move again. Stunned. No injury yet that he knew.

He groped, found his hand on the cat carrier. Still heavy, but he couldn't tell how his cat was. He crouched, stumbled to his feet, walked backward into the wind to the ditch where Rachel lay. He raised his visor and yelled to ask her if she was okay. He couldn't hear himself. She moved, waved arms. He raised her visor. She looked at him, gave a weak smile. He shouted again. She didn't seem to hear. He wished they'd learned sign language. He touched her cheek, put her visor down. He put his own visor down, turned around and knelt with his back to the wind again, wiped his visor, and looked. He could see across the field. Others were moving around. He looked at Jesse beside him, poor dog, flat to the ground, soaked, mud colored. He moved to him, picked him up, and took him to Rachel. He looked again. No Emma to be seen. Still too much noise for her to hear a whistle. Funny. She wouldn't have heard a cannon.

The ground shook and rumbled. But the shaking was less intense.

Mark scuttled to each trench, checking on his friends. He was too wiped out to keep names straight, or to remember if he'd checked on them all. Wind gusted and debris still flew, so they stayed on the ground. He shouted to each to grab their bug-out bag and stay put. Many seemed not to be able to hear. Mark grabbed a bag, waved it in the air, pointed to it. They understood and started to root for their own.

Mark crawled back to Rachel. Nothing to do until the hurricane ended. She was lying on her side in the ditch, with Jesse in her arms. Mark lay down beside her and put his arms around them. They lay there for a long time, rain lashing, trash flying, ground quivering.

Mark woke with a jerk. It was raining but much quieter. Wind, but not hurricane. He hated that he'd slept. Missed something. Didn't watch Rachel. Asleep on duty. Guilt. Acceptance. Mark laughed. That was quick grief. He'd have to sleep eventually. Nothing to guard against that he could do anything about.

Rachel was okay. She had her visor up, sitting with Jesse in her lap, looking at the land above them. Where the farm lay. The old house was gone. They could see the bottoms of the roots of the trees that had stood by it, fallen away from them with the wind. From where they lay, they couldn't see where the wreck of the mobile home had been, but Mark would have put money on the bet it was gone.

People were moving around.

Time to restart the world.

First needs would be shelter, warmth, food.

Mark collected a crew. They grabbed axes, saws, ropes, and tarps from their caches and headed for the trees by the old house site. The trees were walnuts, tall, in full leaf. Lying flat on the ground. As they lay, their branches formed V's with the points into the wind. The crew cut away most of the branches, dropping them to the ground, leaving the large limbs in place. Over these, they stretched and tied large tarps to form lean-to tents. The limbs offered stout anchors for the tarps, which flapped rapidly in the wind but stayed firmly in place.

Surviving 10

It was hard to communicate. Everyone seemed to have the same roaring in their ears that Mark had. But gestures and pantomime served.

The ground was rough. The quakes had brought countless stones to the surface. Moving was awkward.

In an unmeasured time, they had shelters from the wind and rain. At the downwind edge of each shelter, they built fires, using dry wood from a cache and lumber from the remains of the house. Everyone warmed, ate, cleaned up, traded parkas for ponchos from their kits.

No major injuries.

Emma, shaking and grateful, came to the fire.

The sky offered no clue of time. Always the same, not lighter or darker.

The earth seemed more solid.

They selected shifts to keep the fires going. Everyone else slept.

Nothing else was possible.

AFTERTIME, DAY 1
NEW WORLD

The clan rested for the span of a day, although the light didn't change. Rotation hadn't started yet. It was chilly, stuck as they were in the dawn after a nasty night.

As the clan members woke, they moved to the fire. Some were silent. Others wanted to talk. Mark watched them as they worked on the memories, the experience, the trauma. They commented that they were all intact, had come through the train wreck without injury and the car wash relatively dry. It seemed to help that they had known it was coming, that they had prepared.

"Man," Charlie said, shaking his head, "I can't imagine what that would have been like without the parka and the motor cycle helmet. I got hit in the head by a flying branch. Just bounced off. I'd be in major hurt if I hadn't had that helmet on."

They all spoke at once.

"The last bump was quite a jolt, like being in a car crash."

"More like a train wreck."

"No trains now."

"Did you see that piece of tin fly over? Came from somewhere down the hill."

"Anybody looked downhill yet?"

"In this rain? What could you see?"

"How's your dog?"

"Sticking close. Wouldn't eat."

"Mine's just shaking."

"Looks like Emma's back to normal."

Emma, the small terrier, was sniffing at holes in the ground, alert, looking around. A survivor.

The cat howled in his carrier.

"We can't leave him in there forever. And we can't confine him. When do we let him out?."

"We'll there's nothing we can do but let him go. Might as well be now. He'll probably stay near us. Maybe he won't. That will have to be his choice."

Mark opened the carrier, and the cat crept out, complaining loudly, looking around warily.

Donna walked over. Mark smiled at her. "How are the sheep?"

"We lost a few, but we still have the core of the flock."

"Wow. That's great."

"Chickens?"

"Some still alive. They won't be laying for weeks. Fortunately, we have some live roosters."

"Unbelievable."

No hyperbole could touch the experience. But many tried, describing single frames in a long, long movie. Funny. Movie. Might never see another one. These survivors could understand frame and movie. Their grandchildren would have no clue.

So the forgetting has begun.

But, no matter.

Having some idea of what was coming helped get through the shift. The next part of getting beyond the shift would be to have some idea of what was next.

In that, they might as well rely on ZetaTalk, now more than ever recognized as a reliable source.

So Mark talked matter-of-fact about how the rotation would start again fairly soon, that days would come and go, as before. That they were now closer to the equator, so it might not be so chilly. That the rain would be part of every day for a long time to come. That they would now start to figure out how to work, live, plant, grow and prevail in the rain. That light and heat, water and food were life.

The first needs were immediate: firewood, good water, and sanitation. They got to work.

The wood from the skin of the old house was splintered and relatively useless for recycling, so they focused on that supply first. They pulled, cracked, snapped, cut, and stacked all the relatively dry wood they could find and covered it with tarps. Crews spread out to look for downed trees. There proved to be so many that it was unlikely they would have to cut a tree down for a very long time. Most were Douglas fir, but some were oaks. And they had the walnuts that sheltered them.

The water team assessed options.

They had no hope of further electricity to drive the pump, so the well was worthless. Even if they had had a hand pump, it was likely the well casing was gone after all the shaking they'd had.

Plan B was the stream below the ridge. With all the rain, the runoff from the hills above was immense. The stream ran fast and muddy, and new ones appeared in other low spots coming down the ridge. The ridge they were on was nearly an island. They discussed whether the water was polluted by runoff from the tree plantation. Jack had said the company normally used herbicides and pesticides to improve their crop, so the water was likely unfit for drinking. At the least, it would need filtering and distillation.

Plan C was captured rain water, which fell in good quantity. The water team found a tarp with a gash in the middle. They rigged a frame slightly smaller than the tarp and lashed the tarp to it so it hung down in the middle. They put a bucket under the gash and immediately began to collect a fair amount of water. The team used the first water to clean the tarp. As collection continued, Sharon took a sample in a plastic glass, held it up toward the light of the fire at the lean-to. The water was fairly clear, with some stuff floating in it.

Squinting, Sharon said, "Well, there's something in the water we're getting. It could be ash. It could be mud from the tarp. We'll check occasionally to see if it gets cleaner the longer we use the tarp."

She sniffed the water. No smell. She tasted the water. Not much taste. She dumped it out and turned to her team members, saying, "Okay. We'll go with rain water, but we'll boil it, let it sit for an hour, and draw off the top for drinking. Let's get a rocket stove going."

The team went looking for Charlie. They found him near the remains of the old house.

The open fire in the lean-to was really the worst way to heat known to man. Smoke and ash and an incredible amount of wood. So Charlie, Jack, and Greg got to work on better housing, where they could start using the stoves. The Pontiac model had worked well for individual families, and they discussed building a cluster of family sized houses. The Jamestown model, maybe, with a stockade around the whole thing. They also discussed building one large lodge for the entire clan.

One large lodge would keep everyone together, require less firewood to heat, allow shared duties, provide security, and support the current high state of companionship. Even if they did eventually build homes for each family, a clan lodge would still allow everyone to meet together under one roof.

Rachel was skeptical. The group had done well together before the shift, but everyone had some rough edges. In the chaos of Aftertime, those edges would sharpen. She argued for separate huts for each family, tailored to family size. She said people needed space to deal with trauma and grief, and couples needed privacy to enjoy the comfort and reassurance of intimacy.

Mark admitted they had enough tarps for separate huts, and he agreed that one large lodge would likely take as many.

Rachel also pointed out that the ground and air were warm, and she doubted that communal heating would be necessary. She also said that smaller huts would need smaller poles, saving them the effort of collecting "small trees," as she put it, to frame a large lodge.

No one argued with Rachel on the need for separate family huts. But several people felt the clan needed some sort of place to gather to eat and meet out of the rain. In the end, they agreed to ten family huts gathered around a clan lodge. They laid out the space for the huts, and each family proceeded to build a new home.

The Pontiac model had the advantage of flat roof panels, which they could cover easily with the tarps and even plastic sheeting. The family Pontiac house generally had 6 12-foot poles on each side, for a structure 8 feet high, 10 feet long and almost 20 feet wide. They could expand this plan for larger families simply by making it longer. For the clan lodge, they doubled the plan to make a structure 20 feet long. .

They oriented the family huts and the lodge parallel to the coast, so that one wall would be the "south" side to catch sun, if they ever saw it again. The site they picked was near the old house site, hidden by brush and tangled trees. You couldn't see the huts from the only road to the place, so it was unlikely to attract attention.

They would use two smaller tarps at each end and a double layer of clear plastic in the middle. Overlapping the clear plastic and the edges of the other tarps, they would use a third tarp that could be moved to allow light or laid over the plastic during storms. They figured that if the clear plastic worked as a window, they could add more, and they could change the size of the window as weather dictated. They could also turn up the bottoms of the roof tarps to allow ventilation if weather allowed.

Various clan members stopped by as they lashed up the lodge, lending a hand with poles and tarps. The structure went up quickly with the extra help.

The rain was almost constant, and wind storms were frequent, so they had to make one modification to the Pontiac design. To hold the tarps in place more securely, they added a grid of poles outside to hold the tarps down. To keep the structures from flying away in the wind, they added large logs inside and outside the roofs where they met the ground, lashed securely to the frame. They added similar log weights down the center of the huts and the lodge tied by ropes to the peak of the roof.

The benefit of this construction was that all the weight of the structure was firmly on the ground, and anything overhead was relatively light. The structure was water- and wind-tight, but it was also flexible, so the frequent earth tremors that irregularly punctuated every day were of no consequence.

Even with the extra weight and bracing, the Pontiacs shuddered and vibrated in the wind of the frequent storms.

As they used and re-used rope to tie the poles together, they talked about the eventual need to make new rope. The library had several versions of instructions on how to make rope. It was just a matter of time until that work started.

The kitchen team reassembled the kitchen Pontiac, adding more poles for wind resistance and weight. They also included clear plastic sheeting for windows.

Charlie dug up one of the institutional rocket stoves. They'd put a big rock inside it to make it weigh more, and it was still roughly where they'd placed it before the shift. He rolled it over to the new kitchen and set it up.

A major shortcoming of almost any indigenous structure was the relatively crude means of disposing of smoke from fires inside. Freedom from cook-fire smoke was essential to their continued good health. The clan would make extensive use of rocket stoves of various sizes, most with chimneys, which would vent the smoke safely outside the clan huts.

So Greg and Charlie had come up with a metal plate with a stove pipe hole in the middle, with holes around the edges so it could be lashed between two roof-wall poles. Over the hole, they'd built a cupola of poles with a metal roof to keep rain out of the chimney. This approach provided a reasonably weather-tight chimney without any flashing or caulking required. They had roughly a half-dozen chimney plates and cupola roofs they'd used before the shift. Charlie dug up and assembled a set for the kitchen.

The clan gathered for the relighting of the stove. Bobbie dug out beans and rice and started a stew. The aroma was heavenly. No more survival rations for a while. Life was restarting.

Charlie commented that he could see why the early settlers had gone to timber frame structures. Mark agreed but pointed out that heavier structures like timber frames would be more susceptible to damage during earthquakes. They also required a lot of muscle to put up—young muscle that the clan simply didn't have. The Pontiacs were made of poles the older folks could—and did—lift.

Next, Charlie began work on a wash house, a hut almost identical in form to the kitchen. Staying clean was a big part of their plan to stay healthy, so this hut was next most important. They carried another stove to the wash house and set it under its metal roof plate. With some shifting, the 9-foot chimney of a rocket stove went through the hole in the roof plate and stopped about a foot under its cupola roof. They weren't concerned about sparks on the tarp roofs, since the tarps were usually damp, and the rocket stove did not emit much in the way of smoke or sparks anyway.

An additional advantage of the institutional stove was that it totally enclosed the fire, so people moving in a tight space around were much safer around it than they would have been around an open fire. Even if the stove tipped over, which would be hard to do, it would likely not spill enough of the fire to be a problem. Hot water was more of a threat than the fire or the stove sides, but the inherent stability of an institutional rocket stove made spilled water less likely.

Bill filled the pot with water, and Charlie lit the fire. Everyone was pleased by the prospect of being clean again.

The water team requested a similar structure for water purification. Charlie promised to get to it next.

Bobbie stood by her pot of beans. She pointed at the open space in the lodge and called to Charlie. “How about tables and benches?”

Charlie called back to her. “This is a new world. We eat standing up.”

Bobbie chuckled. “Plate in one hand, cup in the other hand, and a fork in...what...your nose?”

Charlie laughed. “Or somewhere else. Yes. Tables would be nice. We'll put some together pretty quick. And benches.”

Progress.

Sharon and Donna walked up to Mark. Sharon smiled and said, “We've checked out the outhouse. The hole is still there—Haw! Some things just don't blow away—but the sides caved in. Do we use it, or dig a new one?”

“What do you think?” Mark asked.

“Dig a new one as soon as we can, and use the old one until then. We've got to deal with shit A-SAP. The cat holes we're using now will flood and poison us in this rain.”

“That's a plan. Can the sanitation team handle that, or do you need help?”

“We can handle it. We'll put up the cover over the old hole, get it back in operation, then figure a new place for the new one.”

That meant more tarps. How many did they have? How many would they need, given the need to do more under cover?

Bill and Mark discussed ways to cover the roof that would free tarps for other tasks.

The standard approach during colonial days, and even later, was shingles made of weather-resistant wood, usually cedar. Making shingles would take time, they'd need nails to hold them down, and flat purlins to nail them to. None of that would happen soon.

Another approach would be to split planks from long logs and ship-lap them on the roof. They might be able to lash the logs to the existing poles, but they wondered how heavy such a roof would end up being.

The third alternative was to salvage metal roofing, siding, and other flat material to use as roofing. They'd seen some metal sheets go flying by during the hurricane, so such stuff was out there somewhere. Metal sheets would be lighter than planks, probably more weather-resistant, and likely longer lasting. They decided to pursue recycling them as soon as other more critical stuff was taken care of.

Charlie came over and joined them. The three of them looked at the trees lying on the ground around them. Charlie said, “It seems to me that we should start planning how to use the wood we have. Some of it is firewood. But other trees are good for building and making stuff. We don't want to burn the building wood.”

“Good point,” Bill replied. “We don't want to burn the walnut if we can avoid it. There's plenty of fir to burn. These downed trees are in the way, so we need to cut them up. Question is: how long are the logs?”

Charlie nodded. “The longer, the better. I'd say, the longest we can move around. We can always cut shorter later. But we might want to have some long beams.”

Mark had made a hobby of working wood the old ways. “Well, if we're going to save the walnut, we need to get the bark off it, so beetles don't take it all.”

That discussion started the Charlie and Bill Lumber Company, as everyone called it, “CB Lumber” for short.

Charlie, Bill, Jack and Greg cleared a space for the lumber lot. The wind had dropped well below gale force, so they built a shed of poles and tarps to provide a dry place to work, and another to store firewood. Soon they would need to be drying wood, whether for construction or fire. They inventoried the nearby trees and sorted lumber from firewood. At times, everyone got involved in lifting, heaving, cutting and hauling wood to the lumber lot.

They settled on a scheme of cutting logs to lengths that four could carry to the lot, where others could work under cover to finish the work. All of the walnuts went to lumber. Jack and Charlie used chain saws to cut logs. Mark and Bill used draw knives from Mark's collection of antique tools to strip bark, showing others who took turns at the work.

The wood team focused on the limbs and branches until they were down to the main trunks of the big trees. They left these for some future time when they had time and energy to deal with them.

They would find in time that it was well they left the trunks where they were.

DAY 4
SALVAGING

Day and night were hard to distinguish without the Earth's normal rotation and views of the Sun. By various watches, they worked, then rested for roughly twenty hour "days." On the fourth day, teams moved out from the clan site, assessing damage, spotting salvage, looking for survivors in the houses up the road. The landscape they found was familiar. Some slopes had slid downhill, erasing any trace of roads and even houses that had been there. Small and large rocks lay everywhere, worked up from underground by the shaking. Some slopes looked unstable. All the large trees were down. Some stands of young Douglas fir were still upright, where they had leaned against each other for support.

They checked a half dozen houses on the road. One house was crushed under trees the shook or blew onto it. They could not be sure whether there had been anyone in it. The others were piles of debris or, in one case, a foundation with debris field beyond. No signs of life anywhere.

When they returned, they gathered around the stove in the lodge.

"Find anyone?"

"No. You?"

"No sign. How about salvage?"

"Not much. The hurricane pretty well scattered everything."

"We found remains of a workshop."

"No kiddin'. How could you tell?"

"Found a vise, a table saw, and an air compressor."

"The vise could be useful."

"Axes? Shovels?"

"Didn't see any offhand. We probably need to go back and take more time."

"Yeah."

"Funny."

"What?"

"Once upon a time, we'd have cared about the air compressor. Now we swoon over the vise."

"True. True. Sign of the times."

The clan gathered. Hot tea and a little coffee, long under rationing.

Mark stood up and walked to the stove, which had become a sort of central altar for the clan.

"I have a question to put to you."

The group went silent and waited.

"Many of you have read *Patriots*, the book about the group that survived the collapse of the U.S."

Nods from a few.

"They made a big deal about not salvaging, which they considered stealing, that it wasn't Christian to steal, unless the person was caught doing something distinctly un-Christian."

Nods again.

"How do we stand on salvaging?"

He stood silent, looking around the group.

"This is a time where I think we need to face the issue and decide as a group. A Compact decision."

Nobody spoke for a while. Mark waited. Tension grew.

Abe was the first to speak. "Well, I'm Jewish..."

The lodge exploded in roaring laughter, cutting off whatever he might have been about to say, and the tension was gone.

"Boy, who writes your stuff?" Donna howled. "Your timing is flawless!"

Abe grinned, then spoke. "No. Really. I don't see a problem with salvaging under our circumstances. I doubt the people who lived here will ever come back. I say let's use what we can. If someone ever walks up here and wonders where his shovel went, he'd find it easier stopping here to claim it."

Donna spoke next. "I don't see a problem. If we hadn't gotten the clan together and I'd stayed here alone, I'd have died here alone. Look at what's left of my trailer in the creek there. If I'd decided to leave, I'd be in chaos somewhere else without a thought to what's here. If somebody came along that could use my stuff, I'd expect them to do it. That's just common sense. Has nothing to do with Christianity. Hell, it's Christian to be charitable."

Alice added, "I think it's about stewardship. It's just stuff we're talking about. We don't take it with us when we die, so it's about how we use it while we're here. We're not talking about owning land any more. We share everything we have. I think we have a moral right to use what we find, provided that we accept that we may have to share with others, if they show up."

"Well," Bill said, "that's fine if we're talking about someone who lived here and came back. If he insists on his stuff, he can have it. And we'll share with others as we can, especially if they join us. But I don't feel obligated to share with just anyone who walks in here, unless they're prepared to work and share as well.

Nods from many.

"So," Mark said, "does anyone else feel differently? It's okay. If you feel strongly otherwise, let us hear."

Silence.

"All in favor of what Alice and Bill and Donna and Abe said..."

All hands went up.

"So be it. It's still raining, and it's going to rain a lot for a long time. If we're going to salvage anything, we'd best do it soon. Anything in the open is deteriorating as we speak. Whacha think?"

Nods.

"Okay. We need a salvage team to make a survey, with help to bring stuff back."

"How about everyone not required for water and wood?"

"Good idea. When?"

"After lunch?"

All agreed. They ate quickly, discussing how to proceed. They decided to check all the houses beyond Donna's on the road past her place. It had been long before the shift that they saw the last people walking by from that direction. None had returned. So it seemed reasonable to start there. Charlie asked that everyone look for clothing, food, building materials, metal roofing, electrical wire, window screening, pipe of any sort, hardware and so on. He basically asked for anything they might have found at a thrift store or a hardware store.

Mark asked them to document what they found, where the found it, at each home site. They'd make a map of the area later, and it would help to have those landmarks.

The salvage crew set off with shovels, axes, and tarps, which would serve to hold the early collection.

They returned in two's and three's over the next several hours and gathered at the lodge to trade stories.

"It's hard to see much in the gloom."

"There's no trace of the place at the bottom of the hill by the stream. Washed away."

"We looked over the workshop site. There's really a lot there. We brought back some hand tools and the vise. Left the power tools for later."

"Why bother with the power tools?"

"The frames, the metal. Maybe the motors can be made into generators. Who knows."

"We found shovels, rakes, a garden sprayer."

"We'll need all the garden tools."

"Well, we know where they are. Brought a few back this trip."

"How about building supplies?"

"The metal roofing is badly bent, but I suppose we could flatten it. Lots of bent pipe, some PVC. Need a saw to get it loose."

"We found a hack saw."

"Cool."

And so it went. They all agreed that everyone who had lived up the road was gone, either before or during the chaos of the shift.

Over the next few days, they appointed a salvage team to locate, map, and recover whatever might be of use and bring it back to the clan site. Everyone else got back to firewood, water, laundry, and whatever else was needed.

They retrieved a surprising amount of stuff that could prove useful, so they erected two new Pontiac huts to hold it all. One would be the thrift store. The other the hardware store. Charlie created shelves out of poles and boards. Over the next several days, they washed all the clothes. They hung the wet clothes everywhere they could, in all the huts, in the lodge, any place under cover. It took days for them to dry. Then the salvage team arranged them on racks in the thrift store. Charlie and Bill sorted and arranged the hardware.

They discussed whether to go down the road out of the hills into the valley. Given the distance and the possibility of being seen, they decided to wait until they could scout out who was left down there.

The water supply seemed settled: rain. Boiling and settling seemed to be enough to make water acceptable for drinking and cooking. Nobody reported any adverse affects, but Sharon kept a sharp eye on water.

During the evening gathering, Abe asked, “Do we need to keep a guard on duty? There's nobody out there, and not likely to be anybody.”

Mark looked around. “Well, I hear you. But I personally think we need to keep watch indefinitely. First, nobody coming with bad intent will warn us. Second, we can assume that predators survived and will gradually move into space once occupied by humans. And they'll be hungry. I think we need to stay alert, especially at night.”

Donna said, “Yeah. I think that's right. There were coyotes and cougars here before the shift. I bet some are still here. I think we need to stay alert. I'll stand my shift.”

Nods indicated the group agreed, so they would continue to stand watch day and night.

DAY 7
FOOD

Alice said, “I think we need to talk about food. We're using up our stored food pretty quickly. We need to have new stuff in mind before what we have now is gone. We don't even know what season we're in or what we can grow. What are we going to do about food?”

Donna said, “We have sheep. And chickens. If we can keep them alive.”

Alice said, “They're not nearly enough. And we can't eat all of them anyway. We need to keep the flocks going. We really shouldn't eat any of them.”

“So what're our choices? Grow and harvest, raise and slaughter, or hunt and gather.”

“Probably all of the above.”

“We can't slaughter yet. So that leaves grow or hunt.”

“Time to hunt? It's quicker than growing.”

Greg spoke from the darkness. “Or fish.”

“Ah. Fish? Where?”

Donna knew. “The lake. Oh. Sorry. Former lake. No dam anymore, probably. The river that made the lake is that way.” Donna pointed across the hills. “There may be some of the lake left, with fish in it. Lots of bass at one time, especially below the dam.”

“That might mean there are fish below us in the mess in the valley.”

“Worth taking a look.”

“What about mercury? I heard the fish in the river weren't safe to eat.”

"That was because of mercury in the water coming down the south fork. Don't think the east fork was as tainted. At this point, who knows?"

"Or cares?"

"Well, Greg, looks like it's time to go fish. Where first?"

Greg agreed with Donna. "Let's try down the hill in the river in front of us. We can see it from the bottom of the hill. If that doesn't pan out, we can try the valley where the lake was. The lake is a hard hike away."

"Who's going?"

"Let's keep the group small," Mark said. "I'd say Greg, with his sons, Brad and Doug, as guards."

"Guards?"

"Yeah. We don't know what's down there. We're exposing ourselves. We need more eyes on the hills than on the fish. We don't want to be seen. If we are, we need to be prepared for an encounter with someone more desperate than we are."

Brad nodded. "Sounds good. Give us a minute to get our stuff."

Brad and Doug returned with rifles. Greg had his fishing gear.

Doug reviewed what they'd practiced. "Go slow. Stop. Listen. Keep to cover. Keep eyes peeled for anything odd. If we see something, freeze. Maybe wait 'til dark to come back. Keep to cover. Maybe alternate route so it's not clear where we came from or where we went. Leave no trash. Avoid foot prints. Cover trail. Basically all the stuff you do to keep the deer from seeing you."

Mark smiled. "Sounds great. Happy fishing, and good luck."

The fishing patrol set off down the hill. Greg had hunted with his sons, so they treated the trip like a deer hunt. They had three rifles between them, and Greg carried the fishing gear. They went down the hill and soon lost sight of the clan compound. The road wound along the edge of a ridge that descended to the valley, flattening out into what was pasture before, wetland now. They stopped at the last tangle of trees and scanned the hills to their left and right and the valley floor in front. They took their time, searching for any signs of human life. There just wasn't any. Nothing but a sea of mud and the twisted remains of trees and the scattered remains of structures.

Doug scanned the valley to his right, then lowered his binoculars. "Whadaya think?"

Brad had been looking to their left. "Don't see any signs of people. There's nothing moving on the interstate. We have to cross the valley floor and get past the interstate to get to the river. The old river channel was beyond the interstate. There's a lot of water this side, but no telling how deep it is or whether there's any fish in it. Dad?"

Greg looked at the interstate. "We can look. But the old river channel is likely best."

Doug frowned. "There's no cover on the road."

Brad pointed. "But the road is raised. If we keep to the north side of that road below the pavement, I think we'll be all right. I don't see any place anybody could be up that way." He pointed to the flat land to the north of the road ahead of them. He pointed to the south. "The town was that way. More folks, anyway. If they're still there, they'd see anybody on their side of the road or on top of it. So we stay north."

They were all using north and south as the land lay before the shift. Out of curiosity, Greg took out his compass, looked at it for a while. He turned and faced up the valley, parallel to the interstate. Looked at his compass again.

Doug smiled. "What it say?"

"Says north is to my right. Says I'm facing west. That means the coast, over there," he pointed to the hills of the coast range, "is roughly south of us now. Son of a bitch. Mark was right. We've had ourselves a pole shift."

"Really? I thought it was just a little storm off the Pacific, with a gentle earthquake for company."

"Right. So do we use old north or new north."

"Let's forget the compass this trip and navigate the way we always did. I don't see it makes much difference until we need to go a long way overland with a map and a compass."

And so they proceeded into the valley.

They saw no one. Greg caught a few fish, noted where more might be had. They returned as they had come, without incident.

"Fish! Somebody kiss this man!"

"How'd it go?"

Greg reported. "Not a hitch. Easy to get there and back. The interstate will be empty for a long time. We saw two bridges down, and the support road to the exit below us collapsed. So there's no way for wheels to get on or off this stretch."

"Good news is the road down and back is passable on foot. So we leave no trail."

"How many fish could we get?"

"Lots. They're plenty down there. Will be more. Nobody else is fishing, and the fish have lots to eat."

The full meaning of that last comment hit everyone almost simultaneously: bodies.

"Oh."

"Okay. So we start a regular fishing business. Greg, do you mind?" Mark asked with a grin.

Greg grinned back, made a mock salute, and said, "If you insist, sir."

"So, we have fish. Let's avoid hunting, lest the sound of gunfire give us away."

Everyone nodded agreement.

"Besides, the longer we wait, the more there will be when we need it."

"How about gathering. What do we gather?"

"There were oaks along the river. The big ones are likely gone now. Not the season to know if the camas are still there or washed away. The walnuts are down, too. It wasn't time for harvesting nuts. Beyond that, we're down to cattails and such. Pretty meager fare at the moment."

"Still, can we do a survey and see what we can find along the river? Same route as the fishing team? Maybe two additional people to go with the next fishing patrol. Same guards. Same drill."

So the next patrol was five.

When they returned, they reported something nobody had expected.

"There are cattle down there. Some of the head from the ranch survived. Just wandering along the edge of the wetland. Happy as clams."

"Did you get close?"

"Close enough. A few females. A few males."

"Ball-bearing models?"

"Huh? Oh! Very funny. Yes. At least one was a bull. Others are steers."

"Let's keep an eye on them. If someone is tending them, we should think about making contact. If they're wild now, we should be tending them. That's too good a find to ignore."

"I think we should check this out right now. The ranch starts across the road. We could be at the ranch house in half an hour. They were good people, managed well. But we haven't see any sign of life over there. Can't imagine they'd have left if there were cattle still around."

"Who goes?"

"I'll go," Donna said. "They knew me. Neighbor, you know."

"Okay. Who else?"

Several volunteers. Donna picked one.

They were gone several hours. The guard on duty announced their return.

"Alive?"

"No. Dead. Recently. Really sad. Two of them. Man and a woman. The owners. Nobody else there. Looks like suicide. Or murder and suicide. Pistol was by his body. The house was solid. Battered but still standing. Must have been a timber frame. It was old. Some windows gone, but basically intact. They had food in the cupboards. Looks like they drank a lot before the end. Empty bottles everywhere. Not long dead, either."

"Crap. No plan. No prep. No hope. Alone. We should have gone over."

"Did you bury them?"

"No, but we should. The place is usable and valuable."

"Well, let's go back and put them to rest. Find out about their help."

"They were Mexicans. Probably lit out when the crunch started."

"Where could they go? Maybe they're dead, too, or they're scared and hiding."

"If so, we need to find them. Let's be sure."

"Yeah, people alone and unprepared are really vulnerable."

Mark and five others returned to the ranch, buried the owner and his wife, cleaned up the house, looked around the grounds. They called out to see if anyone was around. Someone saw the door to the root cellar behind the house open slightly, then close. Donna went over and talked quietly at the closed door for some time.

The door opened, and a man came out. She wrapped her arms around him. He started to cry. A woman and two children came out behind him. The group gathered around them. They talked for a while. The man spoke fluent English and explained that they had all taken to the root cellar when the shift started, that the owner and his wife were stunned by the experience and became increasingly depressed in the time afterwards. The suicides had just happened, and the man and his family were frantic to know what to do.

"Well, we're right next to you. You can join us. We're a family, and you're welcome. We can work out how to keep the ranch going, take care of the herd, and go on with life. You are not alone. You are not alone."

The man and woman started to cry, hugged each other, and sobbed. The children clung to their parents, crying as well. Donna kept saying, "It's okay now. It's okay now."

Donna introduced them. Manuel, his wife, Ramona, and their children, Manny and Rosita.

Through excited talk, Manuel revealed that there was another family, so Donna and Mark made it as clear as they could that the other family was welcome as well. They all went to an outbuilding and retrieved the family. Angel, his wife, Maria, and their son, Alex.

The two families chattered in a mix of English and Spanish. The children clung to their parents, somber and silent.

In Beforetime, Manuel and Angel were aliens, legal but assumed illegal in press and common discussion, often welcome to work but not welcome. But evidently not at this ranch, from what Donna had said. The owners had been good to their staff and treated them like family. Too bad. They would all have fit in the new clan. At least the young families would go into the Aftertime.

Life ended. Life went on.

They all went back to the clan compound. Donna and Alice showed the new families around the lodge, the kitchen, the wash house. Sharon checked everyone's health, talked about washing and sanitation. The whole experience was a bit overwhelming, so Alice settled the families in a quiet corner of the lodge.

They discussed whether to build more shelter with the clan or to have the new people return to the ranch. The ranch had room and food and supplies. But the ranch was known, exposed and obvious to anyone walking the interstate. So they decided to expand the compound, bring everyone to live together in a supportive community. They also decided to drive the herd into the hills to the pasture across the road from the compound. The compound was more obscure and more easily defended than the ranch house complex, and the herd would be out of sight from the valley.

In a few days, they'd moved the herd and brought all the food and supplies at the ranch to the compound. They set up two new Pontiacs for the families. And with some improvised fussiness, they inducted the newcomers into the clan. Mark told the story of the clan's beginning and what the compact meant, asked each adult if they agreed with the compact, which they did, and had them sign it.

With hugs all around, Charlie brought out his guitar, and Mark brought out his fiddle, and they sang and played tunes in celebration.

MONTH 2
CLAN COMPOUND

Life proceeded. The Earth had started to rotate again, sooner than Mark had expected. The sky remained cloudy, with intermittent rain, interspersed with storms. The days were light, but the sun was never visible. The nights were incredibly dark, with no Moon at any time.

It was not cold, not hot. They had no clue as to season.

They gradually rigged raised beds, with good drainage. They erected open sheds over them to provide cover from the steady rain for the vegetables. They knew they would need porous beds so water could run through quickly, rather than drowning the plants. So they added rock to some, twigs and grass to others, to see which worked best. They were inventing as they went along to conduct agriculture in a rainy environment.

Potatoes, squash, carrots, beets. Lots of potatoes. Some things sprouted, and Paula and Alice and others kept constant watch over them. As more sprouted, they became more confident in the covered garden approach. In time, they had roofs channeling water into gutters, lined with rock and logs. They used lots of fir logs to stabilize the land, and grass began to grow. They laid slash—small branches cut off trees—in the paths to cover the mud. In time, the paths became spongy with the mulch, but mud free. Water had always drained well in the volcanic soil. The compound took on a new look that gradually overlaid the old farm of Beforetime.

They also began what would be a long-term practice.

With so much rain, Paula was concerned that the rain would leach nutrients out of the soil. The shed covers over the beds would help, but there might come a time when they couldn't keep the sheds in good repair. Mark had read a book called *1491*, by Charles Mann, a book about the Americas before Columbus. A copy of the book made it through the shift in the clan library.

The book included a section on the Indians of the Amazon. Early explorers had encountered many large villages and cities along the Amazon, but these were gone when later explorers arrived, so everyone discounted the early reports. Many doubted that the jungle could support large populations, because the tropical rainfall would leach the soil and make agriculture impossible. But twentieth-century archaeologists found unmistakable evidence that the early reports were true, that a large population once lived along the Amazon, and that they grew a wide variety of crops in the jungle in great volume.

Their secret was *terra preta*, black earth. The Indians overcame tropical rain with manufactured soil, a mixture of dirt, pottery fragments, fish remains, and the magic ingredient: charcoal. Charcoal held moisture, stored and released nutrients, and stabilized the soil.

So, they started making charcoal using a method Mark had seen in *Mother Earth News* before the shift. They piled slash on the ground, lit the pile, and smothered it with a thin layer of soil. The process was crude, but it yielded charcoal. Paula mixed the charcoal with the soil and waited to see if it helped.

Paula also knew that some sort of fertilizer would be needed with all the rain. The most abundant source of nitrogen, phosphorous, and potassium was currently going into the outhouse with the poop. Urine could be mixed 1 part to 20 parts water to form an almost ideal plant fertilizer. She put the idea to Sharon, to be sure it passed the public health muster. Sharon thought about it and finally agreed that the practice was common worldwide for millennia. So Paula announced her new initiative at the evening campfire. She expected joking and kidding about it. Everyone just nodded and asked where and how.

Welcome to New Plymouth.

Charlie worked constantly to engineer new spaces, new tools, new stoves. They now had a new rocket stove in the center of the clan lodge with a large griddle on top. Charlie patterned it on the Justa stove he learned about Beforetime on the Aprovecho Research Center web site. It served mostly for heating the lodge, and it also worked well to keep tea water hot. They could have cooked large meals on it, but they chose to keep the cooking in the kitchen hut.

The kitchen stood beside the lodge, with counters, storage, a new Justa rocket stove and griddle of its own, and a space to wash utensils. There was plenty of rain water for the garden, so Charlie just channeled the water from the sinks into the already-polluted creek down the hill.

Can't do everything at once. Chaos sets its own priorities.

They had lost a sheep to coyotes, so they built a stockade around the herd pen with 8-to-10-foot poles driven into the ground, well braced, and with rocks placed along the base. They did the same for the garden, and eventually the entire compound. In a few months, the compound had the look of a fortified village at the time of the Romans. The walls curved in a bit at their middles, apparently crude, but done deliberately so the corners formed points. At each corner, they built a sturdy platform, heavily reinforced and barricaded with three rows of logs, with crushed rock in plywood boxes between the first and second rows. The idea was to provide at least some protection from gunfire.

Anyone in any of the towers at the points could see the entire wall to the next tower.

They rigged a large gate near the tower on the corner by the road. The other walls had small doors to provide access to the forest and fields.

The walls did not make the retreat a fortress. They kept out predator animals and obscured the view for humans. But the walls also made it harder for those inside to see what was going on around the place. So they built a watch tower by the lodge, based on a plan from Beard's book, *Shelters, Shacks and Shanties*, so the guard could see over the stockade. They fastened branches to it to make it look like a tree where it appeared above the top of the stockade.

The original fort was now just outside the compound stockade. It still looked like a pile of brush, so they left it in place. They made a door in the stockade wall just opposite the ramp into the trench and piled brush on both sides to hide the door and the ramp.

Since they were providing protection for the towers on the corners, they prepared two similar bunkers inside the compound for protection for everyone else.

MONTH 2
HARRY

One day at midday, the guard called down. “Someone coming up the road. He's got a rifle.”

They'd been months without contact, none except the discovery of the families at the ranch next door.

But they had a plan for what to do if somebody approached, borrowed from the novel *Lucifer's Hammer*, a story about a community that survived a meteor strike. With a few added twists.

Mark yelled. “Snipers. Spotters! Road approach!”

This signaled the sniper teams to deploy to the fort and the three towers that had a view of the road from the valley. Two teams went to the fort outside.

The snipers put their sights on the stranger, while the spotters watched Mark, who walked out the stockade gate and waited clear of the walls for the stranger to come near.

The stranger had a rifle in his hands, like a hunter stalking a deer, ready to raise and shoot. Mark remained silent until the stranger was even with a white-topped fence post at the side of the road. The snipers knew the range to that post, so they had the range to the stranger. Mark knew that the snipers had all adjusted their sights while he waited. Mark noted the wind, and he knew the snipers already had that figured, too.

Mark held up his hand and said, “Please stop there and state your business.”

The stranger stopped, shifted his rifle forward, pointing it down to the road but in Mark's direction.

Mark knew the drill, but his mouth was dry.

"I'm just wandering the valley, going from place to place. Headed nowhere."

Mark looked him over. No pack. No supplies. No gear. Just the rifle. This was no vagabond wandering the valley. He was a scout.

"Bullshit. No pack. No gear. Just a rifle. You're from somewhere, and you plan to go back there. Who are you, and where are you from?"

The man looked a bit ruffled.

"Look. I can go anywhere I want."

"You didn't answer my question."

"I don't have to answer your questions."

"You do if you're standing in front of me with a gun aimed roughly in my direction."

The man shifted his rifle slightly. "Easy. Look, I'm just scouting the valley to see what's left."

"Why'd you come up this road?"

"I'm checking all the roads."

"For whom?"

"My business."

"Not now. It's our business too."

"You're pretty feisty for an old fart. You don't even have a gun."

"Yep. Pretty feisty. And I have five crack hunters with scope-mounted rifles aimed somewhere between your chest and your eyes. One move from me, or one move from you, and you're in pieces."

The man twitched.

"Hey, wait a minute. Hold on. Meant no offense."

"The hell you didn't. Walk in here and tell me you can go anywhere you want, that it's none of my business. Well, it is now. Lay your rifle on the ground."

"No way."

"You really don't have any choice. Put down your rifle. Anything else you do, you're dead."

The man pursed his lips.

"This is bullshit."

Mark yelled. "Greg. One round, the rock to his right."

A shot rang out. The rock shattered. The man flinched.

"Put your rifle on the ground. Now!"

The man quivered. Then he took his left hand off his rifle, knelt slowly, and laid the rifle on the ground. Then he stood up.

"Back up."

The man backed up.

"Now kneel."

The man hesitated, then knelt.

"Now, once more. Who are you, where are you from, and why are you checking roads?"

"From Eugene. Looking for food. Hungry."

"You don't look hungry."

"I am, believe me. Just looking for food."

The guard in the tower called. "Three more on the road with a cart. Armed. Coming quickly."

"Friends of yours?"

"We travel together."

"Hunting and gathering?"

"You might say."

"I might say robbing and pillaging, judging from our early discussion. Stay where you are."

Mark called out. "Each of you sight one, left to right. Spotters! If any one of them raises a rifle towards us, call fire. If anyone fires, all fire."

The man looked frightened. "Shit. Spotters. Who the hell are you? Crap. Why did we have to check this road?"

"Just stay where you are. You might live."

They waited. Mark with arms folded. The man on his knees.

The other men came up the road, saw their fellow on his knees. They hesitated. One yelled, "Harry, what the hell's going on?"

"Tell them to drop their rifles."

"Guys. He's got all of you covered. He says for you to drop your guns."

"And kneel."

"And kneel."

"Harry, are you crazy. Bullshit. Let's take them!"

One of the men raised his rifle. The guard in the tower yelled, "Fire!" Harry, kneeling in front of Mark, threw himself flat on his face and yelled, "No!" Almost simultaneously, a crash of rifles from the compound replied. The men on the road spun and fell. The shot aimed at Harry hit the road behind him.

"Cease fire! Snipers, keep sights on the bodies and this one. Scouts check the guys down the road, but stay out of the line of fire."

Harry was shaking and crying. "No. Please."

Mark approached Harry, walked around behind him and said, "Now, I have a .22 automatic aimed at your head. I suggest you freeze solid while I frisk you." Mark was shaking, his heart pounding. He paused for a moment, took some deep breaths. Then he knelt and took his time checking Harry for weapons. TSA would have been impressed. He found a pistol and two knives, lots of ammunition. He piled everything in the road, told Harry to get back on his knees. The man complied.

"The three guys are dead. The cart had food and stuff in it."

"Harry, what were you all doing?"

"What anyone nowadays does. It's kill or be killed. We were hungry. So we started gathering."

"Gathering means you find nuts in the woods, not food from the hands of people you just killed."

"Same thing. Everybody is doing it. It's your only choice."

"Too bad you think so. So totally untrue."

Greg walked up. "Mark, we can't risk letting him go."

"We can't decide that here. Time for a Compact decision. Let's take him up to the lodge."

Harry looked stunned as he walked through the gate into the throng of people waiting for them. They all crowded into the lodge. Harry looked around, amazed at the lodge, the stoves, the healthy and obviously clean people.

"Who are you people?"

"We're the New Plymouth Clan," Mark said, inventing the name as he spoke. "This is a new world, and we're making a new life dedicated to service to each other."

"A goddam hippie commune."

"You might say that. Now," Mark turned to the clan, "what say you all about Harry, here. Do we let him go, or do we give him the end his companions chose?"

"If he goes free, he'll tell others about us, and they'll come looking for us. No end of trouble."

"But what sort of people are we if we start killing everyone who finds us?"

"We've taken in others."

"But they didn't walk in here like they had a right to help themselves."

"What will he tell others? That they better not mess with us. Might not be all bad."

"I don't want to be part of a group that does summary executions. Let him live."

"So what if he tells others. They come looking to trade and help, fine. They come looking for trouble, they'll find it. But as time goes on, I'm thinking we've got to focus on service to others, not fighting with others."

"You hear all that, Harry?"

"I don't fucking believe this. Are you people real?"

"As real as you are. And our way obviously works better than yours does."

"Is there anyone here who wants to kill Harry?"

Silence.

"Okay, Harry. You remember us. Go. Leave. Tell everyone you meet what happened here. Tell them they're welcome if they come in peace. Tell them if they come to steal or harm, we'll do to them what we did to your companions. Tell them that the selfish in this new world are dying quickly. Those who help each other live, and can live well. Oh, and one more thing, Harry. You can come back here too, if you come in peace, to help and serve. Come back here to harm, you'll hang from a tree down the road as a warning. Got it?"

"Yeah. Can I have my weapons?"

"Harry. Really. I totally don't think so. Now, git. On your way."

Harry staggered a bit as the clan spread apart to let him leave the lodge. He walked slowly out the gate and down the road to the valley, past the bodies of his companions. He did not stop or look at the bodies as he passed.

Mark asked Brad to shadow him for a bit. Brad returned a few hours later and said that Harry had walked over to the interstate, stood for a while looking back into the hills. He'd sat down on the road for a while, then got up and headed north.

Old north, Mark thought. Old north.

So many directions had changed.

When Brad returned, Sara called attention to Harry's companions. "We need to deal with the dead."

The clan as a group went down the road to the bodies. Abe, Jack, Bill, and Charlie carried shovels. There was a section of pasture where the soil was fairly deep. While the men dug the grave, Mark and Sara searched the bodies for any identification. There wasn't any that they could find.

They gathered the men's rifles, ammunition, and other equipment and put these in the cart. When the grave was finished, the men lifted the bodies and lowered them gently into the hole. Then everyone stood silently around the grave.

"Should we say something?"

Mark knew that religious tradition was not strong in the clan, save for a few. So he invited those to speak. "Would anybody like to offer some appropriate words on this sad occasion?"

Shelly had been depressed and sad in recent days. Mark looked at her. She took a breath, looked at him, then at the bodies. "It's really sad that they found us in the mood they were in."

Paula looked glum. "Maybe if they had found us sooner, they might not have gone the way they did."

Shelly nodded. "Now they are gone, and they have put a burden on us, in our hearts."

Charlie pursed his lips. He had his own feelings, but he respected Paula's faith. "They had free will, and they chose to do what they were doing. Free will always has consequences. We had the freedom to surrender, but we chose to resist what we considered evil. It was done well and quickly. We spared Harry. Life goes on for all, and it ends for all. May we pay more attention to how we live, because of this event."

Sara added to his thought. "And may these souls learn from the consequences of their choices, wherever they are now."

Donna was less sentimental. "Well, we had a responsibility to each other to do what we did. We have taken in others, like the families at the ranch. Our hearts are in the right place. I think we did the right thing, and they did the wrong thing. That's all there is to it. Death itself is not terrible. It just is. We're all headed there. We have no idea how many died around us before, during, and after the shift. We couldn't even help them, let alone these three. And what about the poor folks these guys found before they reached us? We just need to keep going, doing what we've been doing."

Mark waited a moment. "Who fired the shots that killed them?"

Hands went up, slowly, not high.

Mark looked at them. Eyes met. Mark spoke kindly. "Thank you for doing what we all trained to do. You did well. Thank you for protecting us. There is no guilt on you for this."

Unrehearsed, the entire clan said, "Amen."

Mark summed up his own feelings. "It's probably hopeful that we're not gloating, and we're not devastated. We'll face many new and unpleasant choices now. This was just one of them. Let's just bury them and go on."

And so they did.

MONTH 2, LATER
CONSIDERING DEATH

Everyone was a bit shaken after the incident with Harry and his companions.

"I worry that he'll come back with friends to take revenge," Alice commented over breakfast. "Still, I think we did the right thing, prudent or not."

Mark finished chewing. "I don't think he'll be back, at least not to get even. Seems to me that revenge is a function of family and society. You get even because you lose something that's really important to you. Well, Harry was with those guys, but he didn't seem overly upset when they went down. I don't think they were family. So I don't figure he'd think about revenge. He'd probably admit that we were unduly fair with him. The shift has demolished so many social structures, especially family. Harry was just coping with life after the shift in the only way that was obvious to him. I don't think he liked it much either."

Mark shifted the conversation. "We are in a very small minority of survivors. We prepared. We had tools ready to restart life. Imagine how we'd have done if we hadn't prepared? For one thing, how would we be doing if we didn't have tarps?"

Alice winced. "Ooh. Not well. Tarps have made a tremendous difference. We certainly wouldn't have decent shelter. I never would have included so many tarps in a survival plan."

"Okay. How about no rocket stoves?"

"Oh, big time bad news. We'd be struggling to find enough wood to keep open fires going. Smoke and soot all over. Bad air. Wheezing. Coughing. Irritated eyes. Maybe pneumonia."

"Right. So we are very rare in this world. Most folks out there might even agree with Harry that the only choice to survive right now is to hunt down and gather from any weaker people who have a little food left. Hell, we might have been more like him if we hadn't been so well prepared.

"Remember that two-thirds of the people who were on Earth at the shift were primarily service-to-self. STS. I'll take what I want when I want it, and to hell with you. So life among the survivors could be, as they say, nasty, brutish, and short right now. The STS types are killing each other off. Over time, the remainder will be more likely service-to-others. The Darwin Effect, again. Undecideds, in the middle, could go either way. I'm hoping that there are other clans like ours, where service-to-other people are clustering and supporting each other."

"It would be nice to know."

"Maybe Harry will tell someone who tells someone, and another someone will come walking up the hill to meet us."

"Maybe Harry will come back himself?"

"Maybe. Service-to-other is a tendency, not a defined genetic condition. There have to be degrees, and some are just borderline. Some may join an STO community because it's their only option. They may be reluctant to share and less likely to spend much time thinking about others. But over time, they might change if they see the benefit—like brushing your teeth—even catch themselves thinking about someone else. What a concept. Practice makes habit. We may encounter a lot of folks like Harry."

Donna walked over and sat down. Abrupt as usual, she interrupted. "Shelly's a mess."

"Oh? What do you mean?"

"She's walking by herself, moping around. Had tears in her eyes. Didn't eat breakfast."

"Do you know why?"

"I suppose her kids. They didn't join us. They were down in California somewhere. Who knows where they are now. Or were."

"Have you talked to her?"

"You know me. I don't cry. No. She's avoiding me."

Alice rose, collected her dishes. "I'll go talk to her."

Mark smiled at Donna but waited until Alice had gone. "So how are the sheep?"

"Pretty good. The new fence helped. They're less skittish."

"Are we going to get any lambs?"

"Don't know. That old male seems preoccupied."

"Can't imagine why. Could you give him a copy of Playram?"

Donna slapped her hand on the table and let out a shriek. The others in the lodge just then turned to look.

She laughed for a bit. "That's good. If you have a copy, I'll give it to him." She cackled again.

"Sorry, I left it at home. So," he paused, "are sheep like chickens that get weird after a trauma?"

"Boy, do they love their routine. The shift was quite the trauma, and they stopped eating. Then we had the coyote take one of them, and that messed them up. Then we've had all the rain, which messed up the ground, and they really like clean pasture. So there's not much happening now they care for. They breed in the fall, and I suppose the ewes are not sure this is fall, or what. For that matter, neither am I. If they're not interested, even Playram won't help."

"So we need to do what we can to establish and maintain routine for them?"

"Something like that. For one thing, more contact with people would help."

"Do you need some help?"

"Couldn't hurt."

"How about the kids from the ranch?"

"Hey, that would be cool. For the sheep and the kids."

"Hokay. How about we get 4-H going again?"

"Say, that's not a bad idea."

"I don't remember enough to do the whole 4-H thing. What was it? Heart, hands, health, and head. Hmm. We could do a lot with those words, especially with the kids."

"I could get excited about that, even though I was never in 4-H."

"My daughter was in 4-H for a few years. I went to a lot of meetings and was a project leader for woodworking and photography. At least we can still do woodworking. Could be a framework for getting kids involved and focused."

"How do we start?"

"Put it to the clan. Tonight?"

"Sure. Lookin' forward."

Donna got up and headed to the sheep corral.

Surviving 10

Mark thought about the kids. There were nine of them. From roughly 5 years old to 18. Maybe the older kids could teach the younger ones. Some couldn't read. If those kids didn't learn to read, the books they'd hauled up the hill would soon enough be used in the outhouse. Much to do. But again, keeping busy was the only way to deal with the trauma of the shift and the chaos that followed.

Then he thought about the old issue of needing a place to go if they had to bug out. They'd talked about having a route to flee into the hills to avoid an approaching legion of STS marauders. That sounded likely when all they had were some tarps over a tree. Now they had a real settlement. The sheep. The garden under cover. The stockade. And the fishing so close. A lot of work to lose and re-do.

There hadn't been any legions yet. Just Harry and his group.

They were well down the south end of the valley. South again. What was it now? Let's see. East. The roads were useless. Nobody would be coming up from California along the interstate, not knowing what might be ahead. Quakes and landslides pretty much restored the mountains to the way they looked before the roads and railroads. Hell, more likely we'd be going there. Anyone coming from California now would come up...along...the coast. That would make them more a problem for folks on the coast than around here.

The coast. What must it look like now? ZetaTalk said we'd gain a thousand feet of elevation. That would bring ocean bottom above the surface. The new coast might be miles further out now.

Mark had a pang of longing to see the coast again.

The other direction? Eugene? Portland? The valley was a wetland again. No roads worth using. The river flowed toward Eugene and Portland, and it was at flood. Anyone coming their way couldn't use the river and would have to slog through the bog. On foot. Without draft animals, they'd have to carry food with them. On their backs. If they had food, why would they move in this direction? It just didn't seem likely there would be hoards of brigands in their end of the Willamette Valley in Aftertime Oregon.

Now, maybe someone had heard about the Plymouth Clan. But they'd also have heard about snipers and spotters, who killed those who threatened them. Why would anyone take that risk for a meal?

No. It was more likely that, if the word got out, anyone coming down the valley to the Clan would be looking to join or live near in some sort of harmony. That would be the only reason to bother with the effort to get to them. A filtering out of the service-to-other folk still alive.

Or the calling of opportunists and con men.

Alice came back into the lodge, saw Mark was still where she'd left him, and sat down at the table.

"Shelly's depressed, sad, doesn't see any reason to go on."

"What did you say?"

"What can anyone say? It's not like there's an identifiable goal to achieve. We're just coping and living a day at a time. People live because, well, they just do. You go on. If you think about it, you might say it's to see grandchildren, or find a husband, or to get a degree, or whatever. But if you really sit down and ponder *why am I doing this?* and all the answers touch on things you've already lost, you wonder why bother going on."

Mark sighed. "In the end, all the problems of the world are spiritual. I used to believe that you could explain everything a person did in his or her life by looking at how they defined death."

"How's that?"

"Well, if you think death is defeat, you hang on to life no matter what, grasp at gruesome medical treatments just to keep on breathing. And if you have the power over someone in a coma, you put them on a ventilator, put in a stomach tube and all that, just because you're terrified of defeat. You can't let go of loved ones, because to do so is defeat. If you lose them, you've really lost them. Death for such a person is absolutely crushing, absolutely terrifying. The deepest grief imaginable, and you never get to acceptance.

"But say you think death is just the end of all things, that the only purpose of life it to indulge until its over. You define life as one long party, gathering all the toys and possessions you can. *He who has the most toys when he dies, wins.* Because that was all there was to life.

"Now, say you think death is a point of judgment followed by either heaven or hell, you torment yourself all your life, wondering if you're getting enough points or believing the right things to make it to heaven. You latch onto somebody or some group that claims they have the right beliefs or know how to get the points, and you live by their rules. If the group judges, you become judgmental. If the group does mission work, you go on missions. If the group prays a lot, you pray a lot.

"A lot of groups that enjoy that sort of control tell their faithful that this life is their only chance. *Do what we say 'til you die, or you'll burn in hell when you do. It's turn or burn, baby.* To allow that a member might have a chance in another life would undermine the group's control. I knew a fellow once who belonged to such a group who told me that my belief in reincarnation was blasphemy. I didn't bother to argue with him, because his idea of blasphemy was defined by his group, and his group had no authority over me because I wouldn't allow it. Blasphemy was just one of their concepts, not anything I considered true.

"But say you think this life is a school, or just one class in a school, that death is just the end of the term, where you get an assessment of your progress during the term, and then you start a new term. You know, reincarnate. If you believe that, you see a lot of things differently. Hell, you see everything differently. Things are, as you yourself said when we were debating whether to salvage, just things. We're stewards of things, not owners. It's not what we have, but what we do with it while we have it, how we care, that matters.

"Now some people think reincarnation means a person can do any damn thing he wants, without consequences, because even when he dies, he just comes back to do it all over again. I've never met anyone like that, but some have a problem with the idea of reincarnation because of that. Everyone I know who believes in reincarnation also believes in karma, that somehow, the good we do matters, that the object is to become a better person, a lighter soul. We don't do good things to get points. We do good things because that's just what we do. Like going to the pound to rescue a dog or cat. It's a natural flowing from who we are.

"I think a lot of service-to-other-oriented people tend to lean this way.

"And if you believe in reincarnation, at some point you become aware of soul families. Souls reincarnate repeatedly together in various combinations, usually to help each other grow spiritually. When you meet some people, you feel like you've known them before. That's because you have. So your soul relationships begin to matter more than mere blood relationships. Or maybe the blood relationships matter only because they are reincarnated from the same soul family. Genealogy becomes less an interest than focusing on those you encounter every day. We're not meeting by accident. We're reuniting. We're all related at the soul level. That also means that, since we see each other repeatedly, death is not defeat, or goodbye forever, or I'll never see you again, or any of that. It's just thanks, friend. I'll see you in a while.

"In all that, if you accept the premise, where would you put Shelly?"

Alice thought a while. "I don't think she's on good terms with death. She assumes her kids are gone, given where they were. It's even worse that she doesn't know for sure. Death for her is defeat. So a lot of time, she's into deep loss."

Mark nodded. "I agree. Do you think there is anything anyone could say to convince her otherwise?"

"Well, for me, I worked that out for myself. You just come to believe some things. You can read one book, and you can just know it's true. You can read another book and know it's not true. The judgment is ultimately internal. You just *know.* And you also come to believe that you alone are the final authority, that no other person or group has any authority over you. Even those who buy everything a fundamentalist group dictates have actually themselves given that group its authority."

Alice stopped for a moment. Mark waited. Alice continued. "I don't think this is something you can just explain to her. She may come to a different view of death herself, or she may stay as she is until she...leaves."

"She's likely to leave sooner if she sees death as defeat, thinking there's nothing around us right now except defeat."

"I suppose. Still, I think that's ultimately her decision."

Mark nodded. "I agree. Well, about all we can do is keep her busy and let her know we care. Keep the hugs going."

"I can do that."

"How's the garden?"

"Good. We're figuring stuff out. The growing sheds are working. We can control the water to the plants, so they're responding. I'm surprised that the sunlight we're getting seems to be helping. Not bumper crops, but still usable."

Mark was glad to hear that. The sky was completely overcast. The sun never appeared. But it was light, and it was warmer in the greenhouse, so there was some solar energy.

"And if the wind changes, we have some defense."

"Wind changes? What do you mean?"

"ZetaTalk said all the volcanoes would go that had burped in the last ten thousand years. That would include South Sister. They also said ash from Oregon volcanoes would blow out to sea with the new trade wind currents. If South Sister is pumping ash, we're not getting much. Hope we never do."

"Oh, great. Thanks for something else to worry about."

"No, really, I think the sheds will be some protection. It will happen or it won't. No point in worrying. Besides, volcanic ash can improve the soil."

"Okay. I'll go back to worrying about other stuff."

"How's Bill?"

"He's loving all the creation and construction and invention."
"Great. We're lucky to have you both."
"Thanks. Same to you."
Alice rose and headed to the garden.

MONTH 2
BARGAINING WITH DEATH

Mark sat alone, looking at the empty lodge. Everyone was out somewhere at task. He reached into his pocket, pulled out the bottle, took off the lid, and poured the pills onto the table. He counted them.

Twice.

Seventy-two.

He'd lost his thyroid to cancer some years earlier. Like diabetics and a host of other patients in Beforetime, he depended on hormone replacement to live. His drug was thyroid hormone. He'd laid in almost a year's supply —it went bad after a year—while it was still available. He was supposed to take two pills a day to continue living normally. One pill a day was marginal. He was taking one pill every other day. Maybe the pills were already going bad. The changes in his hair and skin were obvious to him but as yet unnoticed by others.

During cancer treatment, he'd gone without thyroid hormone for six weeks. He remembered the wild dreams, the sleepless nights, the loss of muscle tone, the muscle spasms. All those were returning.

Or maybe, he had a new cancer. Or something else, entirely.

He felt old.

He'd asked Donna, who had once taken thyroid supplement, if she had any thyroid hormone left. She didn't.

Well.

Seventy-two pills. One every other day was less than half a year, then none at all. He wasn't sure what the terminal stages of no thyroid hormone would be like. Gradual collapse? Something acute and nasty? He really didn't want to find out.

What to do. He chuckled. What would Shelly say? What would he say to Shelly?

Give up, or get going.

So, best get going. Thyroid hormone was natural. All mammals, birds, and fish had thyroids. The earliest treatment for thyroid disorder was a stew of sheep or pig thyroid. So it was theoretically possible to make new thyroid hormone in Aftertime.

He went looking for Sharon. He found her studying *Where There Is No Doctor*, a priceless book Mark had gotten from the Hesperion Foundation. He also had downloaded a copy and printed it as well.

Mark explained his situation. Sharon had been thinking about collecting herbs, learning their medicinal values, and had been reading a book in the clan library on that. The clan was already out of pain killers, and Charlie had depended on ibuprofen in the Beforetime. So she was looking for willow. She loved the challenge.

She called to Greg, who joined them. They discussed Mark's problem, and Sharon finally said, "Well, we just need to figure out a way to find our own source of thyroid hormone. Lots of people, especially as they get older, have low thyroid issues. This could help us all."

Greg was surprised that fish have thyroids. He had no idea what they looked like.

They discussed mammals. The clan had sheep and the cattle herd at the ranch, so if they ever butchered one, they'd be able to save the thyroid for thyroid hormone. But it wasn't reasonable to kill one just for that. Squirrels? Smaller mammal. Smaller thyroid. Not unreasonable to kill a squirrel for a little meat and the thyroid.

Greg said, "Well, we could probably supply a steady diet of squirrel thyroid, if we only knew which of all those gooey things was the thyroid."

Mark smiled. "Ah, well, in Beforetime, I was thinking about this, did a Google search, and found a paper a guy had done on the comparative anatomy of a variety of mammals, specifically for their thyroid and adrenal glands. It includes a description of the location and appearance of the thyroid glands in each mammal."

Greg slapped the table and said, "Time to go hunting. Can I use your 22?"

Mark nodded. "Sure. I have hollow point and solid ammo. Probably best to use solid. You need to avoid the head and neck."

Greg smiled. “I'll be lucky to hit one at all. Take your chances and maybe get lucky.”

While Greg was gone, Sharon read the document Mark had mentioned.

Some hours later, Mark, Greg, and Sharon stood around the table where the dead squirrel lay.

“I wish we had a dissecting kit.”

Mark said, “We have a field surgical kit in the first aid stuff.”

“Hate to use it on a squirrel. What if we need it for one of us?”

“Well, it has a disposable scalpel, but we'll not be disposing it. It's all we have. Just sterilize it when you're done. That's why we have a pressure cooker.”

They knew the pressure cooker was marginal, but it was much better than nothing.

“Hokay. Let's get started.”

Sharon peeled the skin back from the neck, carefully exposed the larynx and removed the two red thyroid masses. She dropped them in a spoon.

They all looked at the tiny blobs in the spoon. Finally, Sharon said, “Now what do we do with them?”

Mark had thought about that. “Well, we can't do blood tests to see what I need, and we really have no way to determine how much thyroid hormone is in those blobs. All we have to go on are clinical symptoms, which is, how do I feel after I take some? I'd been taking 90 to 120 milligrams of natural thyroid for years. The paper we have says a squirrel thyroid weighs about 30 milligrams. Even assuming it's pure thyroid hormone, which it probably isn't, I'd need to take three or four a day for a full dose, so one shouldn't make much of a dent. How about I just swallow it, and see how I feel?”

Greg said, “Now that's pure science.”

Mark chuckled. “Yeah. I think we'll call it a clinical trial.”

Sharon asked, “Do you want to cook it or anything?”

Mark shook his head. “Cooking might damage it. Do we have any tea?”

Sharon retrieved a cup. “Sweetened?”

“Please.”

Mark scooped the spoon into his mouth, took a swig of tea, and swallowed. Took another swig.

“Well, that's thyroid. Just like the old natural thyroid I've been taking. Tastes like a cattle feedlot.”

Greg said, “Looks like I need to do some more hunting. Does it have to be squirrel?”

"No. Almost any mammal mentioned in the paper would do."

Sharon said, "I'll make a balance scale. Then I'll make some weights for it, using one of your 60-milligram pills as the standard. That way, I should be able to track how much you're getting, so we can figure out how much you should have."

Greg smiled. "As I said, pure science. This is cool."

Mark replied. "Welcome to the seventeenth century."

Sharon smiled. "We're gaining. Yesterday, we were in the twelfth. Speaking of the seventeenth century, we need to talk about the outhouse."

"Oh? Problem?"

"Big one. We're about out of toilet paper, catalogs, newspapers, everything. What are we gonna do?"

Mark smiled. Welcome to India. He'd been there once, remembered the terror of his first encounter with the hole in a wet floor, with no toilet paper in sight.

"Most of the world didn't use toilet paper."

"What did they do?"

"They washed. Small pitcher of water in the loo. Clean water. Use water and left hand to wash hind end. It's actually pretty sanitary. More easily done when squatting rather than sitting. Some folks remove all their clothes from the waist down to eliminate the issue of getting clothes wet. Just gotta clear the area to be washed. Squatting works best. If squatting caught on here, we could modify the outhouse. After washing butt, drip and air dry, put clothes back on, and wash hands thoroughly.

Mark chuckled. Note to self: check on soap production.

"Folks in Asia reserve their left hand for sanitation, right hand for eating and greeting. We can as well. If we ever get to making paper, it wouldn't be for the toilet."

"Well, I'm the medic. Guess I'll go try that and then hold a class."

"Learn by doing. That's the 4-H way."

"I'd hate to be the judge for that at the county fair."

MONTH 3
CONSIDERING FAITH

Mark stopped by the medic hut. Sharon and Greg were sitting at the table but not talking. They looked troubled.

"Is something wrong?"

Sharon looked at him, looked at Greg, looked down at her hands.

Mark sat down, put his elbows on the table, rested his chin on his hands. And waited.

Sharon looked up, took a deep breath. "Mark, we've been reading your books in the clan library. This ZetaTalk stuff. You believe it?"

"Yes, more of it than ever, since so much that they predicted has happened as they said. Have you read the material?"

"Yes. Mark, it's all so contrary to the Bible. I've accepted Jesus. He's the center of my life. I've prayed and prayed. Either the Zetas or the Bible is true. They can't both be. I feel the Devil at work, trying to destroy my faith."

Mark looked at Greg. Greg looked at Sharon and then at Mark, pursed his lips, and said, "We were very comfortable in our church. We miss that group. We feel alone here. The Zeta stuff is so contrary to what we believe."

Mark sat without moving. Thinking. This was important.

Faith. Believing something you can't prove and acting on that belief.

Mark knew that she was really struggling with her own mental images of what the Bible said. Didn't we all? ZetaTalk mentioned Jesus with respect but did not support the idea that he was the son of God. ZetaTalk mentioned the Call, as they put it, when a person expressed a desire for help or contact with aliens. They said prayer was a sort of Call. If anything, ZetaTalk was just a fresh view of events described in the Bible, especially in Genesis and Exodus.

And Leviticus might have been the survival manual for Israelites trying to get by after the last shift, 3,600 years ago.

So Mark didn't believe ZetaTalk was contrary to the Bible. It actually lent confirmation to the tales of the Old Testament.

The Anunnaki were more of a problem. Zechariah Sitchin, the great and late Sumerian scholar, documented who they were and what they did. ZetaTalk confirmed Sitchin's work and made Yahweh an extraterrestrial for sure. That would sunder most assumptions of the major religions of the Earth. But even in ZetaTalk, there still is a God. That God is just so much more magnificent, universal, and unknowable than the entity who spoke to Moses.

Out of it all, Jesus shone, and maybe that would be—ought to be—where Sharon and Greg should focus.

There had been a time in his life when Mark was discovering the pieces of what he now considered his faith, when he was eager to cast off the old view of Christianity he had grown up with. Actually, the myths and fantastic claims fell into an historical context. The Anunnaki, the *Nefilim* of Genesis 6, were real, and the Yahweh was just the one of them in command. As Sitchin had said, the Enuma Elish of Babylon appeared clearly to have inspired Genesis, which was just a brief retelling of that much longer and more detailed history the Israelites heard while in captivity. Jesus? A Star Child, according to the Zetas, one of several who have come to Earth over the ages. God? A human construct that combined the Nefilim, spirit guides, aliens, and beyond all that, whatever drove the Universe.

Prayer? A call to whomever was listening: spirit guides, aliens. Mark believed strongly in the work of spirit guides. They were to him sort of like the clerk at the county tax office, a real entity he could deal with, yet in her position a manifestation of government. *Government* was the closest construct Mark could think of to explain *God.* You see evidence of government all over the place. You can meet representatives of government. But you can never actually *see* government. Government isn't a man, somewhere. But it is surely real. God was like that.

So don't bother trying to move government by yapping at government. Discuss your problem with the clerk in the tax office.

Then, too, there was Mark's vision of The Mountain.

It came to Mark in a dream, but one that stayed when he was awake. He saw a mountain with brambles and rocks and trash at the bottom, where holes from some subterranean inferno belched fire and smoke. There were people at the bottom of the mountain being unspeakably cruel to each other. A few were trying to climb up the mountain to get away. Some of these fell or were pulled back, but others got loose of the hateful mob at the bottom. They clawed their way through the brambles, pushing each other out of the way, trying to escape. The way was hard, and there were no paths. A little higher, a few paths emerged, and people clawed and shoved each other out of the way to get to the paths. A little higher than that was the first occasion of someone on a path actually helping another. As the paths climbed the mountain, more and more people appeared to be helping each other. The paths led to a clearing, where there were two churches.

At the church on the right, the minister in front was pulling people in, telling them they had made it. At the church on the left, the minister was handing out cups of water and pointing to the path that continued up the mountain. Mark had known both ministers and could see their faces clearly.

Farther up the hill, the paths were wider and smoother and merged into wide roads. The trees thinned out, broad fields appeared, with green grass and beautiful flowers. The sun shone more brightly than it did lower on the mountain. A throng of people surged on the roads, some carrying others, many arm in arm or holding hands. As the roads neared the top of the mountain, they merged into one road, and then dissolved into a bright, white light at the top.

It was clear to Mark that life was the mountain, that the idea was to climb, to find the path, to help others, to go to the light. It was also clear to Mark that there were many roads up the mountain. The one he was on was not the only one. No path was wrong if it led up the mountain.

His heart went out to this kind couple, Sharon and Greg, who were clearly helping others they met on their road. They were well up the mountain. Now they were deeply troubled. The shift looked like God's judgment on the world, and it brought the Anunnaki and the Zetas—extraterrestrials—into view. Whatever Mark said next needed to help, support, encourage. And point up the hill.

It occurred to Mark that this discussion was suddenly a critically important moment for their community in the Aftertime.

He took a breath, let it out. He had once been a lay minister, had done extensive Bible study, had even preached sermons in church. He knew the Bible well enough. Should he try to re-teach what they got from the Bible? No. He would likely fail at that. Their pastor had been a powerful preacher. His messages were full of emotion. There was a lot of emotion in their faith. And then, trying to undermine their belief in the Bible as they knew it would also be totally stupid. For that matter, the Bible wasn't a bad place to start. It said a lot about a path up the hill

He couldn't think of anything else to do.

So he told Greg and Sharon about his vision of the mountain.

Then he shut up.

Sharon stared at him. Smiled. Tears in her eyes. Greg was quiet.

Sharon spoke. "What about Zetas? Aliens?"

"What about angels?"

She thought about that. Then uttered one sound. "Hmm."

Then, "What about sin? We're told to be perfect."

Ah. That was a subject he'd discussed years ago with a navigator he'd hung out with in Vietnam.

"The Gospel of Matthew: *be ye therefore perfect, as your heavenly Father is perfect.* I studied that one. The Greek word translated *perfect* is *teleios*, which has several meanings. One is *unblemished*, but that is when it's applied to sacrificial animals. When applied to people, it means *adult, complete, not partial,* that is, *impartial*.

"Just ahead of this verse, Jesus is saying *love your enemy, turn the other cheek.* Be adult. Don't take sides. There's nothing in chapter 5 that says you have to be flawless. That's not where he's going. And if you're worried about hell, in the next chapter, Jesus tells you not to even worry about tomorrow. Jesus simply didn't lay a burden of guilt and shame on anybody. Neither should you."

"But he died for our sins."

"Well, I think if you look, you'll find that's Paul, the first of many preachers to claim that. What Jesus said was that where he was going, you could follow. *In my Fathers house are many mansions*, he said, like many paths."

"So you don't believe in Hell?"

"Doesn't matter what I believe. I'm just encouraging you to consider that the message you've believed can have a wider meaning. Maybe consider that the shift, this experience, gives you the opportunity to see through a glass that is a little less dark than before. We're all still very committed to what Jesus himself taught: loving our neighbors as ourselves. That's just another way of saying service-to-others. We all believe that."

"So you don't believe ZetaTalk is contrary to the Bible?"

"Not at all. I could go through the Old Testament and describe how it reflects the same events the Zetas and Sitchin talk about. I could point to the Jesus story as the coming of a Star Child. I pay attention to what *Jesus himself* said. I pay a lot less attention to what Paul and other writers added later. They were humans, and they had agendas.

"I met a fellow in Vietnam, a navigator, who talked about *First-Century Christianity*. He tried to get back to the way it had to have been while the first Christians were still alive, before the story we have in the New Testament was written down. Just think about First-Century Christianity. It would have a small group of people, dedicated to each other, sharing everything, living communally, trying to stay out of sight when the Romans came near. Sound familiar? I really, really encourage you to embrace what we're doing in the spirit of First-Century Christianity. Just focus on the Jesus message in that light and let everything else go. Don't worry about tomorrow, let alone when you die."

"But the Bible is the word of God."

"Well, I've read scholars who say there are maybe ten thousand documented changes in the text of the Bible from the earliest known copy to the most recent. Not to mention many known errors or changes of opinion in translation. With so many changes and errors, it is clearly the product of men. To say they were all inspired is disputed by the fact that some made errors. Verses moved, others disappeared, and new ones appeared over time. So I would not say that God himself wrote it, or that all the real writers were infallibly inspired. That simply is not what the scholarship has shown.

"So what is it? I'd say that the Bible reflects spiritual teachings that are worth embracing. But I take full responsibility for my own understanding and application of those teachings. I'm human with not the most powerful mind. I can only use what I can understand. And I myself am the final authority on what I believe, since I am the one on my path in my life, working out the growth of my own soul.

"But if you want to believe the Bible is the word of God, do so. You also have the authority to do that.

"As far as our clan here is concerned, there are no two of us who believe all the same things. I think what really matters is how we come together, how we care for each other, and how we behave when we're in dire peril. That's the truth the matters. Let your actions speak your truth.

"What we do, how we act, will in any case reflect what we truly believe.

"If I act as you would act, does it matter what I believe that inspires me to act that way?

"If I don't act as you would act, it makes no difference if I say I believe exactly what you believe. I'd be a proven liar.

"There are many paths up the hill."

Sharon sat for a while, reached her left hand to Greg, took his hand. Then she reached her right hand to Mark. Mark put out his hand, and Sharon clasped it. Squeezed. Looked at Mark.

"Let me work on that."

They all stood. Greg shook Mark's hand and said, "Thanks."

Mark left the hut, forgetting why he'd gone there.

MONTH 3
CONTACT

The guard in the tower called out. “Two people coming up the road. They're not doing well. Sick or injured.”

Everyone turned toward the gate. Some walked to the gate to see, since the alert did not suggest any danger. Still, dutiful, the hunters went to the lodge and grabbed their rifles and went to their positions.

Mark went to the gate, stood and watched.

The guard looked them over with binoculars. “They're dirty. No signs of wounds. No weapons. They look sick.”

“Sharon!” Mark shouted.

Sharon was already watching. She'd picked up her field kit and walked to the gate when the guard called out. She stopped and stood by Mark.

“I don't think we should let them in here without checking,” she said.

“Totally agree. Be careful.”

Sharon walked out to meet them.

“Please stop where you are,” she said kindly, “and tell me who you are and why you're here.”

The two men stopped. One of them spoke.

“We're from Eugene. The city was pretty much destroyed by water and quakes when the dams went. We tried to collect in the south hills. Scavenged food. There wasn't any water in the faucets, so we drank water anywhere we can find it. People are getting sick. Some died. We heard about you. Maybe you could help. Joe and I decided to come see.”

“Who told you about us?”

"A guy named Harry. Walked in a while back. Said there was a place down here that might be doing better than we are. Told us where you were."

"Tell me what happens when people get sick."

"God, you name it. Lots of shits and puking. Everyone has that. Some get real hot. Some have nasty sores. The mosquitoes are thick. The valley stinks. There must be a lot of bodies around. It looks a lot better here."

"Do you have bites from insects?"

"Yeah. Fleas, I think."

"Okay. Stay where you are. Do not come closer yet. We'll come to you."

Sharon walked quickly back to Mark.

"They're coming from Eugene. The south hills have a survivor camp. It's a disaster. Symptoms they describe could be dysentery, cholera, malaria, typhoid fever, even typhus. They're swarming with mosquitoes, maybe fleas."

"Sounds like Sumatra post-tsunami. Bad water, no sanitation, bodies. Without drugs, all we can do is public health and quarantine."

"Starting with those two."

Mark thought, then pointed to a clearing near where the two men stood. "Let's put them over there. Keep them outside the stockade."

Sharon nodded. "We'll burn everything they're wearing out there somewhere. Scrub every inch of their bodies. Give 'em shelter, clean clothes, and start what cure we can give. Fresh water, for sure, and maybe just broth to start."

Mark spoke without taking his eyes off the men. "They'll need their own latrine. Over there will do. We can burn it later. That would be it for now. If we can't help these guys, we won't do any good for the ones back in Eugene."

"You wouldn't believe why they came here, to us."

"Oh?"

"A guy named Harry told them about us. Said we had it together."

Mark smiled. "Could be good news or bad news."

"What do you mean."

"Harry cared for someone and is trying to help them."

"That's what I was thinking."

"Or he sent their sickness our way."

"Oh, Mark. Think positive. It don't matter now. They're here, and we'll do what we can."

Sharon hollered for a Compact meeting. The clan assembled. She described the situation and the plan. Then Sharon went back out to the two hapless patients, standing quietly in the rain, which had started again.

While Sharon explained to the men what was about to happen, several men grabbed poles, rope, and tarps, then moved it all to the appointed space, and set up a small Pontiac. Then they dug a shallow latrine, erected a seat from poles, and rigged a tarp over it.

The women retrieved suitable new clothes, quilts, and blankets from the thrift store, broth from the kitchen, a 60-liter pot of hot water, soap, and towels. Charlie retrieved a can full of gas they'd siphoned from one of the vehicles. They took the stuff out to where Sharon waited.

The women dumped the hot water into four buckets set near Sharon, who stood roughly 10 feet from the men in the road, and took the pot back to the kitchen.

Sharon had the men remove all their clothes and pile them in the road. Charlie doused the pile with gas and set it on fire.

Sharon moved the men to the buckets of water sitting in the road, told them to wash and scrub every inch of their bodies, using one bucket for washing, and the other bucket for rinsing. She commanded like a drill sergeant and the men quickly complied. As soon as they were washed and rinsed, she had them move quickly to their Pontiac, where fresh water and dry clothes waited. She had them get dressed and told them to drink as much water as they could stand. She told them about the latrine, how to use it, how to clean afterwards, and really emphasized that the clan was healthy only because it followed strict public health practices. If they did the same, they would get well.

Sharon came back to Mark, who was standing at the gate.

“I think we're gonna need some nurses' aides and housekeepers in this here hospital.”

“Who would you pick?”

“How about the older kids?”

“Great idea. But let's explain the whole business to them, begin their training as public health experts. Our heritage gift to them.”

Sharon collected the kids. Four were 10 or older. They were to ferry water and broth to the men, check that they were clean, call for help if they had been sick. Sharon explained the critical importance of avoiding bodily fluids. She talked about the diseases they might be dealing with.

“If it's dysentery, good water and nourishment will probably get them through it. These guys are still walking, so I don't think it's typhoid fever, but it could be. You remember those villains, Sam 'n' Ella. Need to keep human waste and drinking water totally and forever separate. Got that? So when they clean up from the bathroom, they need to wash in the wash water, not in the drinking water.

"You're the scouts. Keep a sharp eye out for the villains. Make sure they have plenty of both kinds of water. Dump the used wash water in the latrine. It will soak away in this soil. Don't get too close until we've seen some improvement. Stay beyond an arm's reach. And wash your hands after handling anything they handled. Any questions?"

She and the kids talked until she was sure they understood their tasks. Then they went to work.

Sharon went over to the two patients and explained what she had told the kids. She asked their cooperation. They agreed immediately.

She asked Mark if the guards could check the men roughly every few hours. The guards stood four-hour shifts, day and night. They decided to have the new guard coming on duty check the men before relieving the previous guard. That way, the previous guard would stay in position, and the new guard would know the current situation of the men. If anything needed attention, the new guard would get help before relieving the previous guard.

The men were on solid food the second day. In five days they were much improved. Sharon checked their temperatures twice daily with a good old-fashioned glass and mercury thermometer from the medical kit. After some days, it was back to normal.

Sharon considered then that it might be safe to have them come inside the compound. They would never know what bug had caused the men's illness. They had no antibiotics. It was down to staying healthy enough to survive, perhaps carrying a lingering pest for the rest of a life. Malaria would be like that, if it came to them.

She discussed the matter with Mark, and he suggested a Compact meeting.

The clan discussed their situation. They were so far surprisingly healthy. They recognized the value of good sanitation. They had remained isolated from other survivors in the valley. It seemed that their reluctance to be seen had actually protected them from contact with survivors carrying diseases. Did they choose to continue in isolation, or were they willing to mix with survivors outside the group, and if so, on what terms?

For whatever reasons, the clan members voted unanimously to allow contact provided it was under conditions of good sanitation and public health. No admission of anyone exhibiting symptoms of a disease. Isolation until healthy. Bathing and clean clothes before admission to the clan compound.

Mark noted with a chuckle how close those rules were to Leviticus. Sharon was the clan priest.

Charlie raised the idea of a sanitation station for visitors, which everyone thought was a great idea. They discussed expanding the site the two men occupied into a visitors site, and debated ways to sanitize it after an occupation like the one just ending.

Sharon preferred keeping the current site as an infirmary and erecting a new site elsewhere for visitors. That ended up the plan, with fire the disinfectant.

The group left it to Sharon to decide if the visitors were healthy enough to mingle with the clan. A day later, they moved into the compound, but housed in a newly erected visitors' Pontiac, not the lodge itself. Sharon liked the idea of having a separate lodging that could be used as an isolation ward or infirmary if any clan member showed signs of coming down with something.

The men sat at a table at dinner with Charlie and Paula. Mark, Rachel and Sharon joined them.

Mark asked, “Feeling better?”

“Much better. Thank you all for all you've done.”

“Tell us about what it's like where you came from.”

“Well, we were probably the healthiest ones there. Lots of people were so weak from puking and crapping that they couldn't walk. We had no good water and virtually nothing to eat. I guess as weak as we all were, almost any bug could move in. But from what I've seen here, we probably were drinking spoiled water. Nobody did what you do with your latrines. People just pooped anywhere without a thought. All the washing you guys do is probably a real life-saver. And those stoves you use. Damn. I can't believe how clean the air is here. Back in Eugene, there's smoke everywhere. Burns the eyes. Everyone is coughing.”

“Welcome to the new Third World. Did anybody have high fevers?”

“Some. Hard to tell. Nobody was acting like Sharon here.”

“What about food?”

“A few guys had guns. Shot squirrels and rabbits. A few folks tried to hoard for a while, and there were arguments about sharing. One guy shot another. Kind of a mess. In the end, the ones left pulled together without any idea what to do. We went through all the houses and piled up all the canned goods. All that is pretty well gone."

"What's the land like?"

"The city is flooded. From the stink, must be a lot of rotting corpses. The south hills and the buttes have survivor camps on them. Some of the buttes are islands, completely surrounded by water. How deep I don't know. We were able to walk the interstate, which went right by us. It was built high enough, so you can get through the wetlands on it. But bridges are down, so driving is out of the question. You have to climb over or around holes and breaks here and there."

"Do you think the people you left behind could do what we've done here? Is there enough room?"

"Oh, there's no question the south hills are big enough to support a group like yours. But there are more of us there than you've got, there's no food, and there's no leadership. And they're all so weak, I don't think there are enough still strong enough to get started, even if they knew how and were well led."

"I was hoping you two would go back and lead them, do for them what we've done for you."

"Well, we weren't leaders there. We heard what Harry said, and we just decided we had nothing to lose coming looking for you."

"Ah. Harry. Tell us about him."

"He just said there was a group down south that had it together. Told us that if we knew what was good for us, we'd get gone and come down here. Guess he was right."

"Why didn't he come with you?"

"We asked. He wouldn't. Didn't say why. He was in pretty good shape. Just didn't want to come."

"How many people are there in the south hills?"

"I'd guess about fifty still alive."

"Ages?"

"Not too many old folks. Some families. Some couples and lone folks. Mostly younger. Some children. Most of them sick."

"Do they cooperate, or are there some who don't like to help, hoard, argue, act threatening?"

"There were a few bullies. Somebody shot one of them. The other disappeared. Most folks would agree helping each other is better. Even the ones who had tried to hide their food finally came out and added what they had to the pile. I think the children gave them reason."

"Why is there no leader?"

"They were all working stiffs. More labor than management. Nobody knew what to do, so I guess nobody tried to take charge. The ones left are good people. Just sick and weak. We hadn't planned to go back, but I can see that might be the thing to do. Got nothing else to do. But no food there is a problem. I doubt we could accomplish much. Would you help?"

Mark looked at Charlie. Charlie looked at Paula.

Paula said, "We're on this planet to serve. Helping others is clearly what we have to do. Only question is how best to do it."

Charlie said, "They need shelter, rain water catchments, big and little rocket stoves, a good latrine or two in the proper places, and a plan. Food plan. Garden plan. Salvage plan. A thrift store. Having all that focuses work. And a Compact of their own."

Mark looked at Charlie and Paula. "Would you two take that on?"

They both spoke simultaneously. "Absolutely!"

They talked about plans and actions for a while. The two visitors were fading, so they went to bed. Paula left Charlie and Mark alone. Mark smiled at Charlie and said, "I admire what you've agreed to do."

"Mark, this is just like the mission trip I took to Central America years ago. I've done this. I love the challenge. Especially showing them how to build their own rocket stoves. I'd bet there's a leader in those hills somewhere. Just needs to be empowered."

"Bless you. Bless you both."

MONTH 3, LATER

MISSION TO SOUTH HILLS

Mark, Rachel, Charlie, and Paula sat at a table in the lodge. They'd been discussing the mission to the south hills.

Charlie was thinking well down the road. “I think it's important to make sure there are communities around us that not only survive, but thrive.”

Paula had worked with families in crisis and knew the value of getting beyond crisis. “If we can get them out of chaos and into progress, we have hope of trade, safety in numbers, and a wider set of skills.”

Mark had two concerns: viable neighbors and safety in numbers. He could see a time when the valley would again be home to many little settlements that supported themselves and traded with each other, as Native Americans had for a thousand years before white men came. If the settlements grew from groups in some sort of balance, they might be more likely service-to-other. If they were in chaos, they might more likely submit to a service-to-self martinet. If the settlements shared common values, they could cooperate and offer joint support if some danger threatened.

Rachel saw peril in sending key members of the clan to help another group when the clan still had a long way to go. They all agreed that hers was a valid concern. They would all have preferred that this challenge had waited a while.

Charlie saw several reasons to go ahead with the mission. “If ever was there a sign from the Universe that we have a purpose, this is it. Maybe we haven't just been lucky. I feel an obligation to help others anyway, but this is almost spooky. I just couldn't turn my back on this challenge. Also, I agree that we need friendly neighbors. Helping earlier rather than later makes sense. The longer we wait, the worse off and the more vulnerable they'll be. People may be dying there from things we can easily fix. I just think we need to act now."

Mark was always grateful that Charlie had joined the clan back before the shift. Charlie was spiritual before he was religious. In his life, he'd been a Buddhist and an Methodist. Those faiths were just parts of his. He also had many practical skills that had made a tremendous difference as they prepared and as they recovered.

Mark wrapped all the concerns and options into one conclusion. "We don't disagree. We're just weighing the obstacles and chances. Ideally, we need to get them set up and get you guys back here A-SAP. What's the best way to do that?"

"Well, I don't think we should go up there and take charge," Paula said. "We can't run their show or anybody else's. So first, I think we need to establish a clan there, with a compact like ours, and get someone in charge. If they don't do that, we're wasting our time."

"But we need to ensure that they don't think they can just pick up and come down here to join us," Rachel said. "We don't have the room or the food."

"Right," Mark agreed. "They must accept that they have to make it on their own, unless there is some really nasty thing going on in the group. If some were hard STS, preying on others who were more STO, we might end up bringing the STOs down here and wishing the rest of them a good day."

"No," Paula said, shaking her head. "Much as I like the idea of STOs, as you call them, I think a mixed group is better for them and us. We really don't want a small group of STS types up there without anyone to hold them back. They'd just come down here and cause us trouble."

Mark thought about that. "Okay, so we press them to get their act together. Maybe we should explicitly rule out the option of their coming down here."

Charlie held up his hands. "Hey, guys, I really don't think we need to decide all this stuff right now. I say, let's get up there, see what we have to work with and against, and do what we have to do. We agree on the ultimate objective."

"Okay. Without a State Department and satellite communications, that's probably as good as it will get."

Later, Mark walked over to Charlie to discuss an additional matter. “You know, the south hills are really far away by standards of our day. There are—were—a number of towns between here and there. If there are any survivor groups left, we probably need to know about them.”

“I don't want to get distracted,” Charlie said.

“Agreed. South hills is priority. I just think we need to know what's left —who's left—out there. The land between here and there is pretty much like the land here, so it should support lots of survivor groups our size. For their sake and our own, they should be balanced groups leaning toward STO.”

“Okay, Amigo. I'll keep an eye out.”

“And another thing. I told all of you there would be a pole shift. Looks like we had one. But most folks probably don't know what hit them. I think it probably would be best to slide over that discussion and just deal with what to do next.”

“Right.”

Two days later, Charlie and Paula left early with the two visitors. Charlie had a bag of tools, including the hand tools he'd need to make simple stoves. The tools were all spares, and Charlie planned to leave them if they couldn't find like ones in the salvage. Paula had a collection of seeds. They took no tarps, hoping that something of use might be found there. Mostly, they took with them ideas and an orientation. And two witnesses of what was possible.

The trip used to take a half hour on the interstate. Just 20 miles. Now it would take all day, if nothing happened.

They made good progress. Part way, they reached Creswell. It looked like flood and quake had flattened every structure in the valley, so it was hard to tell where the town had been. Mostly, the best clue was the remains of the interstate exit. Charlie looked for signs of life. The most likely sign would be smoke. In the rain and gloom, Charlie didn't see any. They kept going and reached the south hills without incident.

Charlie and Paula toured the settlement, with the two men making introductions.

The shacks were random and variably effective. Most leaked. The people were dirty, hungry, and sick. The fires were more smoke than flame. There were no latrines. All classic problems with totally known solutions.

The people? Fragmented, mostly by family. The early hoarding and food hiding had upset everyone, so there was little trust. No identifiable leader. Too bad. Charlie had known a fellow who lived in south hills and might have made a difference, but he'd moved to Idaho before the shift.

Harry was sitting by himself in a lean-to. Charlie looked at Paula. She nodded, walked away. Charlie walked over to the lean-to and squatted. “Hi, Harry. I'm Charlie. From down the valley. I'm part of the clan you and your friends tried to hit.”

Harry looked down. “Oh, man, I'm really sorry.”

“It's done. Harry, you told these people about us. Why?”

“These folks are lost. Looting didn't work. What we're trying to do doesn't work. But what you people were doing looked like you had your act together. Thought there was nothing to lose talking about it.”

“Harry, you did a beautiful thing. You helped others. That's all that matters to me. Come on, Friend. Walk with me.”

Harry looked up. Stared. And began to sob. Charlie put his hand on Harry's shoulder, waited.

After a while, Charlie said, “Come on, Harry. Let's walk.”

Harry got up, shakily. They moved together through the settlement. Charlie asked questions. Harry explained. No bad apples, it seemed, no bullies left. Just folks trying to make it, alive by accident and fortunate decisions, during and after the shift.

Charlie called a meeting. The group gathered.

“Folks, Harry's told you about us. We live in a good community. We're dry. We're warm. We have clean water. We cook without smoke. We don't breathe smoke at all. We're growing food. And we're really pretty healthy. What Harry told you is all true. And we're here to tell you that you can have the same things, live the same way. We came to show you how to do what we do, if you want us to.”

The group muttered a variety of things, all approving.

“Here's the deal. The first thing we did, and the best thing we have, is our compact. A compact is like a little constitution. In our compact, we formally agreed to work together, to make important decisions as a group. And we all formally signed the written agreement on a piece of paper. When a new person came along, agreeing to and signing our compact was the only condition for joining our clan. We chose whether to call ourselves a tribe, clan, family or whatever. We called ourselves a clan for a number of reasons unique to us. A friend of mine has been our leader by mutual consent, selected and agreed to, according to our compact. So, if you want to be like us, you need to agree to a compact and pick a leader.”

Shelly frowned. “Can't we just learn the stuff you've been doing? Why do we need to be organized?”

“Well, the key to surviving is mostly mental. Loners don't make it. Bullies don't make it. Only people who work as a team make it. There are times when all problems need a group solution. You have to be a group before the problem hits. So, no, if you don't want to organize as we have, then our work here is done. We'd waste our time and mislead you to tell you otherwise.”

Silence. Looks. Mumbles. Whispers.

A woman spoke. “What are we waiting for? We're not making it. What choice do we have?”

And so it was done. Paula led the group through agreement on a compact. It was simple: agree to agree as a group, leave details to the group as needs come up. Pretty much the same as the Mayflower Compact.

The group declared themselves the South Hills Clan and selected a leader.

Paula had them include provision for appointment of teams to handle details like sanitation. So the group had heard the idea before she sprung it on them.

Which she did next. Right after the adults and children over 12—a provision the group added to the compact—had signed the compact. The children—young adults—were particularly excited about being included.

The group selected teams by assent, appointment, and a bit of familial coercion. Sanitation, water, wood, food, cooking, housing, medics, salvage. Some ended up on more than one team. Immediate needs, as ever, were to get the people into better housing with stoves so they could make clean water. All that depended first on salvage.

MONTH 3
SOUTH HILLS SALVAGE

Paula and Charlie assembled everyone and told them to scour the hills for certain items for a radius of several hundred yards.

One of the people said they had already scoured all the houses. There was no food left.

Charlie smiled and explained. The cooking team would focus on cooking utensils and every last item remaining in ruined kitchens. The sanitation team would look for claw-foot bath tubs, soap of any sort, towels, and buckets. The medics would collect clothes, medicine of any sort. The water team would look for anything that could contain water, especially metal or plastic containers with lids. The housing team would look for roofing materials, tarps, sheet metal, pipe, rope, nails, electrical wire, window screening and tools.

The people nodded. They had ignored virtually everything Charlie mentioned. So they went searching with new purpose. They moved slowly, weakened by hunger and sickness. A few were too weak to participate. It would have been ideal to have them get well and then go to work. There was no time for that. In this new world, there would be no healthy help coming in from outside. Paula and Charlie alone could not hope to care for this many people. The sick and hungry had to provide their own rescue.

When they had arrived and gone from family to family, Charlie and Paula had surveyed the ground. The south hills were a prominent feature of the landscape, rising well above the surrounding wetland. The top was level for some distance, and this was where the people had been living.

Much of the space was now polluted by poor sanitation. Moving to somewhere else was essential to a fresh start. So Charlie and Paula had spotted and selected a new area for a new settlement.

The crews brought all they found to the site of the new settlement. There were a surprising number of tarps, often unwound from trees and the ubiquitous blackberry tangles. They brought tools, rope, wire, clothes, dishes, pots, pans, buckets, pipe, and metal cans of any size. They found a couple of claw-foot bath tubs, which they spotted for liberation and relocation.

Charlie had also had them looking for metal barrels of any size up to 55 gallons. They found a half dozen of these and rolled them to the collection site.

Paula inspected the tarps and selected two for rain water collection. Charlie got a crew together to make two large funnel structures with the tarps, with clean barrels to catch the water. They used the first batch to rinse the tarps. After several batches, the water was reasonably clean.

There was many an occasion when someone said, “Why didn't we think of that?”

Housing was priority. Charlie pointed out a well-drained area, a gentle ridge, at the new site and told the group that the new housing should stretch along the highest part. They would build a kitchen, a laundry, a bath, and family huts. He explained the idea of Pontiacs.

To demonstrate the construction process, Charlie, Paula and the housing team quickly cut poles for a Pontiac structure for the kitchen. Charlie explained assembly as they erected it and roofed it with the tarps. The idea caught on, and all the adults went hunting for the right sort of poles.

They ran out of tarps, so they used sheets of metal roofing from the remains of several houses that had once been on the hills. Charlie used a screwdriver to punch holes along the edge of a sheet, like grommet holes on a rigid tarp, and they used salvaged electrical wire instead of rope to lash it to the Pontiac frame. Once shown the approach, several crews quickly completed the rest of the structures. The settlement looked rather imposing compared to the lean-to's and tents the clan had been using.

While construction proceeded, the sanitation team started digging the outhouses at the new site. Paula had them dig two, down the hill from the housing. She wasn't overly concerned about pollution of ground water, as they were going to rely on rain water harvesting for drinking water for the foreseeable future. Charlie assembled a stack of salvaged wood to make the floor when the holes were ready.

Paula recruited a few fishermen to go see if they could catch anything down at the river. They had already done a little fishing and knew how to proceed. She asked them to catch at least two dozen fish, or as many as possible. They departed with purpose.

In fact, everyone was working with purpose. The idea had sparked. The clan was functioning. Charlie and Paula kept up a continuous conversation, coaching, really, with the new leader, a dignified, well-spoken woman roughly 50 years old. She was smart, educated, and she understood people. Once given the mantle, she quickly expanded into the role of her title: Coordinator.

People wanted to move to the new shelters, but Paula asked them to wait until they could bathe and put on clean clothes. All agreed, some more reluctantly than others, that one more day wouldn't matter.

Charlie had sited the bath house and laundry on the edge of a steep slope, so draining water would be easier. They might put a garden there later. As soon as the bath house and laundry were ready, Charlie had a crew retrieve the bath tubs. They placed two tubs side by side in the bath house. They would use one immediately to wash clothes. The laundry hut would be where they dried them.

MONTH 3
VITA STOVES

It would take a few days to build some rocket stoves, so Charlie made three stoves based on the VITA stove design he'd found on the Web before the shift. Each stove fit a pot Charlie selected from those available. The VITA stove was simple sheet metal, but it shared some of the principles of a rocket stove. As he worked, he explained the principles and the construction to the coordinator and the construction team.

A big advantage of the VITA stove, as with the rocket stove, was that it worked best with small sticks and twigs. The wood team was delighted to hear they would not be condemned to a life of chopping and splitting, and they quickly collected a supply of wood. Charlie placed one of the stoves in the kitchen and two of the stoves in the bath house. He had teams fill the pots with rain water and light the fires. Paula coached the cooks, and Charlie coached the laundry team on how to tend the fire.

"Use five sticks for high power. That will boil water. Feed the sticks steadily. When one stick is gone, replace it with another. If you just want to keep water hot, use three sticks."

Charlie and Paula enjoyed hearing the comments.

"That's about as easy as a gas stove."

"Yeah. And look at the smoke."

"What smoke?"

"That's just it. There isn't any."

There was some smoke, but not nearly as much as they had endured since the shift. So Charlie did not try to rig chimneys. The gases from the stove just blew out the ends of the Pontiac huts.

The sanitation crew filled the bath tubs with rain water, which was rather cold, and mixed in pots of boiling water until the water was tolerable.

They brought the families, one at a time, to wash their clothes, blankets and any cloth material they would take to their new dwelling.

The laundry team ferried the wet clothes to the laundry hut, where Charlie had built a large version of the VITA stove with several openings to feed wood. But this stove was tall, went clear through the roof of the hut, like a big chimney. It had metal fins inside, fastened to the sides of the chimney. As the fire got hot, the fins collected the heat and passed it to the metal sides, which soon heated the hut. The laundry team could control the heat by inserting or removing sticks from the fire holes. They arranged clothes on wooden racks near or far from the chimney, shifting, retrieving and folding as things dried.

As soon as a family's clothing was clean and dry, they returned to the wash house to bathe. Then they put on their clean clothes and moved in to their new home.

The bathing, washing and drying took several days. As a family had washed and had clean clothes, they moved to their new lodge. The salvage crew gathered what was useful from their old dwelling and burned the rest.

They all worked on a mutually agreed principle that every thing of use on the hill would be collected, sorted, cleaned, repaired, or recycled. Anything of no use would go to the landfill, down the hill but to one side of the latrines. The children were quickly the primary agents of this work, combing and retrieving from the sites of all the ruined houses.

In two weeks, the South Hills Clan was in new lodgings, clean, essentially smoke-free, and self-directed. It was amazing to see the progress that nearly sixty people could make if they worked together. The fishing crew had done well, so a steady diet of fish was improving nutrition.

Paula had worked with the food crew to scour the woods for supplements to the fish diet. There was a surprising variety of vegetables from ruined gardens, including tomatoes, some fruit, lots of dandelions, and a potato patch that only Paula recognized. These were ideal, as their Vitamin C would be essential to continued health. Paula founded a garden team and began the work of planning a garden on the hill. As they laid out their plots, the construction team erected covers over them, and planting began.

Paula had brought a few seed potatoes, soon to be a staple of the diet. She showed the gardeners how to plant and tend them in barrels, which were proving to be the most effective way to grow potatoes in large quantities.

Charlie and Paula discussed first aid and hygiene with the medics. The new medics understood the basic ideas, but there were no nurses in the group. So for the first time, Paula suggested they come to New Plymouth to spend some time with Sharon. They agreed and decided to return with Charlie and Paula when they went home.

Charlie also decided that it would be easier to show how to make real rocket stoves back at New Plymouth, where they had tools and plenty of examples. And he wanted to work further on the wood furnace he'd knocked together for the laundry drying shack. That might be a nice addition to New Plymouth. So he proposed that some stove builders accompany the medic team as well. They could build a new institutional rocket stove with chimney at New Plymouth and bring it back to south hills.

Sooner or later, they'd need to figure out a way to move goods. Might as well start with stoves.

Charlie and Paula hoped that the exchange would be the beginning of new commerce of sorts in the valley.

The south hills were relatively isolated from the surrounding valley by wetlands and the roaring river. So the group had not had any encounters with coyotes or other predators. Still, there was the possibility that predators might come calling. So Charlie planted the idea that the South Hills Clan might want to start collecting poles for a stockade. The south hills were well wooded, but they did not have the easy access to a Douglas fir plantation that the New Plymouth Clan had enjoyed. So building a stockade would be a bigger project.

Charlie and Paula discussed security with the coordinator. She agreed that her group did not have any real protection from four- or two-footed predators, and she said she would raise the issue and see if there was some agreement. She said she would also discuss with the group whether there were any other groups in the area that might benefit from the sort of help Charlie and Paula had provided. The group had no firearms. Charlie remembered Harry's weapons, which they had confiscated the day Harry arrived at New Plymouth. Charlie thought that returning those weapons might now be in order.

Charlie spoke with Harry regularly during their sojourn in the south hills. Harry was one of many who had been undecided about whether to look out for himself or help others. He'd gone with the flow when the flow was service-to-self. He happily was going the other way now and seemed to enjoy working with several of the teams. There were others like him in the South Hills Clan, almost three-score people thrown together randomly by chaos, a microcosm of what the U.S. had been in its last, nasty days.

The only thing they had in common was they'd survived the shift.

Charlie mulled over the fact that there were no Harrys at New Plymouth. He concluded that Mark had picked the New Plymouth group. They were all like-minded.

Charlie could see that New Plymouth would be the exception in this new world. They would find, Charlie thought, that most of the survivors in the new world would be like the South Hills Clan.

Now a Methodist, Charlie grinned to think that Moses might have had the same thoughts in the Sinai.

And as he and Paula and their companions walked along the shattered interstate back to New Plymouth, he wondered where he and Paula might go next.

MONTH 4
SOUTH HILLS VISITORS

The guard called out, “Travelers coming up the road. It's Charlie and Paula. There are people with them.”

Everyone stopped what they were doing and walked toward the gate. Some went on down the road to meet the travelers.

Everyone bombarded Charlie and Paula with lots of questions. Charlie held up his hand and said, “Let's go to the lodge. We'll tell you all there. We're hungry, thirsty, and tired. Sitting would be nice.”

Various clan members grabbed parcels and baggage, introduced themselves to the strangers, who looked a bit bewildered and very tired.

In the clan lodge, Charlie told the tale of what they'd done in the south hills. He introduced the people from the South Hills Clan and talked about why they had come to New Plymouth. He said he hoped their visit would be the first of many in both directions.

“Some of these folks are going to build rocket stoves. They've brought pots with them, and we're going to show them how to build stoves that fit the pots. We're also going to show them the big stove here in the lodge, so they can build one like it.

“Then we're going to do something really special. They helped me build a new kind of stove for their laundry, because we had an awful lot of stuff to wash, and we needed to dry it quickly. It's really kinda neat. So they're gonna build one for our laundry. How cool is that?”

The clan cheered, and the visitors grinned.

Work started the next day with clanging and banging. By evening of the second day, the visitors had a large institutional stove and a smaller stove boiling water.

The stove crew needed a way to make stove chimneys out of salvaged sheet metal. Charlie had worked with sheet metal tools in Beforetime, but had neglected to buy a metal working shop for the retreat. Failing that, he improvised a way to roll metal into a smooth cylinder.

Charlie selected a log about four feet long, with a diameter roughly the diameter of the pipe they wanted. The crew removed the bark and shaved the log into a smooth cylinder. Along the length of the log, Charlie snapped a chalk line (which he *had* brought to the retreat). Then he cut a slot in the log along the line, about one inch deep, using a hand saw. It took a while. When the slot was done, Charlie inserted the end of a piece of sheet metal into the slot and slowly rolled the log. The metal bent smoothly around the log.

Holding the metal tightly against the log, Charlie marked the metal on both edges where it crossed the slot . Using tin snips, he cut the outside end of the metal sheet to a line one inch beyond the marks. Then they removed the metal cylinder from the log to free the metal in the slot, which now formed a 90-degree bend toward the inside of the cylinder. They inserted the other end of the metal sheet into the same slot, being careful not to unroll the cylinder any more than they had to. It sprang open a bit, which helped.

Then they ran a board through the cylinder and used it to break the metal into a 90-degree bend toward the outside of the cylinder. They removed the cylinder, which had one edge bent inward, the opposite edge bent outward. Charlie put on leather gloves and used his hands to flatten the bent edges back against the sheet metal. Now he had an open cylinder with two edges that had opposing hooks. He hooked one edge into the other and, with a bit of grunting, had a sheet metal stove pipe. He locked the seam by flattening it at both ends with a hammer.

"When we install this, we'll put a screw through the seam to make it permanent.

Bill had watched the whole process without saying a word. Now he smiled. "Wouldn't it have been easier to cut the sheet to the exact length before you rolled it?"

Charlie looked up at him. "Now that you mention it. When we started, I hadn't yet worked out how we'd join the edges."

After some fussing and discussing, the crew took Bill's suggestion and was in production. They used all the sheet metal they'd set aside for the project to make seven lengths of stove pipe.

Charlie smiled. Another new industry. Bring us your sheet metal and a few potatoes, and we'll give you back your pipe.

Mark walked over as they worked, watching the process. Charlie left the crew to their labors and joined him. Mark said, “I see you have another victory.”

“They're doing pretty good. I'm pleased. Lots of ideas to improve the process.”

“Is this something we'll be doing at both places, or do we establish a metal working operation somewhere?”

“I'd say both places to start, using metal scrounged from nearby. We don't have good options for moving stuff very far. But we might have the same people doing it both places, if someone rises to the challenge and proves to be really good at it. New industry.”

“Itinerant pipe makers?”

“Deployable Metal Smoke Evacuation Device Technologists.”

“Portable Pipe Poppers.”

“Moveable Metal Mashers.”

They both laughed.

Over in the medic hut, Sharon was discussing her approach with the medics from south hills.

“We're more about public health and first aid. We're the ones who have to teach and enforce all the reasonable sanitation practices. We need to do everything we can to keep everyone healthy. We don't have any drugs, and we don't have any doctors. So staying healthy is our only option. If somebody gets hurt, we do first aid, which is really the only aid. No surgery is possible. No good outcome for wasting illnesses. We do what we can, and we let go when it's time.”

A young woman asked, “What about broken legs, cuts...the sort of stuff that happens when people climb on rocks and carry axes?”

“We'll talk about wound treatment. I've never set a broken bone, so I don't know how. We haven't had one yet. I know a lot of breaks will heal without even a cast, if the person takes it easy. We'll have to hope we don't have to deal with anything a surgeon used to do. The biggest thing we can do for wounds is keep them clean and let the body heal them.

"Basically, we're going to start with a couple of good references. We only have one copy, and I need to keep them here, but you can study them and make all the notes you want. These references are things we got off the internet and printed out before the shift."

Sharon stopped abruptly. She'd said it. Maybe nobody noticed.

But a young man had. "Before *what* shift?"

Sharon took a breath, let it out. Here we go. "The pole shift."

The man frowned. "Pole shift?"

Sharon realized the medics from south hills had never heard of ZetaTalk or any of that and didn't know what had happened. She really didn't want to go there, so she punted. "We'll explain that in a bit. We were all friends who sort of decided after Katrina and Sumatra that if you live in Oregon, you should be prepared for an earthquake. So we pulled a lot of stuff together. It was sort of like a hobby. I am a nurse, so I approached the project from the point of view of someone going on a mission to a third world country. There were lots of resources for medical teams, and we got most of them."

The young man persisted. "Good thing. We're sure a third world country now. But this *pole shift* thing. You know why we're in this mess?"

"Honestly? Yes. We think we know why. Look. Let's just focus now on the medical stuff. We'll discuss this mess at the lodge after dinner."

Sharon took them through the list of materials they'd downloaded from the Hesperion Foundation:

A Community Guide to Environmental Health
Where There Is No Doctor
Where Women Have No Doctor
A Book for Midwives
A Health Handbook for Women with Disabilities
Disabled Village Children
HIV Health and Your Community
Helping Children Who Are Deaf
Helping Children Who Are Blind
A Worker's Guide to Health and Safety
Cholera Prevention Fact Sheet
Sanitation and Cleanliness for a Healthy Environment
Water for life
Safe Handling of Health Care Waste
Where There Is No Dentist

These formed the core of what they were about. She gave a summary of each document.

The young woman leaned back, shook her head. “We can't learn all this in one visit.”

Sharon knew it was going to take a lot of continuing education. “That's for sure. I think the first thing we need to do become aware of what we need to do, decide what is most important for this trip, and then decide how to cover the rest of it.

The young man leaned forward. “I'd say the public health stuff is our top priority at the moment.”

“Right. That's critical now, as we all know so well. Then we can get to first aid and the deeper stuff on emergencies.”

Sharon agreed, and they proceeded to go through the sanitation material. The mess of their old camp and the changes Charlie and Paula had brought were still very fresh in their minds. By the end of the discussion, the south hills medics were evangelists for public health.

MONTH 4
POLE SHIFT EXPLAINED

At dinner that night, Sharon told Mark that the words *pole shift* had slipped out in her discussion. The medics wanted to know what that was all about. Mark nodded, knowing the subject would come up sooner or later. He said he'd think about how to do it and would be prepared when dinner was done.

With the dishes cleaned up, one of the medics looked at Mark and said, “So what's this about a pole shift.”

Mark smiled. What to tell. How to tell.

“Okay. Folks. Gather 'round.

“I could gloss over the details and leave you with a lot less than what we know here in New Plymouth. But that's what happened 14,400 years ago and caused Noah's Flood. It happened 3,600 years ago, at the time of the Exodus. The Bible describes the events, but the writers then didn't know the cause, and myths and legends resulted. So 3,600 years later, most folks didn't what was going to happen. After generations of telling only a part of a part of a story, nobody knew the whole story, and silly tales replaced it. At least for this generation, let's be dedicated to truth.

“What I'm going to say in brief is well documented, and we have books in our library that go deeper. But this is an overview.

“Here goes. When we went through school, we learned that there were nine planets in our Solar System. From the inside out, we knew about Mercury, Venus, Earth, Mars, Jupiter, Saturn, Uranus, Neptune and Pluto.

Now a few years ago, astronomers dissed Pluto, saying it wasn't a planet. That didn't change the fact that astronomers found Pluto because they knew there had to be another planet out there. They'd studied the orbits of the outer planets and found variations that could only be caused by another planet in the vicinity. That's why they were looking for a planet when they found Pluto. Saying Pluto isn't a planet doesn't say there's no planet out there. Just that Pluto isn't it. Do you know why they fired Pluto? Because probes finally reached it and showed it wasn't large enough to do what the astronomers measured. So, where was the missing planet?

"Actually, they found it in 1983. The news made the papers like a UFO report. I have a photo of the article. Then, the government stepped in, and the news died overnight. A few folks continued to talk about it, and they were savagely attacked. Any astronomer depending on government grants —you can't name one that didn't—toed the line. Total cover-up. Except a fellow named Harrington. He was looking for it when he died suspiciously. His search died with him.

"Meanwhile, a fellow named Zecharia Sitchin is a young Jewish kid in Hebrew school. They're studying Genesis. Chapter 6:6. That's where it says:

> *There were giants in the earth in those days; and also after that, when the sons of God came in unto the daughters of men, and they bare children to them, the same became mighty men which were of old, men of renown.*

"Sitchin looked at the passage in Hebrew. The Hebrew word for *giants* was *nephalim*. Now he knew that *nephalim* didn't mean *giants*. He knew Hebrew and knew *nephalim* meant *they who came down*. So he objected. His teacher scolded him unduly for questioning the meaning.

"That scolding prompted what became Sitchin's lifelong quest for the truth. He spent his life studying the old myths, going back to ancient sources. The biggest source he used was tablets from Sumer, the first and oldest civilization known on Earth. The Sumerian library is huge, thousands of tablets dug up in ancient Babylon.

"According to Sitchin, the Sumerians knew there were twelve planets. They counted the Moon and the Sun, but that still left ten of what we would call planets. They knew about the nine we thought we knew, had a name for each. They knew that Neptune lies on its side. They counted Pluto. They gave each planet a number, counted from the outside in. Earth was number 7. And they knew about the planet we've been looking for, which they called Nibiru.

"They knew that Nibiru is on a highly elliptical orbit, so it swings far out beyond Pluto, coming back to the inner Solar System only once every 3,600 years. Its orbit is contrary to the orbits of the rest of the planets, so when it passes through the orbits of the other planets, it occasionally passes near or even collides with the inner planets. It's the reason there are irregularities in the orbits of the planets. It's the planet that does what Pluto couldn't do, because it's big, roughly five times the size of Earth.

"Now, billions of years ago, Nibiru swung through the Solar System and collided with a large planet between Mars and Jupiter, called Tiamat. Blew it to smithereens. A big chunk of the planet dropped into a lower orbit between Venus and Mars. Today we call it Earth. The Pacific Ocean covers the gash where half of Tiamat was blown away. Oh, that stuff is still out there. We call it the Asteroid Belt, plus a lot of comets.

"So how did they know all this in a time when they had no telescopes? According to Sitchin, *they were told*. Who told them? The Anunnaki. The Anunnaki were a race of extraterrestrials who lived on that Twelfth Planet. Nibiru is inhabited. So what contact did the Sumerians have with the Anunnaki?

"Plenty. The Anunnaki *founded* Sumer. The Anunnaki were here on Earth. They'd been here for hundreds of thousands of years. They'd come a long time ago to mine gold, which they needed for some purpose on Nibiru. When they came, there were no humans on Earth. They tried to get gold from sea water first. When that didn't work out, they started digging. Mines in South Africa are still there, absolutely ancient. But digging gold is hard work, so the Anunnaki asked for help.

"One of the leaders of the Anunnaki group, named Enki, understood genetics. So he decided to make a worker by crossing their DNA with a local hominid, some sort of early ape. *Let us make a worker in our own image.* His sister, Ninti, cooked up several crossbreeds. The early ones were smart enough to work independently, dumb enough to follow orders without question. But they were sterile, like mules. Anunnaki women had to give birth to every one of them. That got old, so Enki and his sister went back to work and made a worker that wasn't sterile. That is, he gave the worker the *knowledge of the tree of life*, the ability to reproduce.

"The Sumerian word for worker was *adama*. Enki's symbol in the tablets was an attempt to draw the double helix of DNA. That's hard to do in clay, so they settled for a snake winding around a stick.

"Does any of this sound familiar?"

The guests grinned, shook their heads. It was bit much.

Mark went on. "Well, things went well for the Anunnaki for a long time. Generally, when Nibiru was far out beyond Pluto, they'd while away their time, watching Adam and his offspring do all the heavy lifting. When Nibiru was close, they'd go home on vacation. So they knew when Nibiru was coming close.

"Sometimes, when Nibiru came into the inner Solar System, it didn't come close to Earth. But other times, it would come close. The Annunaki knew that when that happened, Nibiru, which is five times the size of Earth, would grab onto Earth magnetically. If close enough, it would lock the mid-Atlantic Rift so strongly that the Earth would stop rotating. The core of the Earth would keep going, and the Earth's crust, the outer 20 miles or so, would break loose from the core. The crust would move to a new location relative to the North and South Poles in the core.

"About 14,400 years ago, the Anunnaki knew that Nibiru would come very close. They knew the crust shift would be a bad one. So they decided to leave Earth and ride out the shift somewhere else.

"The head of the Anunnaki group on Earth, named Enlil, didn't much like humans they'd made. Humans bred like rabbits and ate too much. *He repented that he'd made man.* He figured that this would be a good time to get rid of them. They'd all drown when the seas sloshed over all the land.

"But his brother, Enki, was fond of mankind. After all, he'd engineered them. So he told his favorite, Noah, and probably others, to build an ark. Noah did, and the rest is, as they say...Genesis. Here you had two Anunnaki behaving differently with mankind. One wrathful. One loving. At any time, one of these guys was in charge. He was *the* yahweh. *Yahweh* was a title, not a single guy.

"Well, the Anunnaki left, Noah built his boat, and the crust shifted, putting the poles under new spots on the surface. The pole, which had been in what we call Hudson Bay, moved to where it was when we last looked. That shifted the arctic circle north, and the Wisconsin Glaciation ended. There's no such thing as Ice Ages. The arctic circle simply moved. The Niagara River started flowing. Geologists know that Niagara Falls has been cutting its way through that rock for about that long.

"Roll forward two passes of Nibiru, to 3,600 years ago. Not coming as close. The worst effects were iron oxide dust from the mass of dust around Nibiru, its tail, raining red dust on the Earth. The rivers turned red. Earthquakes killed those living in stone buildings, the wealthy, the first born of Egypt, while the Israelites living in tents survived. The planet heated up, frogs came ashore and died, and flies flourished.

"On this pass, Moses and his people got out of Egypt, reaching the Reed Sea just as a tsunami is building from the eruption of Thera in the Mediterranean. That's an eruption triggered by Nibiru's effect on the magma below the crust. That eruption wiped out the Minoan civilization. Thera blew, the water withdrew to fill the hole, which gave the Israelites time to get across the Reed Sea, a spot somewhere on the coast of the Mediterranean northeast of Egypt, then returned as a classic tsunami to wipe out the Egyptians. Geologists figure that Thera blew up around 1,500BC. That's pretty close to 3,600 years ago.

"So the Exodus and the end of the Minoan civilization happened at the same time, triggered by the passage of Nibiru.

"Well, count with me. If Nibiru loops through the Solar System every 3,600 years, and the last loop was 3,600 years ago, we come down to what just happened. Again.

"Nibiru passed by us some months ago. If you were lucky and looked up when the sky was clear, you saw it. It caused a major crustal—pole—shift. This one was really bad. As Nibiru came close, it caused earthquakes, sinkholes, and landslides all over the planet. It brought our civilization to its knees before the crust shifted. Nibiru came very close, stopped our rotation, and tipped the Earth on its side. We had long days, long nights, and the Sun rising in the West. Not that we could tell with all the clouds. But we knew it was dark for a long time. Then the crust broke loose and rolled over the core for about an hour. We remember that. And we remember the train wreck when it slammed to a stop.

"Sources we had before the shift indicate that the coast of Oregon and California is now running east-west, parallel to the equator. We've checked a compass. What was north before is east now. The old west coast of Alaska is now right on the Equator. We're going to be warm here the rest of our lives. The North Pole is now off the bulge of Brazil, and the South Pole is off the tip of what's left of India. Central America is gone. The ice-covered islands that made up Antarctica are now sitting right on the equator. Ice is melting like mad, and in a few years, the seas will rise 600 feet.

"Roughly 90% of the people on Earth died in the shift or shortly after. We are the remnant of mankind."

Mark stood there and looked at the faces of the visitors from the south hills. He tried to gauge whether this was all a shock or sensible or what. He waited.

A young man from South Hills asked, "What happened to the Anunnaki?"

Mark decided to tell more of the story.

"They left. Around 700 BC. You can see where in the Bible, when God stops speaking and men start being judges and kings. They left, and they won't be coming back."

The young man came right back. "Why'd they leave."

Mark smiled. Here we go.

"They were told to leave."

"Who told them?"

"The Council of Worlds is a good enough name. Composed of civilizations all over the Universe. The folks who drive UFOs. The folks who did all those crop circles. They got really upset at how the Anunnaki were exploiting mankind on Earth. Told them to leave us alone. The *Prime Directive*, just like in Star Trek. Leave a primitive civilization alone to develop without interference."

Someone uttered a common expression of shock. "Jesus!"

Mark took that as an opening. "Oh, Jesus was a Star Child. But he came later."

A young woman asked, "How do you know all this?"

"If you're with me this far, I can tell you that gray aliens from Zeta Reticuli, part of the Council of Worlds, told us. A web site called ZetaTalk had been on the internet since 1995. The site explained everything in excruciating detail. Told the whole story, and predicted what was going to happen. Around here we subscribe to what ZetaTalk said, because everything they said would happen did happen exactly the way they said it would."

The young man was doubtful. "Aliens ran a web site? Give me a break."

"No, a woman ran the site, but she was, she said, in telepathic communication with them.

The man shot back. “I don't believe it.”

“Well,” Mark said, “it is fantastic and unbelievable, but it is the only explanation for everything that's happened. It reconciles everything from the months of earthquakes we went through to the contradictory personality of Yahweh in the Old Testament.”

He paused.

“There is one more thing to say now. The rest can wait. The most important thing is that those who survive and prevail now will do so because they care for each other. We say that such people have a service-to-other orientation. The service-to-selfish are already dead or will die shortly. Those who pull together for the sake of others will not only survive, they will prosper. Look at us. Remember what we've been through, how we worked together to get this far. Look at what we're accomplishing. Imagine where we're going. And believe that you can do that, too.”

Charlie stood up and said, “Amen, Brother.”

One of the visitors stood, scratched his head. “I'm going to have to think about all of this.”

The young woman rose, looked at Mark. “You said you had books?”

“A whole library. You're welcome to pile into it. Take notes. Spread the word.”

There were many more discussions that night and the next day. A few wanted to stay to take it all in, but the visitors as a group decided they needed to get home.

They were, after all, now in service to others.

MONTH 5
HURRICANE

The days rolled on. Still gloomy, with fog, mist, and rain nearly every day, interspersed with storms.

Mark could imagine the Earth settling down in all its particulars: land, water, wind. Earthquakes were common, most more rumbles and tremors than real quakes. There were a few real quakes that would have fractured solid houses. But the light structures of New Plymouth rode them out. Occasionally a rope around a few poles might come loose. Just pick up, tie up, and go back to work.

The storms were a problem. Some near hurricane force. There was no withstanding them. All you could do was hide. The last one had shredded tarps, blown over stoves, soaked clothes. They might have tied down more, had they known it was coming. The problem was that, without weather forecasting, there was no good way yet to tell when another thunderstorm was going to be a hurricane.

Before the shift, nobody in Oregon ever experienced a hurricane, let alone much of a thunderstorm. They knew that in the winter, the wind came from the south, and it rained. When the wind shifted and blew from the north, the rain stopped. So it was, year after year. Now, the wind came from the coast—that was roughly new south now—and it rained all the time. If there were clues now that a hurricane was coming, they were new to everyone.

In any event, they decided to build a storm shelter, to have one ready when needed. The trunk of the walnut tree that had sheltered them after the shift was still where it fell. The limbs were gone, but the huge trunk remained, mostly because they had not had the need or the time to dismember it.

They carried some heavy logs over to the trunk and laid them in a V, to form a triangle with the trunk as one side. With some effort, they stacked the logs four feet high, held by poles on both sides, connected by heavy wire. When they were done, they had a storm fort twelve feet on a side, where they could collect when a full storm hit.

Donna was their best forecaster. Her weather vane was her herd of sheep. The sheep and her dogs behaved differently before a real storm, and she learned to notice when they did.

So it happened that the signs spelled storm. “Mark, I think the sheep are saying we're in for a bad one.”

The sky was swirling, so nobody argued for waiting. One team removed tarps from the Pontiacs, used them to wrap clothes, tools, the library—anything that water could harm significantly. They hauled all the bundles into the storm fort. Another team checked the stockade around the sheep, got the chickens into the coop, corralled the clan dogs, put leashes on them, and brought them to the storm fort. The surviving cats were pretty much on their own.

They had no hatches to batten, but they battened everything else. As the rain and wind grew strong, they donned rain suits or ponchos and climbed into the fort.

The storm was nearly as strong as the one during the shift. The wind blew rain so hard it stung. Debris, sticks, and even small rocks pelted the fort and the clan within it. After an unmeasured time, the wind slackened. When the storm had faded to little more than the normal daily rain and wind, the clan climbed out of the storm fort and started to put things back together. The bare frames of the Pontiacs had hardly moved during the storm, and the tarps were safe. Reassembling the clan structures took only a few hours. So, the clan all felt the storm fort and their other preparations had proved effective.

Except for the garden.

They could hardly find it. The rain had hammered every plant flat and washed them all away. All that remained was sopping mud in the wooden frames of the raised beds. The potato barrels were full of water.

Alice and Paula hugged each other. Paula sobbed. All their effort. All their hopes that the clan would have more than fish to eat. All their concern about vitamins, especially vitamin C.

Lost.

With the fish at hand, they weren't facing starvation. But they were facing the prospect of impaired health from a limited diet.

It was hard to judge the seasons. Could they plant again? Would they lose again to another storm?

The gardeners gathered in the lodge to assess and plan. It was not hot, but it was not cold, either. If they were now closer to the equator, they might be able to grow all year. They had no real alternative. They still had seeds. They were using planting methods they had found in the book Square Foot Gardening by Mel Bartholomew, so rather than sow a lot of seeds and thin later, they sowed only as many seeds as they desired plants. This meant their seed supply would last for many seasons. The raised beds should drain quickly. They dumped the water out of the potato barrels. Maybe the potatoes and beets would survive if they did not stay so wet too long.

They had removed the tarps covering the beds to save the tarps, and they had lost the beds. So they discussed what to do differently for the next storm.

While inspecting the remains of the garden, they found a few plants that had survived by benefit of a slight amount of protection: a post, a stump, a log. They also found that the soil in the beds was muddier in some places than in others. Examination showed a difference in the amount of sand, rock, and charcoal.

They decided to do two things to weather the next storm: make the soil in the raised beds even looser, so it drained quickly, and build low fences of long poles lashed to long stakes. They would drive these fences into the ground along the sides of the beds facing the coast. These would work, they hoped, like snow fences, to lessen the blast and give the plants some protection.

Over the next few weeks, they assembled several different types of shelters, planning to see which worked best.

They collected sand and rock from the streams and turned it into the soil.

Charcoal required some work. The rocket stoves did not produce much charcoal, and the production by burning slash in the bed did not work well. They decided to start manufacturing charcoal for use in the garden.

Charlie rolled a 55-gallon drum over to the garden and removed the lid. He punched a number of holes in the other end of the drum and set it up on some bricks. Then he built a small fire in the drum and quickly added a lot of kindling and small sticks, until the drum was full and beginning to blaze. With the fire going fully strong, he dropped the lid on the drum, leaving a small gap on one side, and shoved dirt around the base to block most of the air going in through the holes in the bottom.

White smoke billowed from the drum. Charlie knocked on the sides of the drum a few times to mix up the fire inside, and more white smoke poured out. After a while, the smoke became more blue than white. That was the sign that the charcoal was starting to burn, so Charlie moved the lid to seal the gap at the top and then piled dirt to seal all the air intake at the bottom.

They left the barrel to cook and cool for a day. When Charlie removed the lid, there was a thick layer of charcoal in the bottom. He poured this into a bin in a soil-making area Paula had arranged in the garden. Paula started mixing it into soil for the beds, and Charlie started another batch.

It occurred to Mark about that time that they would also need a supply of wood ash shortly to start making soap. The rocket stoves hardly made any. And the charcoal furnace didn't either. So he suggested to Charlie that they construct a fireplace where they could enjoy an open fire occasionally. Some of the wood would burn to ash, which they could use to make lye for soap. Some of it would become charcoal, which they could add to the garden. Everyone liked the idea. There was something about an open fire that they missed with all the efficiencies of their rocket stoves.

So they built a new circular structure near the lodge, based on the Pawnee Hogan in *Shelters, Shacks, and Shanties*. In the center, they built a raised fire ring with a smoke hood suspended above. With a mind to the next hurricane, Charlie made the structure of poles nearly 6” in diameter, tied together by long bolts he'd salvaged from downed power poles. The smoke hood was sheet metal, as was the roof, lashed to the poles with electrical wire.

The clan inaugurated the new fire ring with a feast of fish, stories, and music around a fire that blazed for hours.

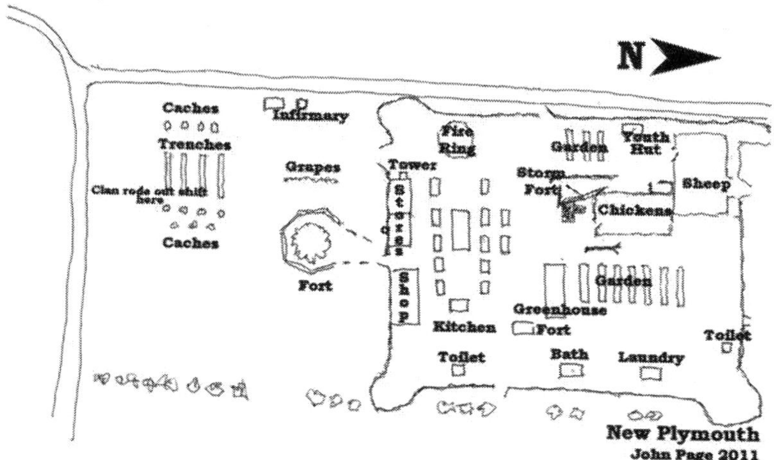

"When can we do this again?"

"How about every Friday?"

"When is Friday? Is this Friday? Do we still have weeks?"

"Well, this is Fireday."

"Cool. Let's do this again next Fireday."

"Is that seven days from now?"

"Maybe we need more charcoal than that."

"Let's do it every four days."

"Why four?"

"We get more weekends that way."

"Hey, I've finally achieved the four-day week."

And they laughed.

Life was not all grim. There were victories. They made progress. They were healthy. They were not hungry, even if they were sick of fish.

And they had managed to come out of a hurricane with a new tradition that drew them closer.

MONTH 6
SCHOOLING AND ARCHIVES

Life settled into a natural rhythm after the hurricane. Perhaps it was the last of a season as new climate cycles took charge of the New Earth atmosphere. Perhaps another would come. Life went on. They had prepared for a disaster and come through it as they had planned. Being able to absorb disaster without collapsing was a mark of civilization.

Fish prevented starvation. A few deer added variety and more fat for soap.

When he wasn't fishing, Greg hunted a steady stream of squirrels and other small animals to supply Mark with thyroid tissue. The rest of the animal remains went into the pot. He was becoming an excellent shot with the .22 rifle, and they had over a thousand rounds in the arsenal, but he was beginning to consider trapping to save ammunition for pest control.

Bobbie experimented with seasonings to make food at all interesting. Mostly, she used the wild onions and garlic that had grown wild in Beforetime. The stash of spices from the survival cache helped a little. They didn't have enough pepper.

Alice and Shelly roamed the hills around New Plymouth to collect and catalog whatever grew there. They hoped to find edible plants in the tangle. They spread out what they brought back and compared it to books in the library. The ferns and dandelions were welcome in the kitchen, so the clan organized the children to begin gathering them.

Paula and Sara watched the garden, where recovery was slow. She worked on ways to make the soil more porous, ways to grow root crops in a rainy climate. She might have gone entirely to hydroponics had she had enough containers to hold the beds. She knew little about hydroponics, and the clan library had only a few documents on the subject.

She checked the blackberry bushes around the compound. They had flourished in Beforetime Oregon. In time she would know if they liked the new climate as well. If they did, New Plymouth would have a source of fruit with many uses.

The men and children collected and recycled building materials of every sort. Their focus was on more permanent roofing. They often discussed how to construct a better structure than the Pontiac or Pawnee huts. Charlie and Bill were experienced carpenters, but with Beforetime tools and materials. The only lumber now was salvage. The only nails now were pulled from ruined structures and straightened by hand, save a few caches recovered from destroyed houses. Charlie had brought his air compressor and nailers to the retreat, but they had no way to power them. Swinging hammers to drive slightly bent nails did not sound like a viable plan, especially to old men. They were nearly all in their 60's.

Greg and his sons hunted. The children helped with the sheep and cattle.

Rachel and the mothers took the children in hand. Every day had a little school, a little play, the rest useful work. Their intent was to get beyond the trauma, establish a livable daily life, and make sure the children grew up knowing how to prevail on their own. The children who were learning to read needed to learn well, so they could use the clan library and even add to it.

Mark, Rachel and Jack talked often about how to prepare the children—six boys and three girls, aged 5 to 18. In the long run, they would need to combine with others their age to survive into adulthood. Before that, they needed the mental and spiritual preparation to prevail and contribute to the New Plymouth Clan now, and to a clan of their own making later.

Jack had come to the project as a Native American with an abiding interest in the old ways, as well as the father of three daughters, none of whom were with him. Mark and Rachel had raised four daughters between them, with a renaissance mixture of scholarship, music, foreign languages, and foreign travel. All the girls grew into young women with passionate concern for the Earth and their fellow humans. So Jack, Mark and Rachel worked out a plan to blend the best of all they could do to truly educate the children still with them.

The plan included reading, writing, drawing, and music. They assessed where each young person was in the subjects of math, biology, botany, history, and foreign languages. The younger children came from Spanish-speaking families, so the clan committed to becoming bilingual. The children 12 and older learned to shoot the .22. The oldest learned to shoot the .30-06. All the children worked at crafts, helping with woodworking, metal working, clothes construction, leather working, trapping, fishing, gardening and gathering from the forest—all skills they generally observed their parents and other adults doing every day.

Mark and Rachel both felt the clan needed to decide formally on one point: would all the children learn all the skills, or skills defined by conventional gender roles. Would the boys learn to hunt while the girls learned to sew? The clan unanimously decided to have all the children learn and work at all the skills. If any wanted to focus on one or another for mastery after that, they were welcome to choose. But all would cook, sew, hunt, fish, garden and gather.

The children built their own Pontiac hut to learn how it was done. They used the space as their own for school, recreation, and to have a bit of refuge from all the adults.

Jack sang and played guitar and banjo. Mark played fiddle, mountain dulcimer, guitar and mandolin. Charlie played guitar and sang. Rachel played fiddle. Donna sang.

If the clan could get 12-volt electricity going, they might use their inverter to resurrect Rachel's electronic keyboard, which remained wrapped in its waterproof bundle. So they had musicians to teach and accompany. The clan library included a pile of books full of tunes and songs. Music and dance would be part of their clan life.

In the back of the parents' minds was the enormity of their situation: knowledge and civilization depended on the continuity of learning and tradition from parents to children.

Now 23 adults hoped to pass on to 9 children what they needed to know. Exactly what was that? The books in the clan library would help, but they were mostly about survival skills, gardening and such. There were a fair number of books on American history. A dictionary. A Bible. Only one book on science, *Caveman Chemistry*, Kevin Dunn's fascinating volume, which might prove to have been the best book to have if you could only have one. None on mathematics, astronomy, geology, botany, biology. So much knowledge from 20 centuries of civilization would simply evaporate.

But was that a tragedy? Or an opportunity?

What would these adults pass on to these children that had real meaning? What was truly important?

The parents and interested adults gathered to discuss their challenge.

"So much of what we learned had to do with being able to work in industry. There isn't any now. We didn't learn then so much of what we've needed to know since the shift."

Jack leaned forward on his bench with his arms on his knees. He looked at Mark and said, "What kids need now are life skills, immediate skills, how to survive."

Sara jumped into the conversation. "And how to rebuild. We're the seeds of a new Earth."

Mark nodded. "Okay. Then what do we want to see sprout on this new Earth?"

Sara spoke first. "Somehow, we have to avoid as long as possible the corruption and pollution of Beforetime."

Charlie brought up a common subject in their discussions. "Well, you know that comes down to what service-to-self people do to each other and the planet."

Bill scowled. "Yeah, study biology so you can modify the genes of plants, then patent the life form."

Charlie snorted. "*Patent life forms*. God, that's obscene."

Mark broke in. "So do we teach values?"

Brad replied immediately. "Absolutely. Service to others in all things."

Charlie leaned back and smiled. "Yeah. Have you noticed we haven't needed money?"

Bill chuckled. "Hah. Nothing to buy."

Charlie shook his head. "No. No need to buy. We have plenty. We have *enough*. We have what we need. Share. Help. Support. Assist. Even with the folks up in the south hills."

Donna could see that the adults agreed. But what about the kids? "Are any of the kids not STO?"

Rachel had spent some time with them. "Not really. They're good kids, and they pitched right in. Example helped."

Sara nodded. "I'd like to see us make a big deal about STO. Make it the center of our tradition. Tell stories to support it."

Mark was grateful for her support. “So we tell them about the last days of Beforetime? Why we were in that mess.”

Charlie replied with some emotion. “Absolutely. Most of them remember it. We have to talk about it, so what we do now goes on from that.”

Mark leaned forward. “I have a huge collection of documents about the last days on my computer. I called it *millennium*. If we get 12-volt electricity going, we can pull it up and teach it.”

Rachel sighed. “Wish we could print.”

Mark pointed to the tubs that held the library.. “Well, fortunately, we did print a lot before the shift. A tub full of paper, printed both sides. Some of the historical documents are in there.”

Donna looked at the tubs. “We need an archivist.”

Mark and Donna had discussed that. “Well, we really need a university. One or two people who focus on all the resources of learning we have. All the books. All the paper. The printed music. The songs. And we need to start adding to the library. Anybody know what today's date is?”

Rachel snorted. “Does it matter?”

Mark smiled at her. “It has always mattered. When do you plant? When do you harvest? What will the temperature be two months from now? The answers to all those questions come from records of dates, weather, temperature. We need to start recording.”

Alice could see the point. “A new Farmer's Almanac.”

Mark nodded. “Right.”

Alice looked at Mark. “Mark, you and Rachel had good educations. You brought almost all the books in the library from your house. The computers are yours, and you printed all the paper in the tub. So I'd say you two should be our university.”

Paula broke in. “I bet the folks up north—uh—west...in the south hills —gee, what will we call them now? I bet the folks in the South Hills Clan would be interested in all this. There are a lot of kids up there.”

Sara thought about her daughter, Ashley. “Well, I feel strongly enough about this that I want to take our own direction on educating our kids. I wouldn't want to compromise if those folks wanted something else.”

Bill thought of his son, just Ashley's age. “Agree. We establish our course. They can join if they're going our way.”

Alice also thought about their son. “Right.”

Paula summarized the consensus. “So, it seems we allow Mark and Rachel to focus on knowledge and learning, like scribes in an Irish monastery, while we till the fields to feed the monks?”

Mark smiled. “The Irish saved Western Civilization. Now it's ours to lose.”

Rachel knew Mark had read a book on how the Irish had saved a lot of ancient literature. “Well, we probably already have, because we don't have any books on Greek or Roman poetry, history or philosophy.”

Mark had thought about that, and he mused on how much from Sumer had been lost as well. It was always so. Only a fraction ever survives. “Probably more important what we write now than what we read. Every generation learns the same lessons, makes a lot of the same mistakes. Look at how the conservative Right in the last days was trying to undo Teddy Roosevelt's work of a century earlier. From trusts, to anti-trust, and back to trusts again. If we take responsibility for where we go now, and go there with the intent to be of service to others, we'll do humanity more good than if we pass on some ancient poems.”

Charlie grimaced. “Sadly, I agree.”

“Okay,” Rachel said, accepting a task she had long thought about. “If we're going to focus on the history we write instead of the history we read, I think we need to all get involved in that. I'd like to see everyone start writing and sharing around the fire. Make writing and story telling a tradition here. If these children see us doing it, it will more likely be something they get into themselves.”

Abe protested. “I don't write.”

Rachel wouldn't back off. “If you can talk, you can write. If I can learn to fiddle, you can learn to write. Nobody escapes me.”

Everyone laughed.

Alice asked, “How do we start?”

Rachel smiled at her. “How about this: your life story in one page. Two hundred and fifty words. Write it down so you can read it aloud. I'll have the children do theirs as well. Oldest to youngest will recite, starting at the fire tomorrow night. We can start then. May take several nights to hear 'em all.”

Mark grinned. “Who's the oldest?” I'm 66.”

Abe chuckled. “I'm two weeks older than you are.”

Mark smiled a wicked smile. “Good!”

They worked out the order of readers, and everyone started thinking about their homework.

The next night, everyone gathered by the fire. Word had gotten out to the rest of the clan. Some grumbled, but nobody argued. The Old Ones, as they were humorously called, rustled their papers, ready to speak. Jack started the evening with a group sing, the first they had tried, and the clan proved to resemble a bag pipe: robust melody, occasional harmony, and a few drones. Then Jack, Charlie and Mark played a few tunes while the group drummed on the tables. Rachel sat with the youngest children and encouraged them to drum in time. Tunes she would teach them floated in her mind.

The recitations began. Unknown stories. *He never told me that. Who knew?* Tales of events that shed light on personality and preference. Successes. Failures. Happy and sad. Curiously, in all of the stories, a theme of helping others, taking care of others, serving others began to emerge. Making the point without stating it.

The clan was developing traditions
And a personality.

MONTH 6, LATER
TRADE AND SEX

Charlie and Bill had greatly refined their first attempt at making stove pipe by wrapping it around a log. They now had a workshop where they could produce stoves, stove pipe and a dozen other appliances, all under a roof.

Salvaged heat ducts, forced-air furnaces, kitchen stoves, old refrigerators, yard sheds, barn roofs, and many other sources supplied the metal they cut, chopped, and bent into new uses.

The rocket stoves especially were in great demand, as everyone found new uses for them. Rocket stoves heated tea water and soup during the day for workers in the garden, wood teams gathering poles in the forest above the compound, and the cattlemen at the ranch, so they could stay where they were for lunch.

Several stoves powered the water stills. Two stoves based on Charlie's invention at South Hills heated the hut where they hung clothes to dry. Other stoves heated water for bathing, cooking, washing, soap making, and canning.

Many stoves served the clan, all with virtually no smoke. Those tending one or another of the stoves commented regularly on how lucky they were to live without the smoke from open fires. They also appreciated that the stoves used small sticks—the wind produced a steady harvest in the forest—so they did not have to expend the tremendous labor that would be required to cut down, saw, and split trees for traditional firewood. The children proved to be effective wood gatherers, freeing adults for other tasks.

Charlie and Bill had also built their first, light timber-frame building—their shop—to re-invent how it was done and see if their building could survive the random quakes and storms. They filled in the spaces between the posts with wattles—frames of woven sticks—which they plastered with a mixture of mud—which they had in abundance—and grass. To simplify the joinery, they used salvaged electrical cable rather than wind braces to keep the structure from racking.

The wattle-and-daub walls reduced the need for tarps, at least for that purpose. The walls also allowed them to incorporate real windows, salvaged from houses and vehicles nearby. The roof would be covered by tarps until they found the time to prepare some slightly mangled barn roofing for a metal roof.

The South Hills Clan was busy as well with salvage. The south hills had more houses than the hills around New Plymouth, so they had a greater supply of sheet metal and wire. Those houses yielded a fair set of tools, so the settlement was beginning to resemble New Plymouth.

Commerce grew between the two settlements. Sometimes an individual, often a group on a mission, and sometimes a family made the trip up or down the ruined interstate. Charlie and Bill rigged a light cart from plumbing pipe and bicycle wheels that could carry a fair amount of bulky material in either direction. It was common for sheet metal to travel to New Plymouth, and for stoves and stove pipe to make the return trip. Crops were uncertain, so there was little in the way of produce in the trade.

The two groups talked about investigating the remains of the towns between them. These were clogged with mud and silt from the tsunami-like flood that followed the failure of the dams. Much of the best stuff, like the metal in the old saw mills and shops, was so encased in debris that it might have to wait for archaeologists in a future world to chip it out.

Mark and Greg did make a circuit of one town site to check the drug store there for anything of value to the settlements. Sadly, they found that water had covered the shelves long enough that most of the labels had fallen off their bottles. Mark and Greg bagged what they could, noting that the most valuable find left in the place might be the metal shelving.

They checked the wreckage of the grocery store out near the airport. The water had washed away the labels or soaked and mulched the cardboard boxes. There were few of either, because the panic before the shift had pretty much cleared the shelves. The remaining cans were rusting.

They made a note to send a crew with the cart to salvage the refrigeration and air conditioning pipes and useable metal from shelving and the kitchen.

The airport was a mess, as it was near the river. The relatively flimsy hangars were gone, as were the planes. Whether they'd gone before the flood or during it was unknowable.

Mark and Greg concluded as they walked back to New Plymouth that their best sources for salvage would ever be the houses, barns, farms, and such in the hills above the valley floor.

So it happened that salvage surveys became a regular event for both communities. Salvage teams went after specific items, noting new finds for later recovery. Sadly, they never encountered people living alone or in groups anywhere between New Plymouth and South Hills. In Eugene, there was now no sign of any survivors from groups that the South Hills Clan had known were on other hills just after the shift.

Every few weeks, teams from both sites would meet to discuss what was where and who needed it. Moving anything by cart took some effort, so generally the teams didn't move something until they knew where it would end up. After a number of these trips, the teams had worked out a route between the two groups that was smooth enough and wide enough for wheeled carts to navigate easily.

Abe liked hiking and traveling, so he made it his contribution to organize a freight company to do the moving. He acquired tools, rope, a winch, and a derrick made of poles to facilitate heavier lifting. He worked with Charlie and Bill to improve their *truck*, as he called it. Then he began a regularly scheduled service up and down the interstate, one day's travel in each direction, plus a day to load at each end.

Sometimes people accompanied the truck to look around or visit new friends at the other site. One increasingly regular visitor was Jeff, roughly 17, who had taken an interest in Sara's daughter, Ashley, who was the same age. She appeared to be as equally interested in him.

Mark watched them from a distance, waiting to see if their interest became serious. When the hand holding started, he decided to discuss the matter with Sara.

"Looks like your daughter has a boyfriend."

"Uh, huh. She's pretty happy about it."

"Nature does have Her way, doesn't She?"

Sara grinned. "Yes, She does."

"I've admired from afar your relationship with her. You seem supportive rather than controlling. Rachel was the same way with her daughters."

"I'm proud of her and happy to see her moving on with life as though she has a future."

"I presume you've talked to her about sex?"

"Yes. Early on and often. Not to just say no, but how to be safe."

"What do you tell her now?"

"I doubt we have to worry about disease. Getting pregnant could be a problem."

"Especially as we're a little short in the medical area. We're probably a little short in the condom area, too."

"She knows about the rhythm method and other ways to have fun without ending up pregnant."

"Well, there's one more issue that Rachel was strong about as well."

"Oh?"

"I don't like the idea of them trying to sneak off into the woods for a tryst. We've got coyotes and maybe bigger stuff out there. It's gonna happen. If we make a stand to forbid it..."

"I won't do that. Doesn't work. People who think it does just fool themselves."

"I agree with you. Rachel convinced me of that. Would just drive them to the woods. I think we need to be sure they're safe."

"What do you have in mind?"

"I think we need to tell her to stay in the compound. Tell her if she really wants to roll with him, go to her family hut, and we'll politely leave them alone. Tell her it's okay if she does, okay if she doesn't. I think in this new world, the woman should have the say and the support. If she thinks things are getting out of hand, she can say no. If she says it loud enough, we'll be there."

"That's the way I would do it."

"Well, I think in this new world we should be open and honest about sex, babies and parenting. I'd like to see us tell the clan that this is how we intend to handle birds and bees. Ask her to tell you when it might be getting to that point. When it does, tell the young man that this is the way we handle it, that it's okay if she says it's okay. Not okay if she says no. It's up to her. But sex is one thing. Getting pregnant is another. Could be a death sentence. At the very least, it means sharing responsibility for the child. There are risks, and no need to take them before they're ready."

"Oh, Mark, I totally agree. Thank you. I'll go talk to her now. Where are they?"

"Over there." Mark pointed.

"Do you think we'll get flak from anyone?"

"Don't know. Our clan is pretty progressive. This is a new world. We stress caring for each other rather than controlling. This seems to me to flow from that. But in my mind, in any event, it's you're business as her mother, and it's your call."

Sara hugged Mark, smiled and went looking for her daughter. Mark went looking for Jeff.

Sara had found the young couple first and had asked for a moment along with Ashley. Jeff was sitting on the trunk of a downed tree, waiting.

"Hi, Jeff. How ya doin'?"

"Okay. How're you?"

"Good. Hey, it looks like you and Ashley are getting close."

"Yeah. We kinda are."

"Well, Jeff, you know this is a new world. We're starting over. A lot of things are different now."

"Yeah."

"One of them is sex."

Jeff looked down, uneasy.

"What have your parents said about sex and marriage?"

"Look, we're not that serious."

"It's okay. I'm just curious. What did your folks teach you about sex? And marriage?"

"Well, the usual stuff. Wait. Use protection."

"Do they approve of sex outside of marriage?"

"I'd say so. Both my mom and dad had lived with others before they got married. They told me about protection. I guess they figured I'd get to that before marriage."

"Did they have children with other partners."

"No. They took precautions. I guess. I'm their only child."

"Wow. How do they feel about you coming down here?"

"Times have changed. They're okay with you folks, and I travel with Abe, so it's not like I'm going out on my own to be a mountain man or something. I hang out with Charlie and Bill some, when Ashley's doing chores. Jack's even teaching me to play guitar. And we all sleep together in the lodge. Big family."

"We'll, we're okay with you, too. Happy to have you with us. So, about sex. Here's the deal. Our deal. Jeff, we remember and understand what it's like to be young, to find an attractive friend. There's nothing wrong or dirty about feeling attracted and excited sexually. Hell, that's why we're all here. And aren't we glad?

"But there are problems. One. Sex is a problem when it's not wanted by one of the people in the couple. Two. Sex is a really big problem when it results in a baby too soon. And three. In this new world, sex can also become a tragedy if the couple is rolling in the woods and gets eaten by something hairy."

Jeff laughed. Nervously. *Where was this old guy going with this?*

"Jeff, I discussed this with Ashley's mother, we agreed, and she's talking right now to Ashley about what I'm going to tell you. Our position in New Plymouth is that exploring sex is okay in the right spirit and in the right way. Only if you both want, especially only if she wants. Only if you honor her wishes and respond immediately if she changes her mind. Only if you are responsible and avoid pregnancy. And only inside the New Plymouth compound."

"You're kidding."

"No. We're saying it's okay to be a responsible adult here in this new world."

"In your compound?"

"Yes. We'll respect your privacy. We'll come running if called. And you'll be safe from hairy things."

Jeff failed to suppress a grin. "I don't believe this."

"Take your time. Don't rush. Don't push. Look out for Ashley, and take care of her. Be a friend. And no babies."

"Oh, right."

"No. Really big deal. Look. We don't have a doctor, or even a trained midwife. In the old days, before medicine, women died early, often in childbirth. We're not ready to deal with pregnancies and deliveries."

"Well, I don't have any condoms."

"So? Do you know ways to enjoy sex but avoid pregnancy besides condoms?"

"Yeah. I do."

"All I'm saying is be responsible. We here are dedicated to service to others. Our new world is a service-to-each-other world. That covers everything from wood gathering to sex. Sex is a beautiful thing when it brings beauty to the life of your partner. Explore that idea, and you will enjoy a better world than the one we left behind."

"Wow." Jeff blushed.

"Okay. It looks like Sara is done with Ashley. Why don't you go sit down together and talk openly and honestly about what you're ready for. Be friends."

"Okay. Thanks. I don't know what to say."

"What matters is what you do. *Service to others.* Now go."

Mark watched Sara walk back to the kitchen. He joined her there. She started making tea.

"How'd it go."

"Fine. She's not ready to get into sex."

"That's good, actually. Better we bring it up and face it than pretend it isn't there. I don't think our talking about sex will drive them to it. Might just do the opposite."

"Right. I do think we need to get the clan up to speed on this."

"Let's bring it up privately with the adults, so we don't embarrass the two young people right off the bat. In the long run, we probably need to find a way to get the message to our young people when they're ready for it."

"A youth group?"

"Maybe part of our 4H thing. It fits: Head, Hands, Health and Heart. The sheep herd is finally into sex. It's not like it's a secret. We might actually succeed in making sex natural and healthy again."

"Hmm. Welcome to life in the country."

"The *new* country."

MONTH 8

ELECTRICITY

Mark, Charlie, and Bill sat at a table in the lodge.

Mark looked at Charlie. "Either of you know anything about automotive electrical systems?"

Bill smiled. "You're finally tired of living without electricity?"

Mark looked at the fleet of vehicles lined up at the edge of the compound.

"There are 9 vehicles just sitting there, plus all the equipment at the ranch. Maybe a dozen batteries in vehicles, plus the deep-cycle batteries we brought. Plus all the voltage regulators in all the vehicles. Back in Beforetime, I figured we'd generate power by something that rotates, use it to charge batteries, then use batteries and inverters to drive the laptops. I didn't bother with solar panels, because I figured we'd live with too much gloom after the shift. Now it looks like we might have enough solar energy to generate power, but that's moot. We don't have the panels. What can we do with the alternators?"

Bill looked at the trees in the plantation above them. "We have a fair amount of wind some of the time. We have a lot of flowing water. I'd vote for water power. Anybody done it?"

Charlie put his hands up. "Not me. Or wind, either. This is all new."

Mark nodded. "Agreed. Suppose we break down the problem. Focus first on an alternator and voltage regulator. See if we can isolate the parts, put them in a frame, get it to generate current. That would tell us we have the generator. Then we can focus on driving it somehow."

Bill needed some inspiration. "Do we have anything in the archive on hydro generation?"

Mark looked away a moment. "There are some documents from VITA. Let's take a look."

They walked over to the library hut. A half hour later they found the sheets Mark had printed Beforetime that contained the VITA material about a 1-kilowatt river generator. The document was scant. They studied the diagrams for a while. Charlie finally summarized. "They're using multiple water wheels connected by pulleys and belts to drive an alternator. We don't have nearly all the stuff they used."

Mark leafed through the box that held the printouts of his archive. "I also have a document on using a bicycle to drive an alternator. Simpler arrangement. Maybe we come up with our own, using these for inspiration."

Bill looked at the bicycle rig. "What alternator do we use?"

Mark smiled. "Well, I checked on various models Beforetime. From what I could tell at the time, my Dodge didn't have a voltage regulator and relied on something called a PCM to control it. Probably out of the question to use it now. But Toyotas were straightforward, so I saved the documentation on them. And here it is."

Bill asked, "Why do we need a voltage regulator?"

"It's possible to drive an alternator fast enough to overcharge a battery and kill it. The regulator prevents overcharging."

"Gee, I could have used one of those when I had credit cards."

They all laughed. Then they all looked at each other. They'd forgotten. Thousands of dollars in credit card debt between them. All history. They grinned and gave each other high-fives.

Mark handed the sheets on the Toyota system to Charlie, whose Toyota pickup sat along the fence with the others.

Charlie glanced at the document. "I'm on it," was all he said as he got up and headed for his workshop.

Bill said, "I'll focus on some way to mount it. We can use Donna's old bicycle for the Mod One generator."

Mark left them to it for a day.

When he checked back, they had a wooden frame set up, holding Donna's bicycle with the rear wheel raised. Charlie had removed the fender and the tire from the rear wheel and had a belt from it driving the pulley on the alternator. Bill was pedaling furiously, while Charlie checked the output of the alternator with a volt meter. “We have power.”

Mark grinned. “All we need now is a reliable source.”

Bill howled. “Okay, Critic. Your turn.”

Mark laughed. “Wouldn't do nearly as well as you. Where'd you get a belt that long?”

“It's the serpentine belt from a Dodge van.”

“Uh. I had the only Dodge van here.”

Charlie grinned and bowed from his waist. “Thank you.”

“Oh, well. Life goes on. What's the next step?”

Charlie went to a table nearby and picked up a drawing. “We're working on the other end—the water wheel—next. We need a rig that turns a shaft at least as fast as Bill has been pedaling. If we can do that, we're in business.”

Mark looked at the drawing. “Undershot wheel.”

Charlie nodded. “Yeah. We pull water out of the stream over there.” He pointed to the edge of the farm, where the stream ran swiftly down the ravine toward the valley below. “We'll use some irrigation pipe Donna had. Just stick the end in the flow for the first test. Water comes out the other end and hits the wheel. The wheel is mounted in a sluice box. The water flows under it. The water comes out the end of the sluice and heads downhill.”

“What's the wheel?”

“Our first one will be two disks of plywood, reinforced with sheet metal, with wooden blades between, all screwed together. About 36 inches in diameter. We'll use pipe flanges for the axle.”

“How will you control speed?”

“That's clearly a function of water. We'll work on ways to control how much water flows. And we'll work on a better wheel to survive being in the water. The plywood will de-laminate pretty quickly.”

“The old mills used wood that lasted for years. Mostly oak, and we have oak downhill from here.”

“We'll need something. Wood or metal. The wood wheels never turned as fast as we'll need, so we'd need some gearing.”

“Or pulleys.”

Over the next days, they built a frame to hold the bicycle generator rig, the sluice box and the water wheel. The sluice was a box with a wood bottom about a foot wide, sides about 3 feet high, about 8 feet long, open on the downhill end, all reinforced with metal straps and bolts. The up-hill end had a hole in it to take the end of a piece of irrigation pipe. The wheel rode just in front of the end of the irrigation pipe so that the water discharge hit the wheel blades on the low side of the wheel. The wheel rode on a shaft of pipe screwed into pipe flanges bolted to the wheel. The axle rested on wooden blocks made out of oak. One end of the axle was fastened to the pedal crank on the bicycle frame, which drove the rear wheel with the sprocket chain.

They still had a bicycle generator, only the water wheel was pedaling.

The irrigation pipe was flexible, so they rigged a crane to lower the pipe into the flow of the stream. They could control the flow of water into the pipe by raising or lowering the pipe.

On the first try, they allowed just a little water to come down the pipe. The wheel started to turn, the bicycle sprocket turned, the rear wheel turned, and the alternator generated a little power. There was a fair amount of rumbling and shaking, so Charlie commented that he was glad they'd kept the pedal sprocket and gears of the bicycle in the mechanism. The water wheel would come apart if it turned too fast. Charlie experimented with inlet pipe height and gear selection on the bicycle until he had a fairly agreeable combination of water flow, wheel velocity and gear settings.

They let the rig run for a while to charge the deep-cycle battery, housed in a battery box. Charlie kept testing to see if they were gaining. After a while, the indicator showed that the battery was indeed picking up a charge.

The test was good enough to confirm that they could generate power. Now it would be a matter of building a more permanent rig with a better wheel.

Over the next few hours, all the clan came down to watch the water wheel pedal the bicycle. The kids played in the water gushing out of the sluice. Charlie had to yell at them to get away from the wheels. Without OSHA to worry about, he hadn't rigged any guards on the shafts and belts.

When the indicator showed the battery was charged, Bill raised the pipe out of the stream, and the wheel stopped turning.

Bill and Charlie unhooked the battery, ran a pole through the handle on the battery box, and hauled the battery up to the lodge. Mark was waiting for them there with the inverter and his MacBook laptop. They connected the inverter and plugged in the laptop. Mark pressed the power button and waited. In a moment, the unmistakable music of a Mac booting up sounded, greeted by cheers from the clan. Mark hoped to leave the laptop connected long enough to recharge the battery. He hoped it would hold a charge after being dormant so long.

When the computer was fully up, Mark browsed forgotten folders, finally found what he was seeking: a copy of James Burke's TV show, *Connections, Episode 1*, which Mark had found on YouTube. In it, Burke talked about what would happen if civilization ended. Great speculation and well done. The children crowded in front of the computer, with adults ranged behind. They all watched in the growing darkness of early evening as the computer, freakish relic of a time now gone, displayed the images and played the sound. They were silent, each gauging how close Burke had come to the way things turned out.

Of course, Burke left out the part about the pole shift.

Mark looked around the group, their faces lit by the glow from the screen. The electronic magic seemed out of place, now that they were so used to Aftertime sights, sounds and smells. Sounds around them now were natural—asymmetrical—from birds, children, axes, hammers, pots, sheep, dogs, water and wind.

Nothing throbbed with the consistency of industrial objects. Mark first noticed that while listening to the machinery of the water wheel and the bicycle generator. Sounds of the old life, the old values, the old industry of Beforetime.

He noticed that Charlie watched for a few minutes, shook his head, and walked away.

Mark was glad to have access to the computer again. There were more documents to study that they hadn't printed. They had no printers any more—the toner was gone in the laser, and the ink had run out in the ink jet. If they wanted a paper record of anything now lurking only in the computer, they would have to copy it like scribes into notebooks. At least they had several cases of those left, and they were gearing up to make new paper.

So they still had computers—the MacBooks that Mark and Rachel had used. Rachel's had a copy of everything Mark had, and they had a backup drive with it all, and a network hub to connect it all. For as long as they would work.

There were days of music and hours of video to watch. Images from Before. Electronic copies of many of the great classics. Forty years of

Mother Earth News. Two years of *Home Power Magazine*. A complete copy of the ZetaTalk site.

But Mark knew what Charlie was thinking.

He wasn't sure he wanted to go back.

To Beforetime.

He wasn't even sure he wanted to hear the water wheel.

But there it was—human ingenuity applied to make work easier and allow time for other things. Without the structure and strictures of Beforetime, how would they choose to spend that time?

The next day, Mark rose early to watch the light come. The sunrise was always cloudy, but the play of light, mists, rain, trees, hills, the air—it was all beautiful and fresh. As he walked out of the lodge, he came up behind Sara, Alice and Shelly, sitting in lotus pose facing the light.

They had done yoga together Beforetime.

There had been good in Beforetime. They were sifting through it and pulling it through to Aftertime.

He felt better about the water wheel.

ONE YEAR AFTER
MARK

Mark was tired. More tired each day. He'd been taking the thyroid tissue instead of his pills, to see if it worked. Truth was he didn't even know if the tissue he was taking was thyroid.

His leg itched. The skin was scaly. His nails were turning a dull yellow.

He knew the signs.

He pulled out the bottle. 24 pills left. 48 days. And not good days at that.

What then? ZetaTalk mentioned that survivors in the new world would need to face letting go when health failed and there was no medicine. Mark thought about diabetics who might have survived the shift, only to die shortly after their last insulin was gone. He'd read a novel once about people from the twentieth century who were sent back to the seventeenth century. A newborn baby was too weak to survive. The twentieth-century mother was overcome with grief and anger. Her seventeenth-century husband tried to comfort her by giving her the gift of acceptance, which was common in his time.

Acceptance. Easy to say. Hard to do.

What about responsibilities? What about his wife, his beloved Rachel? She had supported his efforts to prepare for the shift. Invaluable support. What a life they had led! What adventure! She depended on him. The thought of not being there to care for her sometimes left him unable to speak.

What about friends? They were all here because of him. He had given them so many of the things that had gotten them through and into a new life in a new world. He could look around and see his influence.

His legacy.

They would be all right.

Or they wouldn't.

It was time to accept.

He asked Rachel to go for a walk. They went up the road a bit to a point where they could look down on the compound and beyond to the valley. It wasn't raining, so they could see clear to the Coast Range. They found a rock, arranged their ponchos to keep dry, and sat down.

“Quite the trip it's been, Love.”

“Yes. Unbelievable. You should be proud of all that you've done. There are a lot of people alive here because of you.”

“I know. You've been wonderful.”

They sat silently for a while.

Rachel focused, struggled.

“Mark, are you saying goodbye?”

“Is it that obvious?”

“You don't look well. I've been worried about you but didn't want to worry you.”

“Either the squirrel thyroid isn't working, or something else is taking me down. I have 24 pills left.”

“What happens when they're gone?”

“Don't know for sure. You remember how it was when I was clear off thyroid hormone. The hair, skin and muscle problems. Not being able to sleep. The weird dreams. Some of that is back. I researched what comes after those symptoms back when we had internet, just to know. Weakness. Slowed speech. Maybe slow thinking. Heart issues. Maybe heart attack. Or a coma. Eventually death.”

“Well, you should let go of things here and take care of what's left of you.”

“Yeah. As tired as I am, that sounds rather nice.”

“We can also try more of the squirrel, or maybe something else.”

“I'm not counting on it. I will not be a burden. Our friends have enough to do taking care of each other.”

“I know. But they owe you.”

"Well, maybe, but in our new world, I owe them, too. We don't have medicine to speak of. When staying clean and eating well is no longer enough, we need to accept and say our goodbyes. I feel like I need to set an example."

Rachel was quiet for a while. Mark waited.

"I hate this, Mark! God damn it, I hate this."

"We've known this would happen. Thyroid hormone was always an issue, even in Beforetime. And I've had cancer. My mom died of it. And my dad died of heart disease. I could just as easily have a heart attack without warning and never have the time to just accept and hang onto each other. It was never a question of *if*. It was always a question of *when* and *how*. At least we have some inkling, and we have some time."

They sat together, holding hands. Rachel leaned into him. He put his arm around her and kissed her head and breathed. Her hair smelled like her, good, as it always had.

Finally she spoke. "What do you want to do?"

"Well, let's get the clan together and tell them that I'm fading and need to let go. Let's not say that the squirrel thyroid isn't working. Jim has tried so hard to supply it. I don't ever want him to think he failed. Who knows. Maybe he didn't. Maybe I'm just shutting down. Or maybe I have some other kind of cancer. No way to tell now. Then we can spend our time together. There are books in the library we brought with us that I've never read."

"Okay." She was quiet for a moment. "I love you."

"I love you, too."

They walked down the hill to the compound.

Charlie was by the gate and smiled as they approached. "Hey, you two. How are you? Mark, you don't look so good."

"I'm not, Charlie. We need to talk. Would you gather everybody?"

"Sure. Now?"

"That would be fine."

Charlie looked at him sadly. He knew. "How about the kids?"

"Maybe not."

Charlie collected the clan, and they all went into the lodge. Mark and Rachel shared their situation with the group. .

They asked how long. Mark said he didn't know. He just wanted a good transition, and he asked for everybody to accept the way life is in the new world. Then Mark and Rachel left the group and went to the kitchen to make tea. They sat there together for a while, feeding sticks into the fire in the stove, just enough to keep the water hot.

Charlie came in. He'd been crying. They rose to greet him. He put his arms around Mark and Rachel. They just stood there.

Finally he spoke. "Looks like I'm the new leader."

"Not surprised. Good choice."

"God, I never wanted this."

"Best we all just accept. In our turn."

Charlie coughed.

Mark smiled at him. "Thanks, Charlie. For everything."

Rachel patted Charlie on the back. "We kept the water hot. Would you like some tea?"

Charlie didn't want tea. He didn't want to stay. "That would be nice. Thanks."

Others came to the kitchen. It was not easy. How could it be if you cared for one another?

Rachel made many cups of tea that night. Mark just fed the sticks into the fire in the stove.

Mark and Rachel walked over to their hut. They lay down together and slept.

The weeks went on. The pills were all gone. People came and went. Visitors from South Hills. Quick visits, hugs. Mark tried to play his fiddle but was too tired to lift it. Rachel took it, remembered a tune, and played it. That was good. Maybe she would teach others to play fiddle.

The clan had music evenings. The singing was better. Jeff was there, playing guitar, better every time as Jack taught him. Ashley looked happy. Mark didn't ask Sara how Ashley and Jeff were doing.

Life continued. Wood gatherers gathered. Fish catchers caught. Gardeners gardened.

The clan met, discussed, voted, coped.

The life of the clan swirled in Mark's head as reality floated, parted, folded, and flew. When he was aware, Rachel was there. He ate little, partly because he wasn't hungry, and partly because he didn't want to take from others still alive and working, needing the energy. Starving to death? Maybe. The dreams were all good.

An unmeasured time passed. Rachel shook Mark. He woke.

"Sweetie. Look. The sun. The sun is shining!"

Mark turned his head where he lay, looked, saw, and smiled.

He looked at Rachel and whispered, “I love you.”
She gripped his hand. “I love you too.”
“See you soon.”
He closed his eyes and was gone.

AFTER MARK
NEW PLYMOUTH

Rachel sat at a table in the lodge, chin in her hands, staring at nothing.

Alice sat down next to her on the bench and put an arm around her.

"How are you?"

"Mark used to ask, How's your heart?"

"Well?"

"Sad. Very sad. It's so much worse than I ever imagined."

"I know. I am so sorry."

"There's nothing left. No reason..."

They sat silently.

Alice spoke. "Would you like some tea?"

"No."

"Please..."

"Okay."

Alice brought a cup with the herb tea they all drank. Rachel sipped. They sat together, silent.

Little Alex came into the lodge. He was the 8-year-old son of Angel and Maria Garcia, one of the families from the ranch. He stood motionless for a moment, clutching a piece of paper. He looked around, saw Rachel, and came over to her, stood at the end of the table.

Rachel looked at him. "Hi, Sweetie."

"Hi. I wrote something."

Rachel smiled. Mother instinct. "What did you write?"

Alex handed her the paper.

Rachel read the few sentences. Alex had helped his father when a calf was born the previous night. He wrote that he had helped the mother, and he knew, or had heard his father say, that it was good to have a new calf. The herd was growing.

"Tell me about it."

Alex erupted with a stream of run-on sentences all connected by *and* about what had happened, where the mother was, how they found her, what she did, what his father did, what Alex did, what the calf did, what it looked like. His eyes sparkled.

Rachel laughed. "Wow. That was pretty exciting! Do you think you could draw a picture of it?"

"I don't have any more paper."

Rachel looked at him. "Well, let's see if we can find some."

She rose, patted Alice's arm, put her hand on Alex's shoulder, and the two of them walked over to the library hut to find some paper.

Alice stayed sitting at the table. Moist eyed. Bill came in, sat down beside her.

"You okay."

"No...just trying to keep going."

"Yeah."

"How about you?"

"Same." He sighed. "Charlie and I are about ready to put the metal roof on the shop. I came over to see if anyone was around to help lift."

"I'll come. Jack's up in the garden. I'll get him and be right over."

"Thanks, Darlin'."

She touched his arm, and he left.

She watched him walk away.

When would she have to say goodbye?

Minutes unwind like sand falling in an hour glass. Each one gone forever. What matters is how it was spent. Life is a long play, filled with scenes of lounging, laughing, loving, longing, living. Most of the time, the audience of the mind isn't watching, and the scene ends unnoticed. The death of someone dear is like a gong that wakes the audience.

Watch. Pay attention. Life is on the stage.

Alice smiled, took a breath, got up, and headed for the garden.

Surviving 10
ABOUT THE AUTHOR

John Page was born in California, grew up in a suburb of Washington, D.C., graduated from college in Ohio with a degree in Economics, and served four years in the United States Air Force, including a tour in Vietnam. He left the Air Force in 1970 and began a career in computers, sold computers for eight years, then worked for an accounting firm in their data processing department for ten years. In 1989, he founded his own consulting and programming firm, which he managed for the next 15 years. During ten of those years, he taught systems analysis and database concepts at the college level.

A navigator friend in Vietnam introduced him to spirituality. He went on to investigate other mysteries, including UFO's and unexplained phenomena. At some point, he read *Worlds in Collision*, by Immanuel Velikovsky, his first encounter with the idea of catastrophism in Earth's history.

He also studied the Bible in great detail, taught Sunday school, became a lay minister, and even preached a sermon or two.

In the 1990's, he read all of Zecharia Sitchin's books. Sitchin was a scholar of the libraries of Sumer, which Sitchin showed contained accounts of the Anunnaki, extraterrestrials from Nibiru, the as-yet-unannounced "Planet X" in the solar system. The Anunnaki came to Earth 450,000 years ago, bred mankind to do their heavy lifting, and inspired much of the Old Testament.

By 1998, Page was giving lectures on the material in Sitchin's books. When Sitchin announced a seminar in 2000 to certify lecturers on his works, Page attended, met Sitchin, and received his certificate.

Shortly after that, Page discovered ZetaTalk, a vast web site that tied together all the earlier work of Velikovsky and Sitchin. ZetaTalk was clear that Nibiru does exist, that it is close and will pass near Earth before December 2012, and that its passage will trigger a devastating pole shift.

By 2004, Page was convinced that ZetaTalk was largely believable, that a pole shift was indeed coming. So when the chance came in 2004, he and his wife moved to Oregon, predicted by ZetaTalk to be a "safe location" before and after the pole shift. Their sojourn in Oregon introduced Page to the work of Aprovecho Research Center, a non-profit organization involved in making life better for people living in the developing world. He spend time in India and China and met real-world experts in alternative technologies and learned first-hand the considerable difference between armchair theory and effective practice on the ground in the developing world.

Page recognized that survivors of a pole shift would dearly need the technologies now being generally recommended only by knowledgable experts in the developing world. In his view, many of the existing 'survival fiction' or preparedness sites did not address this need or emphasize the skills that would actually be effective in a post-shift survival community. (But then, virtually none of those books or sites even mentioned a pole shift.)

Page studied how local authorities responded to the Indian Ocean earthquake and tsunami in 2004. He believed that what local authorities actually did showed that his view of appropriate technology for the Aftertime was largely realistic.

He wrote *Surviving 10* to fill gaps he saw in other works dealing with the end of the world. Topics he emphasized in *Surviving 10* include public health and sanitation, lightweight shelter, and using improved cook stoves based on rocket stove technology rather than open fires. He also foresaw that pre-shift disasters would exhaust stockpiled food before the shift happened.

Most importantly, Page saw service-to-other orientation as the keystone of survival communities, and he felt the need to offer a possible way to reconcile Sitchin and ZetaTalk with traditional Christian beliefs.

Page and his wife now reside in another safe location in the Appalachian Mountains.